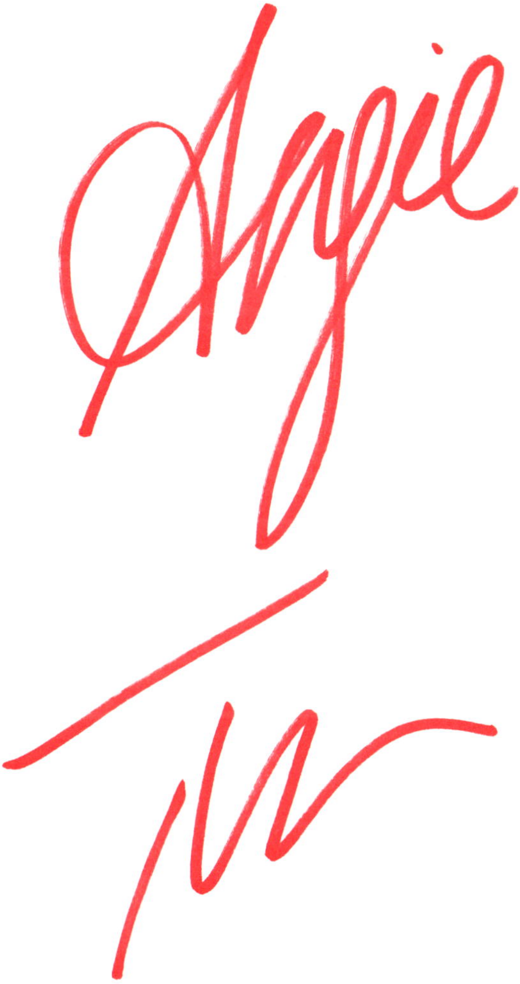
Angie

CONCRETE ROSE

Also available from Angie Thomas

The Hate U Give

On the Come Up

Find Your Voice: A Guided Journal for Writing Your Truth

CONCRETE ROSE

ANGIE THOMAS

BALZER + BRAY
An Imprint of HarperCollins*Publishers*

Balzer + Bray is an imprint of HarperCollins Publishers.

Concrete Rose
Copyright © 2021 by Angela Thomas
All rights reserved. Printed in the United States of America.
No part of this book may be used or reproduced in any manner whatsoever
without written permission except in the case of brief quotations embodied
in critical articles and reviews. For information address
HarperCollins Children's Books, a division of
HarperCollins Publishers, 195 Broadway, New York, NY 10007.
www.epicreads.com

Library of Congress Control Number: 2020946928
ISBN 978-0-06-284671-6 (trade bdg.) — ISBN 978-0-06-305653-4 (int.)
ISBN 978-0-06-304678-8 (special ed.)

Typography by Jenna Stempel
20 21 22 23 24   PC/LSCH   10 9 8 7 6 5 4 3 2 1

First Edition

For all the roses growing in concrete.
Keep blossoming.

PART 1

GERMINATION

ONE

When it comes to the streets, there's rules.

They ain't written down, and you won't find them in a book. It's natural stuff you know the moment your momma let you out the house. Kinda like how you know how to breathe without somebody telling you.

If there was a book though, there would be a whole section on streetball, and the most important rule would be at the top, in big bold letters:

Don't get your ass beat in front of a fine girl, especially if she *your* girl.

But that's exactly what I'm doing. Getting my ass beat in front of Lisa.

"It's okay, Maverick," she calls out from a picnic table. "You've got this!"

Straight up? I ain't got nothing. Me and King got zero points to Dre and Shawn's eleven. One more point and they win. Big as King is you'd think he'd block Shawn's lanky ass or something. Shawn getting by him like he don't exist. Posting him up, shooting jumpers in his face, all that. Got the homies going wild on the sidelines, and got King looking like a fool.

I can't be mad at King. Not with what's going down today. My head not in the game much either.

It's one of them perfect August days where the sun real bright yet it's not too hot to play ball. Rose Park full of King Lords in gray and black—seem like all the homies came to get a game in. Not that King Lords need an excuse to come to Rose. This our territory. We handle business here, chill out here, get our butts kicked on the court here.

I check the ball to Dre.

He grin extra wide. "C'mon, Mav. You going out like this in front of your girl? Lisa should've played instead of you."

"Ooohs" echo along the sidelines. Dre never go easy on me 'cause I'm his younger cousin. He been dunking on me since I was big enough to hold a ball.

"Worry 'bout this whooping you gon' take in front of *your* girls," I say. "Keisha and Andreanna won't wanna claim you after this one."

There go more "Ooohs." Dre's fiancée, Keisha, is over at the picnic table with Lisa, laughing. Keisha and Dre's daughter, Andreanna, is in her lap.

"Look at li'l homie, trash-talking," Shawn says, grinning with his gold grill.

"We should call him Martin Luther King 'cause he got a dream if he think he winning," Dre says.

"I have a dream," Shawn try to sound like MLK, "that one day, you may step on this court and get a goddamn point!"

The homies laugh. Truth is, Shawn's joke could've been whack and they'd laugh. That's how it is when you the crown of the King Lords, the Caesar of Rome. People do what they supposed to in order to stay on your good side.

One of them yell out, "Don't let them punk you, Li'l Don and Li'l Zeke!"

It don't matter that my pops been locked up for nine years or that King's pops been dead almost as long. They still Big Don, the former crown, and Big Zeke, his right-hand man. That make me Li'l Don and King Li'l Zeke. Guess we not old enough to go by our own names yet.

Dre bounce the ball. "What you got, cuz?"

He start right. I follow and run straight into Shawn's chest. They running a pick-and-roll. Dre get away from me, and King go after him, leaving Shawn open. Shawn gun for the hoop. Dre toss the ball up and—

Goddamn! Shawn dunk on King.

"What!" Shawn yell as he hang from the rim. He jump down, and him and Dre do the handshake they've done since they were kids.

"They can't mess with us!" Shawn says.

"Hell nah!" Dre says.

I won't *ever* hear the end of this one. Thirty years from now, Dre gon' be like, "Remember that time me and Shawn didn't let y'all score?"

King slam the ball against the concrete. "Shit!"

He take losing to heart for real.

"Ay, chill," I say. "We'll get them next—"

"Y'all got beat *down*!" one of the homies, P-Nut, laughs. He this short dude with a thick beard, and he known to have a big mouth. There's scars on his face and neck 'cause of it.

"We should've stopped calling you Li'l Don a long time ago. You an embarrassment to the OG, balling like that."

The homies on the sidelines laugh.

I clench my jaw. I oughta be used to them kinda jabs. Let a lot of fools in the set tell it, I ain't as hard as my pops, ain't as street as my pops, ain't as good at anything as him.

They got no clue what I'm doing on the low. "I'm more like my pops than you think," I tell P-Nut.

"Could'a fooled me. Next time, big boy there oughta put as much effort into the game as he do into eating."

King step toward P-Nut. "Or I could whoop your ass instead."

P-Nut step toward him, too. "What it is, then, fool?"

"Whoa, whoa, whoa!" I say, pulling King back. He real quick to fight. "Chill!"

"Yeah, calm down," says Shawn. "It's only ball."

"You right, you right. My bad, Shawn," P-Nut says with his hands up. "I can be a bit temperish."

Temper-what? I swear, P-Nut be making up words to sound smart.

The way King nostrils flare, I got a feeling this 'bout more than ball for him. He shake me off and march across the park. Shawn, Dre, and everybody look at me.

"He got a lot going on, that's all," I mumble.

"Yeah," Dre add in, and lower his voice to Shawn. "You remember that situation with him, Mav, and ol' girl that I told you about? They find out today."

"No excuses, Dre. He always popping off," Shawn says. "He either get that temper in check or get checked."

In other words, a beatdown. That's how the big homies keep us li'l homies in line. See, there's levels to King Lords. You got youngins, badass middle schoolers who swear they got next. They do whatever the rest of us tell them to do. Then you got li'l homies like me, King, and our boys Rico and Junie. We handle initiations, recruitment, and sell weed. Next is the big homies, like Dre and Shawn. They sell the harder stuff, make sure the rest of us have what we need, make alliances, and discipline anybody who step outta line. When we have beef with the Garden Disciples, the gang from the east side, they usually take care of it. Then there's the OGs, original gangstas. Grown dudes who been in this a long time. They advise Shawn. Problem is, there ain't a lot of OGs left in the streets. Most of them locked up like my pops, or dead.

A beatdown by the big homies is no joke. I can't let King go out like that.

"I'll talk to him," I tell Shawn.

"Somebody better," he says, and turns to the others. "Now who wanna get whooped on this court next?"

King nearly out the park. I run to catch up with him. "Dawg, you can't be going off on folks. You tryna cause us some problems?"

"I ain't gon' let nobody diss me, Mav," King growls. "I don't give a damn if he a big homie."

I glance back at the courts. We far enough that Shawn and them won't hear me. "We gotta keep our cool, remember?"

For the past six months, me and King been slinging behind the big homies' backs. Like I said, li'l homies can only sell weed, but there ain't nearly as much money in that as there is in the other stuff. On top of that, we gotta give most of our dough to Shawn and them 'cause they supply the product. One day King decided to do his own thing on the side and get his own supplier. He brought me on real quick. Our pockets stay fat.

We gon' be in deep shit if Shawn and them ever find out. This almost as bad as taking their turf. But ay, my momma work two jobs. She shouldn't have to get me kicks and clothes when she struggling to keep a roof over our heads. Real talk.

"Let P-Nut or anybody else say whatever the hell they

want," I tell King. "We doing our thing, and that's all we need to focus on. A'ight?"

I hold my hand out to King. At first he stare at it, and I don't know if that's 'cause of Shawn and P-Nut or that other situation we got going on.

He finally slap my palm. "Yeah, a'ight."

I pull him into me and hit his back with my fist. "Don't worry 'bout that other thing. It's gon' work out like it's supposed to."

"I ain't tripping either way. It is what it is."

That's the same thing he say 'bout his parents getting murdered when he was eleven and 'bout everything he went through with his foster families. I guess if he wanna leave it at that so can I.

He head out the park, and I head over to Lisa. She looking finer than a mug. Got on a shirt that show her belly button and some shorts that got my mind wandering.

I stand between her legs. "We garbage, huh?"

Lisa wrap her arms around my neck. "Y'all could use work."

"Like I said, we garbage."

She laughs. "Maybe, but you're *my* garbage."

She kiss me, and that make me forget everything else.

It's always been this way with Lisa. I spotted her at a basketball game freshman year. Her team was whooping the Garden High girls' asses. Honestly, she do play better than me. I was there to watch Junie play afterward when Lisa caught my eye.

She could ball, and she was fine as hell. Plus she had a ass. Can't lie, I noticed that thang from jump.

She did a layup, and I hollered, "Hell yeah, shorty!" She looked my way with them pretty brown eyes and smiled. That was it; I had to talk to her. Once she gave me a shot, it's been on ever since.

I messed up big-time. Knowing what I know make me stop kissing her.

"What's wrong?" she ask.

I play with her braids. "Nothing. Mad that I lost in front of you."

"Daddy beat you!" Andreanna says.

Nothing like a three-year-old calling you out. Andreanna look like Dre, which mean she look like me. Everybody say me and Dre practically twins. Our mommas are sisters and our dads are cousins, so it make sense that we got the same wide eyes, thick eyebrows, and dark brown complexions.

"You should've cheered for me." I tickle Andreanna. She squirm and giggle in Keisha's lap. "You shouldn't have cheered for your daddy."

"Heck yeah she should've cheered for her daddy," Dre says as he come over. He scoop Andreanna up and fly her around like an airplane. Can't nobody make her laugh the way he do.

"Y'all going to the party tonight?" Lisa ask.

Shawn throwing a house party like he always do at the end of summer.

"You already know Dre not going to no party," Keisha says.

"Heck nah. We gon' have all the fun. Ain't that right, baby girl?" He kiss Andreanna's cheek.

"Dag, man. It's Friday night," I say. "You can't stay at home."

Never mind, this Dre. He don't go nowhere anymore. Having Andreanna changed him big-time. He stopped partying and hanging out. I think he'd stop being a King Lord if he could.

Ain't no getting outta King Lords. Unless you wanna end up dead or damn near dead.

"I'm where I wanna be," he says, smiling at Andreanna. He look at me. "You sure you going to the party?"

Dre know what's going down today, the thing that might change my life. Problem is, Lisa don't know. He bet' not say nothing either.

"I'm sure," I say.

Dre stare me down the way a big brother do a little brother who up to no good. It get on my nerves and make me feel like shit all at once.

I look at Lisa instead. "Nothing stopping us from going to the party. Gotta get one in before school start soon."

Lisa drape her arms around my neck. "That's right. Just think, a year from now we'll be at college and going to all the parties."

"Fa'sho." The parties the main reason I'd go to college. If I go. I ain't sure yet. "At tonight's party? Everybody gon' notice you when you walk in rocking this."

I take the necklace outta my pocket. The pendant spell out

"Maverick" in cursive. It's made outta real gold with li'l diamonds along it. I got a dude in the mall to make it the other week.

"Oh my God!" Lisa gasp as she take it. "It's beautiful."

"Okay, Mav," Keisha says. "I see you spending dough on your girl."

"Hell yeah. You know how I do."

"Them necklaces cost big money," Dre says. "Where you get dough for that?"

Dre don't know I sell more than weed with King, and I wanna keep it that way. It took a lot to convince him to let me sell weed in the first place. Even though Dre sling himself, he was on some "do as I say, not as I do" crap for the longest. I told him I wanted to help Ma out, and eventually he gave in. He only let me sell enough weed to pay a bill or two. If he find out what I got with King, he'll have my ass.

"I did odd jobs around the hood like I always do," I lie. "Saved up enough to get it."

"Well, I love it," Lisa says. She know what I do. She a real one for changing the subject. "Thank you."

"Anything for you, baby girl." I kiss her again.

"*Eww!* Don't be doing that in front of my baby." Dre cover Andreanna's eyes, making Keisha crack up. "Gon' scar her for life."

"If she ain't scarred from looking at your face, she a'ight," I say as a horn blare in the parking lot from a rusty Datsun.

One of the windows roll down, and this muscular, light-skinned dude call out, "Lisa! Let's go!"

She roll her eyes with a groan. "Seriously?"

That's her older brother, Carlos. He never liked me. First time I called Lisa, he interrogated me like he was the police. "How old are you? What school do you go to? What kinda grades do you get? Are you in a gang?" All kinds of stuff that wasn't his business. When he met me, I was wearing gray and black, which proved I'm Kinging. Fool turned his nose up at me like I was a bug under his shoe. He home from college this summer, and I can't wait for his ass to go back to school.

"What he doing here?" I ask.

"Momma asked him to take me school shopping," Lisa says. "I have to get more of those ugly Saint Mary's uniforms."

"Ay, you be looking fine as hell in them plaid skirts."

Lisa fight a smile, and that make me smile.

"Whatever, those skirts are still ugly." She hop off the table. "I better go before Captain Nosy causes a scene."

I laugh and take her hand. "C'mon. I'll walk you over."

She say bye to Keisha and Dre and cross the park with me. Carlos give me an evil eye the whole way over. Hater.

Me and Lisa stop beside the car. "I'll come scoop you up at eight," I say.

"See you at eight fifteen, then." She smirks. "You're never on time."

"Nah, I'm gon' be early tonight. I love you."

First time I said that word to her, it tripped me out. I'd never told a girl I love her before, but I'd never had a Lisa before either.

"I love you too," she says. "Stay safe, okay?"

"I ain't going nowhere. You can't get rid of me that easy."

She smile and give me a quick peck. "I'm holding you to it."

I open the passenger door for her. Carlos glare at me so damn hard. I flip him off when Lisa not looking.

"Why are you tripping?" Lisa asks, and I hear Carlos say something 'bout a "gangbanger park" as he pull off.

They only gone around a minute when an old Camry with a sunroof turn into the parking lot. Ma used to drive a Lexus. The Feds took it when they took Pops.

"Uh-oh!" P-Nut call out. "Li'l Don in trooooouble. Got his momma rolling through on a disciplitarianship."

A discipli-what?

Forget P-Nut. I open Ma's passenger's door. "Hey, Ma."

"Hey, ba—" She cover her nose. "Damn, boy! You ripe! What you doing so musty?"

I sniff myself. I ain't *that* bad. "I played ball."

"Did you wrestle with pigs too? Good Lord! You gon' clear the clinic out."

"If we run by the house real quick, I can shower—"

"We don't have time for that, Maverick. We told Iesha and her momma that we'd meet them at two. It's already one forty-five."

"Oh." I ain't realize my life might be changing so soon. "My bad."

Ma must catch the dip in my voice. "We need to know the truth. You get that, right?"

"Ma, what I'm gon' do if—"

"Hey," she says, and I look at her. "No matter what, I've got you."

She hold her fist out to me.

I smirk. "You too old to be dapping folks up."

"Old? Boy, please! I'll have you know I got carded when me and Moe went out last Saturday. Bam! Who too old now?"

I laugh as she crank up the car. "You. You too old."

"Ay, hold up!" Shawn call out. He dash across the parking lot and run around to Ma's side. "I gotta say whaddup to the queen. How you doing, Mrs. Carter?"

"Hey, Shawn," Ma says. "You making it?"

"Yes, ma'am. Looking out for your boy."

"Good," Ma says, and this time her voice dip.

No mother want their son in a gang, but no mother want their son dead either. Pops made so many enemies in the streets that I need somebody to have my back. He told Ma I had to join. Kinging run in my blood anyway. Ma's brothers claimed it, then Pops and his cousins. It's like a fraternity for us.

Ma think I'm an "associate" though, aka somebody who only claim it and don't sling or put in work. She say this whole King Lord thing is temporary. She drill it into my head all the time—get my high school diploma and go away to college so I can get the hell away from all of this.

"We've got an appointment to get to," she tells Shawn.

"Be safe out here, baby."

"Yes, ma'am." Shawn look at me and nod. "Good luck, li'l homie."

I nod back.

Ma pull outta the parking lot, and I watch the homies in the rearview mirror. They ball on the courts without a care in the world. I wish that could be me again.

Instead, I'm headed to the clinic to find out if King's son is actually mine.

TWO

The free clinic real busy for a Friday afternoon. Everybody in the Garden would rather come here than go to County 'cause folks who go to County rarely go home. Some man on crutches talk loud as hell on the pay phone like he want all of us to hear that he need a ride. Somehow, he ain't woke up the lady in the wheelchair beside us. A girl around my age chase after this snot-nosed kid and call after him in Spanish.

Wild to think that could be me in a couple years.

This whole situation kinda complicated. King got this homegirl Iesha. She not his girlfriend, nah. They mess around a lot, if you know what I mean. Iesha known to mess around with a lot of dudes though. No disrespect, but it's fact.

Around a year ago, Lisa broke up with me after Carlos claimed he saw me talking to another girl. A bald-faced lie but

Lisa believed that fool for whatever reason. I went to King's crib, stressed out 'bout it. He asked Iesha to get my mind off things. I wasn't sure at first, 'cause it seemed wrong, like I was cheating almost. Once me and Iesha got into it, I forgot right and wrong.

At some point, the condom broke.

Now I'm at the free clinic waiting for DNA test results on Iesha's three-month-old baby.

Ma's leg won't stay still, like she wanna run out this waiting room. She glance at her watch. "They should've been here by now. Maverick, have you talked to Iesha lately?"

"Not since the other week."

"Lord. We gon' have our hands full with this girl."

Ma always talk to God. Usually it's "Lord, keep me from hurting this boy." Guess it's nice she talking to him 'bout somebody else for once.

She claim I got her aging early from stress. She keep her hair in finger waves and got a couple of grays she shouldn't have at thirty-eight. That ain't my fault. It's from them long hours she work. Ma check people into a hotel during the day and clean offices at night. I always tell her "I'm gon' take care of you."

She smile and says, "Take care of yourself, Maverick."

For weeks it's been "Take care of your son." She convinced I'm his daddy.

I'm not. "Don't know why we doing this," I mumble. "He ain't mine."

"Why? Because you were only with that girl one time?" Ma asks. "That's all it takes, Maverick."

"She swear he King's baby. They even named him after King."

"Yeah, and who does he look like?" Ma says.

Maaaan . . . a'ight, she got me there. When King Jr. was first born, he didn't look like anybody. All newborns resemble aliens to me. After a couple of weeks, he got eyes, nose, and lips similar to mine. King was nowhere to be found. Baby boy don't resemble Iesha either.

That's why King stopped dealing with Iesha altogether. She wanna prove to him that I ain't the father and asked me to take a DNA test. So, here we are. Unless I got the worst luck in the world, ain't no way that baby mine.

My beeper go off on my waist, and Mr. Wyatt's number appear. That's our next-door neighbor. I cut his front yard every week. He probably want me to do it today. I'll have to hit him up later.

Ma watch me with a smile. "You think you something 'cause you got a pager, huh?"

I laugh. I bought this joint two months ago. Got it in that blue ice you can see through. Flyer than a mug. "Nah, Ma. Never."

"How's business going?" she asks. "How many yards are you doing now?"

Ma think I make money by cutting grass around the

neighborhood. I do, but I make even more by selling drugs. The whole yard-cutting thing help to keep her in the dark. When she see me rocking new kicks or clothes, I act like I got them for cheap at the swap meet instead of the mall. I hate that I can lie to her so good.

"It's fine," I say. "I'm at around ten yards right now. Tryna get as many as I can before it gets cold."

"Don't worry, you'll find something else to do. Lord knows babies aren't cheap. You'll figure out how to make it work."

I won't have to. That baby ain't mine.

The clinic door open, and Ms. Robinson come in. She hold the door open for somebody else. "Bring your fast behind in here!"

Iesha walk in, rolling her eyes. She got a baby bag on her shoulder and hold a car seat in her hand. Li'l man asleep inside it. His fist rest against his head, and his eyebrows all wrinkled, like he thinking something deep in his dreams.

"Hey, Faye," Ms. Robinson says to Ma. "Sorry we late."

Ma goes, "Mmm-hmm." It ain't approval or judgment. Then she look at me, like she expect me to do something. I stare back, all confused.

"Boy, give Iesha your seat," Ma says.

"Oh! My bad." I hop up. Ma stay on me 'bout being a gentleman.

Iesha take my chair and set the car seat at her feet. Ma suddenly starstruck.

"Aww, look at that little man," she says in a voice she only use on babies. "He knocked out, huh?"

"Finally," says Iesha. "Kept me up all night."

"Ain't like you had nowhere to go," Ms. Robinson snips. "Miss I-Skip-Summer-School-to-Chase-Some-Boy."

"Oh my God," Iesha groans.

"He'll sleep through the night soon," Ma says. "Maverick didn't sleep through the night until he was five months old. It was like he needed to know what was going on all the time."

"He the exact same way," Ms. Robinson says, eyeing me.

She can look at me all she want. That don't make him mine.

Li'l man whine in the car seat.

Iesha sighs. "What now?"

"He probably wants his pacifier, baby," Ma says.

Iesha put it in his mouth, and he suddenly good.

I study Iesha real hard. She got bags under her eyes she didn't have before. "Anybody helping you with him?"

"*Help?*" her momma says, like I cussed. "Who supposed to help her? *Me?*"

"C'mon now, Yolanda," says Ma. "This is a lot for anyone to handle, let alone a seventeen-year-old."

"T'uh! She wanna act grown, she can deal with this like she grown. By. Her. Self."

Iesha blink real fast.

I'm feeling real bad for her all of a sudden. "If he is mine, you won't be doing this alone no more, a'ight? I'll come over and help as much as I can."

Five seconds ago, she looked ready to cry. Now she smirk at me. "Oh, word? Your girlfriend gon' be cool with that?"

I don't know how Lisa gon' react. I figured if the baby wasn't mine, she didn't need to know 'bout any of this. If he is mine . . . "Don't worry 'bout her," I tell Iesha.

"Oh, I ain't worried. *You* should be. Her stuck-up ass gon' drop you quick."

"Ay, don't talk 'bout her like that!"

"Whatever. All them girls at Garden High who drool over you, and you go for the bougie Catholic-school girl. It's all good. My baby ain't yours. Soon as these results come back, I'm taking him to his real daddy, and we gon' be a family. Watch."

"Iesha Robinson!" the nurse calls.

We all look that way.

This is it.

"Go on," Ms. Robinson tells Iesha.

Iesha get up, sighing outta her nose. "This so stupid."

"What's stupid is that two boys could be the daddy!" her momma calls after her. "That's what's stupid!"

Well, damn. Do me and Ma get into it? Hell yeah, all the time. But not in public like this.

Iesha come back and shove the envelope into her momma's hand. "Bet I'm right. Bet!"

Ms. Robinson take the papers out and read over them. By that smug look she get, I know what they say.

"Congratulations, Maverick," she says, staring at her daughter. "You're a father."

Shit.

"Jesus." Ma hold her forehead. Saying he mine and knowing it two different things.

Iesha snatch the papers. She look them over, and her face fall. "Shit!"

"Damn, why you mad?"

"This should be King's baby! I don't wanna deal with your ass!"

"I don't wanna deal with your ass either!"

"Maverick!" Ma snaps.

My son cry in the car seat.

Ma cut me a hard glare and pick him up. "What's wrong, Man-Man? Huh?" She don't have to know you long to give you a nickname. Ma sniff near his butt, and her nose wrinkle. "Oh, I know what's wrong. Where are his diapers?"

"In the baby bag," Iesha mumbles.

"Grab the bag, Maverick," Ma says. "We'll handle this."

Suddenly, I got a son and he got a dirty diaper. "I don't know how to change a diaper."

"Then it's time for you to learn. C'mon."

Ma go into the women's restroom and act like I should follow her in there. Hell nah. She come back to the door. "Boy, c'mon."

"I can't go in there!"

"Nobody's in here. Until they put changing tables in the men's room, c'mon."

Damn, this ain't cool. I follow her in. Li'l man cry his head off. I get why. That diaper stank. Ma hand him to me so she can search his bag, and I hold him away from me. I ain't tryna get diaper doo on me.

"They sure got a lot of clothes in here," Ma says. "Let's see if she's got some changing pads. If she doesn't—never mind, she does." Ma put one on the table. "All right, lay him down."

"What if he fall off?"

"He won't. There you go," she says as I lay him down. "Now unbutton his—"

I miss the rest for staring at him.

Before when I'd look at him, I was in awe that something so little existed. Now I look at him and he mine, no question.

Worst part? I'm his.

I'm scared. I messed up. I only been seventeen for a month, and now I gotta take care of another person.

He need me.

He depending on me.

He gon' call me Daddy.

"Maverick?"

Ma touch my shoulder.

"You've got this," she says. "I got you."

She don't just mean the diaper.

"A'ight."

I change my first diaper with her help. This nurse come in and see us struggling—it's been a while since Ma did this—and give us some tips. Li'l man still fuss even though he clean. Ma hold him against her shoulder and rub his back.

"It's okay, Man-Man," she coos. "It's all right."

He soon calm down. Guess that's all he needed to know.

I grab his bag, and we go to the waiting room. My son's car seat on the floor with the DNA papers lying inside it. Ms. Robinson is gone.

So is Iesha.

THREE

"That trifling heffa! And I don't mean Iesha," Ma says. "I mean her momma!"

Ma ain't stopped fussing since we left the clinic.

At first I thought Iesha and Ms. Robinson stepped outside. Nah, they left. One of the nurses said she pointed out they were leaving the car seat. Ms. Robinson told her, "We don't need it anymore," and shoved Iesha out the door.

We went straight to their house. I banged on the doors, looked through the windows. Nobody answered. We had no choice but to bring li'l man home with us.

I climb our porch steps, carrying him in his car seat. He so caught up in the toys dangling from the handle that he don't know his momma left him like he nothing.

Ma shove the front door open. "I had a funny feeling when

I saw all them clothes in that diaper bag. They shipped him off without a word!"

I set the car seat on the coffee table. What the hell just happened? For real, man. I suddenly got a whole human being in my care when I never even took care of a *dog*.

"What we do now, Ma?"

"We obviously have to keep him until we find out what Iesha and her momma are up to. This might be for the weekend, but as trifling as they are . . ." She close her eyes and hold her forehead. "Lord, I hope this girl hasn't abandoned this baby."

My heart drop to my kicks. "*Abandoned* him? What I'm supposed to—"

"You're gonna do whatever you have to do, Maverick," she says. "That's what being a parent means. Your child is now *your* responsibility. You'll be changing his diapers. You'll be feeding him. You'll be dealing with him in the middle of the night. You—"

Had my whole life turned upside down, and she don't care.

That's Ma for you. Granny say she came in the world ready for whatever. When things fall apart, she quick to grab the pieces and make something new outta them.

"Are you listening to me?" she asks.

I scratch my cornrows. "I hear you."

"I said are you *listening*? There's a difference."

"I'm listening, Ma."

"Good. They left enough diapers and formula to last the

weekend. I'll call your aunt 'Nita, see if they have Andreanna's old crib. We can set it up in your room."

"*My room?* He gon' keep me awake!"

She set her hand on her hip. "Who else he's supposed to keep awake?"

"Man," I groan.

"Don't 'man' me! You're a father now. It's not about you anymore." Ma pick up the baby bag. "I'll fix him a bottle. Can you keep an eye on him, or is that a problem?"

"I'll watch him," I mumble.

"Thank you." She go to the kitchen. "'*He gon' keep me awake.*' The nerve!"

I plop down on the couch. Li'l Man stare at me from the car seat. That's what I'm gon' call him for now, Li'l Man. King Jr. don't feel right when he *my* son.

My son. Wild to think that one li'l condom breaking turned me into somebody's father. I sigh. "Guess it's you and me now, huh?"

I hold my hand toward him, and he grip my finger. He small to be so strong. "Gah-lee," I laugh. "You gon' break my finger."

He try to put it in his mouth, but I don't let him. My fingernails dirty as hell. That only make him whine.

"Ay, ay, chill." I unstrap him and lift him out. He way heavier than he look. I try to rest him in my arms and support his neck like Ma told me to. He whimper and squirm till suddenly he wailing. "Ma!"

She come back with the bottle. "What, Maverick?"

"I can't hold him right."

She adjust him in my arms. "You relax, and he'll relax. Now here, give him the bottle." She hand it to me, and I put it in his mouth. "Lower it a little bit, Maverick. You don't wanna feed him fast. There you go. When he's halfway through it, burp him. Burp him again when he's done."

"How?"

"Hold him against your shoulder and pat his back."

Hold him right, lower the bottle, burp him. "Ma, I can't—"

"Yes, you can. In fact, you're doing it now."

I hadn't realized Li'l Man stopped crying. He suck the bottle and grip my shirt, staring up at me.

I look at him. I mean *look* at him. Yeah, I see me—ain't no denying he mine. More than that, I see my son.

My heart balloon in my chest.

"Hey, man." For some reason this feel like I'm meeting him for the first time. "Hey."

"I'm gonna throw his clothes in the washing machine," Ma says. "Who knows what kinda germs they've got at that house."

Don't nobody hate germs like Ma. She got asthma, and the weirdest stuff can set her off.

"Thanks, Ma."

She go back to the laundry room. I watch my son, and I gotta admit as much as I'm in awe I ain't never been this scared in my life. He a whole human being that I helped make. Got a heart, lungs, a brain partly 'cause of me, and now I basically gotta keep him alive.

This almost too much. Definitely not how I planned to spend my Friday ni—

Oh, dang. The party. Ain't no way Ma gon' let me go.

I stop feeding Li'l Man long enough to dial Lisa's number on the cordless phone. I hold it to my ear with my shoulder. It ring a couple of times, then she go, "Hey, Mav."

I always forget that her momma got caller ID. "Hey. This not a bad time, is it?"

There's a muffled sound like she moving around. "Nope. Just putting an outfit together for the party. Why? What's up?"

I *really* feel like shit now. "Umm . . . I can't take you out tonight. Something came up."

"Everything all right?"

"Yeah. My momma want me to stay home and take care of stuff here."

That ain't a lie. It just ain't all of the truth. This baby in my arms ain't exactly a phone conversation, you know?

"Sounds like my momma," Lisa says, and I can practically hear her roll her eyes. "I could come over and keep you company if you want."

"Nah!"

I startled Li'l Man. His face scrunch up.

"My bad," I tell him and Lisa, and bounce him a bit. Please, God, don't let him cry. "You ain't gotta spend your Friday watching me do chores. I'm a'ight."

"Okay," Lisa says. "See you this weekend?"

"Nah. I'm not allowed to go anywhere."

"Dang. What did you do?"

That's a loaded-ass question. "You know how it go. I'll holla at you."

We tell each other "I love you" like we always do, and I hang up with a deep breath. "Li'l Man, you almost got me in trouble."

He stop sucking his bottle long enough to stretch his mouth and yawn. He clearly don't care.

He halfway done eating. Guess I gotta burp him now. Ma said hold him against my shoulder and gently pat his back. I pat once, twice, three times—

He hiccup. Something warm ooze down my back.

"*Ill*, man!" I hop off the couch. This boy puked on me. He cry, and shoot, I wanna cry. "Ma!"

"What now, Maverick?" she says, and come to the doorway again. She got the nerve to smirk. "Welcome to parenthood, where clothes never stay clean."

"What should I do?"

"Put a towel over your shoulder next time. For now, finish feeding him and burp him again."

"I gotta sit here with puke on me?"

"What I tell you? It's not about you anymore. You gon' learn. Looks like you got the best teacher."

He could've kept this lesson to himself, for real.

The doorbell ring. Ma peek out the front window first. After the Feds bust into your house, you'll always be careful. She open the door. "Hey, Andre baby."

"Hey, Auntie. Did y'all get the test—" He notice me and my son, and his eyes get wide. "Yooo! He really is yours?"

"Yep. He mine."

"Daaaang," Dre says as he step into the house. "He do look like you, so I shouldn't be real surprised."

"Mmm-hmm. And he's already putting Mav through it." Ma chuckle.

Glad somebody think this funny. "Man, I burped him, and he puked on me."

Dre crack up. "Gotta have the towel at all times, cuz." He come around to see Li'l Man as he rest against my shoulder. "Hey, itty-bitty cuz. I'm Dre. One day I'll teach you how to ball since your pops can't."

"Forget you," I say.

"I only speak facts. You keeping him overnight or something?"

I sit on the edge of the couch, get Li'l Man situated, and feed him again. "I don't know. Iesha and her momma bounced."

Dre lower the bottle I'm holding. "Don't feed him fast. What you mean they bounced?"

"We took him to the restroom to change him, came back, and they were gone."

"Shit—shoot." Dre try not to cuss in front of Ma. "Did y'all look for them?"

"We went by the house, and nobody was there," Ma says. "I shouldn't be surprised that Yolanda's trifling behind would pull something like this."

"Dang," Dre says. "Well, hey, if y'all need a crib, we still got Andreanna's old one in storage and her stroller. I can bring them over later."

"That's sweet of you, baby. Thank you." Ma grab her purse off the couch. "I'm gonna go pick up some dinner from Reuben's. Lord knows I am not in the mood to cook. Y'all behave while I'm gone."

"Yes, ma'am," we both say. Even though Dre twenty-three, he do whatever Ma tell him.

She leave, and Dre sit beside me on the couch. He watch me feed Li'l Man.

"Damn, Mav. You really a father."

"I still can't believe it."

"I get that. Fatherhood is a trip, but I couldn't imagine my life without my baby girl. Even as bad as she is."

I laugh. "She can't be that bad. She only three."

"Shiiid. She think she know everything, and she get into everything. People say twos are terrible. Nah, three. Three is next level." He get quiet for a second. "I'm gon' miss her li'l bad butt after I drop her and Keisha off."

A couple of years ago, Keisha moved outta town to attend

Markham State and took Andreanna with her. It's only two hours away, and Dre visit every weekend. He stay in the Garden to help Aunt 'Nita with Uncle Ray after Unc had a stroke last year.

"Hold tight, man," I say. "Before you know it, Keisha will be graduating and y'all will be saying your vows in July."

"If I can survive all this wedding stuff." He grab the back of my neck. "You good?"

Hell no. My life got thrown into a blender and I'm left with something I don't recognize. On top of that, I'm suddenly somebody's pops and I wish I had *my* pops.

Nah, man. I can't freak out. I gotta handle mine, on some G shit. "I ain't tripping."

"You know it's okay to be scared, right?"

"Scared of what? A li'l baby?"

"Of all the stuff that come with having a li'l baby," Dre says. "First time I held Andreanna, I cried. She was so beautiful, and she was stuck with me for a father."

I look at my son, and damn, I feel that.

"I decided I was gon' be the kinda father she deserved," he says. "I had to man up. That's what you gotta do, Mav. Man up."

"Fool, I'm a man already," I say.

Dre put his hands up. "My bad. You a man. You such a man that you slinging behind me and Shawn backs."

I almost lose my grip on my son. "What?"

"You heard me. You buying your girl expensive necklaces,

rocking new sneakers every week. I know how much money you pull in, working for us. I made sure it's just enough so you can help Auntie Faye out a little bit. Where you getting this extra money from?"

I hold my son against my shoulder and burp him again. "I told you I do odd jobs."

"Yeah, right! Don't bullshit me. Who put you on? Where you getting your supply from?"

"I ain't no snitch, Dre."

"Ohhhh, so you *are* doing something on the side."

"Nah, I didn't mean that!" I say.

"Yeah, you did. I bet it was King, wasn't it? Yeah, he seem like the type to go rogue."

Shit, shit, shit. "Dre, I can't—"

"I won't rat you out to Shawn," he says. "You claim you a man, prove it. Men own up to their shit. Own up to yours."

Damn, he had to put it like that. I gotta admit I felt real bad hiding this from Dre. He the big brother I never had. We never keep secrets from each other. And even if I don't admit it, he gon' find a way to get the truth. That could be real bad for King.

I set my son back in his car seat as he fade off to sleep. I can't let my homeboy get in trouble. I gotta take this one for the team.

"A'ight, yeah," I say. "I been selling other drugs on the side. Nobody helping. I found a way to get it myself."

Dre sighs. "What the hell, Mav?"

"I wanna make money! You and Shawn wouldn't let me sell nothing but weed."

"'Cause we looking out for you and the li'l homies. Selling that other shit is dangerous in more ways than one. You don't need to be doing that."

I just look at him. "Fool, you do it!" For real, he got some nerve lecturing me.

"I'm smart with mine, unlike you," Dre says. "You probably careless enough to lead the cops right to you. You honestly need to leave this dealing shit alone, period. Weed, rocks, pills, powder, whatever. Let it all go."

"What? See, now you tripping."

"I'm serious, Mav. You got a son to think about now—"

"You got a daughter."

"Yeah, and I want you to learn from my mistakes and be a better father than me," Dre says. "I hate that this how I gotta provide for Andreanna, but I'm too caught up to get out. You not." He poke my chest. "We could get you a regular job like Wal-Mart or Mickey D's—"

"That ain't no kinda money!"

"It's *clean* money," Dre says. "I can talk to Shawn 'bout letting you out the set, too."

"Oh, you tripping for real," I say. "Shawn can't just 'let me out.' You know that. You saw what happened to Kenny."

Kenny is this King Lord who once played football for

Garden High. He got a full scholarship offer to one of them big universities and decided he wanted out. Guess he didn't want the school discovering his gang ties. There's only a few ways to get out the King Lords—you either put in some major work like taking a charge for somebody, or you get jumped out. Kenny got jumped. The big homies beat him so bad he ended up in a coma. When he woke up, he was too banged up to take that football scholarship anyway. Getting out ain't worth it.

"Maybe we could figure out a different way for you," Dre says.

I shake my head. "Quit lying to yourself, man. Why should I get out anyway? Kinging in our blood, remember?"

"You could break the cycle," Dre says. "Be better than me, Unc, all of us. Do things the right way."

"Yeah, that's easy to say when you driving around in a Beamer," I say. "You a hypocrite, dawg. You also a damn fool if you think I'm walking away from this money, especially now that I got a kid."

"It's like that? A'ight," Dre says, nodding. "Either you give it up or I tell Auntie and Uncle Don."

"Then you'd have to admit to them that you let me sell weed."

"I'm willing to own up to mine like a man. I'll also tell Shawn what King doing."

"I told you, King not involved."

"Yeah right," Dre says. "This got his name all on it. You

don't have to admit it. Me and Shawn will look into it and handle him ourselves."

"You said you wouldn't bring Shawn in this!"

"No, I said I wouldn't rat *you* out to him. I didn't say I wouldn't rat out King. So what's it gon' be, cuz? Let drug dealing go completely or let you and your boy both get in trouble?"

"This blackmail!"

"It's your choice to see it that way," Dre says.

"It is that way! How I know you still won't rat King out?" I ask.

"I trust you to talk to him and remind him of the consequences that come with doing shit like this," Dre says. "I promise if I think you back at it, I'm snitching on him and you."

"Dre, c'mon. Please?"

"This on you, Mav. Your call."

I fold my hands on top of my head. Goddamn! This 'bout the worst way this could go. I wanna keep making money, but I don't wanna get in trouble with my folks. I don't want King to get hurt either.

I ain't got much of a choice. "A'ight," I say. "I'll stop selling drugs."

Do Dre tell me he proud of my decision? Do he give me props for looking out for my boy? Nah, he sit back on the couch and go, "That's what I thought. Now go get me a soda. I'm thirsty from dealing with your li'l hardheaded behind."

FOUR

I finally got Iesha on the phone Saturday night.

"I need a break, Maverick," she said, and her voice was real rough. "I been crying all the time, and my head get in these real dark places. He don't need to be around me."

It sounded like what Keisha went through after she had Andreanna. I think Ma called it "postpartum depression."

"You seen a doctor?" I asked Iesha.

"I don't need a doctor."

"Nah, for real. Dre's girl dealt with that and—"

"I said I don't need a doctor, Maverick! I'm handling it myself."

"Fine." Wasn't no point in arguing. "How long you think you need?"

The phone line got real quiet. Next thing I knew, I got the dial tone.

I told Ma what happened.

"That poor child. Postpartum is rough," she said. "Yolanda's probably not getting her any help either. Jesus. We may need to prepare to have the baby for a while, Maverick. Might need to call Cousin Gary and discuss some options."

Maaaan, that fool is the worst. He a lawyer and live in the suburbs with his white wife and their kids. Ask me when he come around the fam? Never. He think we ghetto and want his money. Cornball ass. Don't nobody want his money.

I don't want his help either. Iesha need a little break, that's all. I pray to God I'm right, 'cause it's only been two days, and this boy putting me through it. That first night was hell. He wanted to be held most of the time or else he'd cry, so I basically kept him in my arms. When I put him in his crib, he woke up every hour. That meant I had to wake up and feed him or change his diaper. I never seen so much poop in my life.

Saturday and Sunday, it was the same thing. Crying, pooping, peeing. Crying, pooping, peeing. I'm exhausted after one weekend.

Today finna be real interesting. It's Monday, and Ma going back to work, meaning I gotta take care of my son by myself. At least this weekend Ma was here if I messed up. I told her that and she was like, "Being a parent usually means there's nobody who can come fix things. That's now *your* job."

That's scary as hell.

Ma run around the kitchen, checking the cabinets and

refrigerator as she jot down a list. Dre gotta make some runs for Aunt 'Nita later and offered to take me to the grocery store. We need all kinds of stuff for my son. Of course, Ma thinking of fifty-leven other things she want.

"I'm adding cornmeal to the list, Maverick," Ma says. "Make sure you get the big bag. Moe wants to fry some catfish this weekend. Oh, and get some of that creole seasoning. You know she'll have a fit if there's no creole seasoning."

Ma's best friend, Moe, come over and cook for us sometimes. She can throw down on some catfish. "Yes, ma'am," I say, through a yawn. Li'l Man kept waking up last night. Surprised he asleep now.

"Now, if something comes up today, call me at work," Ma says. "Also Mrs. Wyatt is next door, and your aunt 'Nita is only a phone call away. Your granny told me to tell you she's a call away." Ma shake her head. "That woman's a fool for you."

Granny live out in the country on the family land, thirty minutes away. She'd probably make that a fifteen-minute drive if I called.

I ain't gon' do that to her or nobody else. "I won't need help." I say what a man should. "I got this."

Ma stare at me for a second. She come and kiss my forehead.

"You'll be okay," she murmurs.

Soon, she crank her car up in the driveway. The engine hum and hum till it fade away, and I'm all alone with my son.

I peek in on him real quick. I had to move my stereo and all my CDs to fit his crib in my room. Man, that was hard. I got the best CD collection in the neighborhood, bet that. Hundreds of joints. Had them stacked in a tower shelf in alphabetical order. Now they scattered over the dining room table.

All that for Li'l Man. He knocked out in his crib with his arms stretched above his head. His eyebrows wrinkled like they always be. I think he dream of ways to solve all the problems in the world.

I watch him for a minute. Tired as I am, I love him more than I can say. It's kinda wild, since I only really known him for a few days. I turn on Andreanna's old baby monitor and give his forehead a kiss like Ma gave me.

I throw myself across the living room couch. I think the hardest part of all of this is not knowing when it's gon' end. Either Iesha gon' come get our son or he'll chill the hell out. School start the week after next, and the thought of going there while dealing with him don't seem possible.

I grab the cordless phone. I kinda wanna call Lisa since we didn't talk all weekend, but that might mean telling her what's going on. Instead, I dial King's beeper. I need to holla at him 'bout this drug situation, plus I wanna make sure we cool. He gotta know the baby mine by now.

I page him. Knowing King, it'll take a while before he get back to me. I stretch out on the couch and pull Ma's throw blanket over me. Right as I start to fall asleep, the phone ring.

I can't catch a damn break. I snatch it off the coffee table. "Hello?"

"Hello!" an automated voice says. "You have a collect call from—"

"Adonis," his voice cut in.

I sit up. Pops never call in the morning. Only in the evenings when Ma home. Something gotta be wrong. I press *1* to accept the call. "Pops?"

"Hey, Mav Man!" Somehow his voice always light when he talk to me, like he on a business trip and not in prison. "What mess your momma cook today?"

I crack up. Pops swear he a better cook than Ma. He is, honestly. His biscuits so legendary, I dream of them mugs. "Nothing this morning. You a'ight? What you doing calling this early?"

"I'm fine. Got some calling time and decided to take advantage of it. Is Faye there?"

"Nah, she just left for work," I say.

"Damn, I should've known. How she doing? She not working too much, is she?"

"She all right. You know she off on weekends now. Moe convinced her to take them off."

"Moe." The way Pops say her name kinda throw me off. They never met. Ma and Moe ain't become friends till a year or two after he went away. "Guess I'm glad somebody convinced her to take time off," he says. "Anyway, how you doing? What was you up to this weekend?"

Last time we talked I was waiting on the DNA test results. I told Pops the baby wasn't mine, and he took my word like he always do. Now I gotta tell him he a grandfather.

"Umm . . ." It's real hard to speak all of a sudden. "I was taking care of my son."

The phone get extra quiet. The call ain't dropped—there's voices in the background.

"Damn," Pops says. "Well, it is what it is. How you handling it?"

I rub my eyes. I ain't sure if they burning 'cause they tired or I'm relieved Pops ain't coming down on me. That ain't really his style no way. Whenever Ma is pissed, I can always count on Pops to hear me out.

"I don't know how I'm handling it," I admit. "He cry all the time, barely sleep, always need a diaper change or a bottle. It's a lot, Pops. I'm ready to crack after one weekend."

"Oh yeah. I remember them days. He pissed in your face yet?"

"Maaan," I groan as Pops laugh. "A couple of times."

"Good. It's payback for all them times you pissed in *my* face. You'll be okay, Mav Man. You gotta find your groove. Don't get me wrong, it won't be easy. Everybody gon' have an opinion 'bout how you do things. What I always tell you? Living your life based off what other people think—"

"Ain't living at all," I finish.

"You damn straight. Let 'em talk. Long as you take care of yours, that's all that matters, you feel me?"

"I feel you."

"Damn. A grandson," he says, in awe. "What's his name?"

"Iesha named him King since she thought that was his daddy."

"Aw nah, man. You gotta change it," Pops says. "Zeke named King that in honor of the set. I got nothing against it or your homeboy, but your son oughta have something of his own. A name with purpose. I was real mindful when I named you. Maverick Malcolm Carter."

Maverick mean "independent thinker." Malcolm come from Malcolm X. Guess Pops wanted me to be a leader from jump.

"Don't throw something on your son," Pops go on. "Give him a name that tells him who he is and who he can be. The world's gon' try to do that enough."

Dang, I'll have to think it out. "Yeah, a'ight."

"Man. If I was home, I'd be the freshest granddaddy you ever saw. Have my little buddy riding around in the drop-top. Make sure you put him onto the Lakers ASAP."

Pops a fool for the Lakers. He worshipped Magic and Kareem back in the day. He made sure I was a fan. "Fa'sho. I'm gon' get him a jersey soon."

"That's what I'm talking 'bout. They got something special in the making, I can feel it," he says. "That boy Kobe gon' be a force. Mark my words."

For a moment, we just father and son, talking basketball. Pops don't feel a world away. "You think we'll get a championship?"

"A couple of championships," Pops says. "Kobe and Shaq gon' ball out, no doubt. How things around the Garden?"

"It's real calm lately. No turf wars or nothing," I say. "The Garden Disciples ain't tripping."

"Good. Shawn, Dre, and them looking out for you?"

I guess that's what Dre call that stunt he pulled. "Yeah. Sometimes they do it too much."

"No such thing. Be glad somebody got your back. You may not always be so lucky."

I got a feeling Dre gon' always be a pain in my ass.

"Well, look, man, my time's up," Pops says. "Make sure you tell Faye I came down real hard on you regarding this baby business, a'ight?"

I laugh. She gon' know I'm lying. "Yeah, a'ight. We'll see you soon."

"Looking forward to it," he says, and I can hear his smile. "Love you, Mav Man."

"Love you too, Pops."

I hang up, and my pops is a world away again.

The doorbell ring. I hop up real fast 'cause I don't want it to wake up Li'l Man. I peek out the front window first like Ma do. It's King.

I greet him with a palm slap. "Damn, man. Didn't expect you to roll through."

He slide in past me. "Phone call's a waste of time. I was around the corner with a customer and figured I'd stop by. What's up?"

What ain't up? Part of me don't know how to start any of this conversation. I stick my hands in my pockets. "Iesha holla'ed at you yet?"

King plop down on my couch and prop his feet on the table. Mi casa always been his casa. "Yeah, she told me. Where your Sega controller? I'm tryna play some *Mortal Kombat*."

"Man, look, I'm sorry, a'ight?" I say. "I thought fa'sho Li'l Man was yours."

"I told you shit happens. It's all good."

"You sure? You named him after yourself. I could see how this might make you feel—"

"Gah-lee, Mav! You sound like a female. Chill. I ain't stressing that girl or her baby." He pull my Sega Genesis controller from between the couch cushions. "Less for me to have to worry with."

"A'ight. Long as we cool."

"For life, homie." He hold his palm out to me.

I slap it. "Fa'sho, except for when you rooting for the sorry-ass Cowboys."

"Take your hating ass on somewhere." King laughs. "Like the Saints gon' do shit. My Cowboys gon' whoop them like I'm gon' whoop you on this game."

"You wish. I need to holla at you 'bout something else."

King blow into my *Mortal Kombat* cartridge in case it don't wanna act right and put it in the Sega Genesis. "What's up?"

Li'l Man wail in my room before I can speak. "Shit," I hiss. "Hold on."

Ma claim that one day I'll be able to decipher his cries. Today ain't that day. She told me to always check his diaper first thing. It's clean, so he must want a bottle. Ma made a couple before she went to work. She think I pour too much formula. For somebody who claim that my baby is *my* responsibility, she help out a lot. I ain't complaining. I rush to the kitchen, grab a bottle outta the refrigerator, and go scoop Li'l Man outta the crib.

It ain't easy to feed a crying baby. It's like he so hungry he mad, and he so mad he don't wanna let me hold him with all the squirming he doing.

"Chill, man," I tell him. I don't know how I get the bottle in his mouth. At first he don't latch on to it, and I'm two seconds away from calling Ma at work.

Finally, he start eating.

"Man," I sigh. "You love to stress me out, huh?"

I carefully walk toward the living room and sit on the couch with him.

King play my Sega, keeping his eyes on the TV. "Iesha left him with you?"

"Yeah. Said she needed a break."

"Oh." That's all King say at first. Then, "You gotta feed him within like a minute of him waking up or he'll act a fool."

"What?"

"I used to go over and help Iesha with him."

"Oh."

We quiet for a moment.

King look over at me and Li'l Man. "Yeah," he says. "He do look like you."

King can say it's all good if he want, but there's this look in his eyes that got me thinking otherwise. "Dawg, I'm sorry."

He focus on the TV again. "Told you, it's all good. At least with you he got a family, you know?"

"King, man—"

"You said you wanted to holla at me 'bout something else?"

I hate this situation, for real. I clear my throat. "Yeah, umm . . . I can't sling with you no more."

He do a double take. "What? Why?"

"Dre figured out what we up to."

King hop up. "What the hell? You told him?"

"Nah! I wouldn't do that. Dre figured it out on his own and convinced you involved. He want me to quit."

"Let me guess, he only want you selling weed for him and Shawn for pennies."

"Nah, man. He want me to quit drug dealing period. Said if I don't, he'll rat you out to Shawn."

"So? I can't believe you letting him punk you."

"I was tryna look out for you!"

"I don't need nobody to look out for me! All I need is this money! Don't you?"

Our arguing make Li'l Man fuss. I rock him a bit. "Of course, but I don't wanna get in trouble. Dre threatened to tell my parents, King."

"So you gon' leave me hanging?"

"Man, you know it ain't like that. I'm saying you oughta consider dropping your side—"

"I ain't dropping shit!" King says. "Mav, we could find a way to do this if we work together. You really gon' let Dre and them get in the way of your money?"

It ain't Dre I'm worried 'bout. If Ma find out I sell drugs, I might not see another day.

"I'm sorry, King," I say. "I'm out."

He glare at the ceiling like he could cuss. "Man, fine," he says. "You do you, but I ain't quitting. They can come at me, I ain't scared."

I swear, King never give a you-know-what. I think I care more 'bout him than he care 'bout himself. "I won't tell them. Hold on, I'll get my stash. Can you—" I motion at my son.

"Yeah, I'll hold him," King says.

I place him in King's arms. Li'l Man whimper at first, but King bounce him and shush him. He probably done this before.

I go to the bathroom. Ma made it my job to keep it clean

every week, making me the only one who go under the cabinet. I get down on the floor to look under there real good and move around the cleaning supplies. They help hide the space in the back between the wall and the pipe that's just big enough for me to slide a Ziploc bag of drugs into.

I take it out, go to the living room, and I give it to King. He give me my son in return.

"We cool?" I ask.

"Yeah," he says. "Even if you is acting like a li'l punk right now."

"Fool, you have met my momma, right? I got good reason to be scared."

"Yeah, yeah, yeah. I'll holla at you later. I got work to do." He look at my son. "Take care of him, a'ight?"

I nod.

King hold out his fist, and I dap him up. Then he gone.

FIVE

Dre swing by the house around noon to take me and Li'l Man to the store.

His ride fly as hell. It's a '94 BMW, but Dre keep it so on point it look like a '98 or a '99. He found it at a salvage yard and fixed it up himself. Added candy paint, twenty-inch rims, and a sound system in the trunk. Oooh-wee! I can't front: I like to be seen in it.

Dre help me get my son's car seat situated—I don't know what the hell I'm doing—and we head to Mr. Wyatt's grocery store. It's around the corner, on Marigold. Dre roll all the windows down, lean back in his seat, and drive with one hand. He nod along to that "1st of tha Month" joint by Bone Thugs-N-Harmony that's playing on the radio.

I'm too tired to nod along. Right after King left, I put my

son back to bed and tried to get a nap. Couldn't for thinking 'bout that conversation with King.

Dre glance over at me. "You good, cuz?"

I rest my head back. "King rolled through earlier. I told him what you said."

"How'd that go?"

"How you think it went? He was pissed, but he said he'd stop," I lie. I gotta look out for my boy.

Dre nod. "Good. That's all that's bothering you?"

"Dawg, when did Andreanna start sleeping good?"

He laughs. "Don't tell me you worn out already."

"Hell yeah. I ain't sleep worth shit this weekend."

"Come with the territory, playboy. Be glad you got nothing else to do, like school. You told Shorty 'bout him yet?"

He mean Lisa. My baby only five two, but she ball like she six feet.

I twist one of my cornrows at the root. Last week, I sat between Lisa's legs on her front porch as she braided me up. Fireflies flashed around us, and cicadas hit high notes. It was the kinda peace I needed.

"Nah," I say. "I haven't had a chance to go over there. I can't tell her on the phone."

"You gotta tell her or the streets will."

"Ain't nobody finna tell her."

"Shiiiid, a'ight," he says. "Put it off if you wanna. It's gon' bite you in the ass."

He act like this gon' be easy. Lisa gon' be hurt, for real. It don't matter that we weren't together when I messed with Iesha. I messed with Iesha, period. "I ain't ready to break her heart, Dre."

"It'll hurt her more if she hear it from somebody else. Take it from me. After some of the stuff I did, I'm lucky Keisha deal with me now."

Dre been with Keisha since around seventh grade. Hard to imagine them not together. "Man, get outta here. Y'all stuck with each other."

He laughs. "I hope you right. I'm more than ready to make it official."

"Still can't believe you getting *married*." The word don't feel right coming outta my mouth. "I love Lisa, but I can't imagine letting a girl lock me down."

"You say that now. One day, it'll be a whole different story. Watch."

"Nope! I'm a playa for life."

Dre crack up. "Yeah, we'll see."

"Hail Mary" by Tupac start on the stereo. That's my joint right there. 'Pac the greatest to ever do it. Hard to believe he been gone almost two years now. I remember when the radio announced he got shot in Vegas. I figured he'd be a'ight—he survived getting shot five times in New York. Dude was invincible. A few days later, he was dead.

At least that's what they said. "Yo, did you hear? 'Pac alive."

Dre laugh. "Get outta here! Next you gon' tell me the world ending in the year 2000."

People already bugging over this Y2K stuff, saying the year 2000 gon' bring the apocalypse. We gotta make it through '98 first.

"I don't know if that's true," I admit. "They said on the radio that 'Pac living in Cuba with his auntie Assata. The government had a hit on him."

"C'mon, Mav. Bill Clinton wouldn't put a hit on 'Pac."

Ma say Bill Clinton the closest thing we may ever get to a Black president.

"Shiid, I don't know, man. 'Pac's family full of Black Panthers, and he spoke so much truth. Word is he'll come back in 2003."

"Why 2003?" Dre says.

"It's seven years after he faked his death," I say. "'Pac got all these connections to the number seven. He was shot on the seventh. He died seven days after that, exactly seven months to the day that *All Eyez on Me* dropped."

"That's a coincidence, Mav."

"Hear me out! He died at 4:03 p.m. Four plus three is seven. He was born on the sixteenth. One plus six, seven."

Dre rub his chin. "He was also twenty-five when he died."

"Right! Two plus five, seven. Then the name of his last album. That Makaveli joint."

"*The Seven Day Theory*," says Dre.

"Exactly! I'm telling you, he planned this."

"Okay, let's say he did," Dre says. "Why he focus on the number seven?"

"Apparently, it's a holy number, I don't know." I shrug. "I'll have to look more into that."

"Okay. Well, I'll admit it, all that do seem planned out. But 'Pac not alive, Mav."

"You said it seemed planned out."

"Yeah, but only cowards hide and fake their deaths. 'Pac wasn't a coward. I don't care if the government wanted him dead, he would've gone out in a blaze of glory."

True that. 'Pac was the definition of a rider. He wouldn't be hiding from nobody.

"A'ight, you got me there."

Dre pull into the store parking lot. Wyatt's Grocery 'bout as old as the Garden. Granny used to send Ma in here when she was a kid, back when Mr. Wyatt's pops ran it. You can buy everything from fresh vegetables to dishwashing liquid.

Dre help me figure out the stroller—why everything with babies so damn complicated?—and I push my son into the store. For a spot in the hood, Wyatt's Grocery is real nice. Mr. Wyatt make sure that the floors always shine and the shelves stay neat.

He at the cash register, bagging up some old lady's groceries. Mrs. Wyatt right beside him, talking to the lady. She retired last year and always in the store nowadays. Except when she across the street, getting her nails done. She keep them painted pink.

Her eyes light up when she see us. "Maverick, you brought the baby!"

Mrs. Wyatt love babies. She and Mr. Wyatt used to be foster parents, and they'd get babies and kids all the time. I always had somebody to play with thanks to them.

Mrs. Wyatt come bend down to look in the stroller. "Chile, you couldn't deny this boy if you tried. He look *just* like you."

"Yep," Dre says. "Even got Mav's big apple head."

"Man, shut up!" I say.

Mrs. Wyatt laughs. "Be nice, Andre." She grunt as she pick Li'l Man up. "Ooh Lord, you a big boy. They feeding you good, huh?"

"I'm in here to buy formula now," I say.

"I see why." Mrs. Wyatt smiles at him. He give her a gummy grin right back. "Faye told us you're taking care of him by yourself today. Everything okay so far?"

Leave it to Ma to give the Wyatts a heads-up. They been our next-door neighbors so long that they family. "Yes, ma'am. I got it."

Mr. Wyatt says goodbye to the other customer and make his way over to us. He got this thick mustache, and he always wearing some kinda hat. I think he losing his hair. Today he got on a straw hat to cover it.

"Careful, Shirley," he says. "Hold him too long, and you'll get baby fever."

"There's nothing wrong with that. Ain't that right, baby?" She kiss Li'l Man's cheek.

Mr. Wyatt grab my shoulder firmly. "You not putting this baby off on your momma, are you, son?"

"No, sir," I say. It's always "yes, sir; no, sir," to Mr. Wyatt. He drilled that in my head since I was little. "I'm handling it."

"Good. You made him, you take care of him. School starts soon, right? You ready? Don't let having a baby make you drop the ball on that."

"Clarence, let the boy breathe," Mrs. Wyatt says.

He'll never do that. Mr. Wyatt stay on my back. As much as he gets on my nerves, I know he care. I remember when the Feds took down Pops. It was straight chaos in our house. Cops everywhere with guns. They made my folks lie on the floor, and an officer escorted me outside. I cried for Ma and Pops, begged the cops to let them go. They almost put me in a car to take me somewhere. Mr. Wyatt came outside and talked to them. Next thing I knew, he put his arm around my shoulder and took me to his house. He and Mrs. Wyatt kept me till the cops cleared Ma that evening.

"Breathe nothing. He's got responsibilities now," Mr. Wyatt says, his eyes set on me. "You need to take care of this baby financially. What you plan on doing jobwise?"

"He actually looking for a job," Dre butt in. "You know anybody hiring, Mr. Wyatt?"

"As a matter of fact, I am. My nephew, Jamal, had to cut his hours down to part-time due to his schedule at the community college. I'm looking for someone to fill in the gaps."

I see where this going, and aw hell nah. Mr. Wyatt stay on my back now as my neighbor. I become his employee? Man, I won't be able to do shit without him watching. "That's okay, Mr. Wyatt."

"What? You got something else lined up?"

"Nah—no, sir. I uhhh . . . I know you can't pay me a whole lot."

"I can pay you the same thing them other jobs would," he says. "What's the problem?"

"Nothing," says Dre. "That sound good, don't it, Mav?"

I swear to God if he don't shut the hell—

"If you're worried about childcare, I can help with that," Mrs. Wyatt offers. "I wouldn't mind keeping the baby during the day."

"For a fee," Mr. Wyatt adds. "Nothing's free around here."

"Clarence!" Mrs. Wyatt scolds.

"Well, it ain't! He's gotta learn that now."

"I'm good, Mrs. Wyatt," I say. "Li'l Man gon' be back with his momma soon." I hope.

"All right," Mr. Wyatt says. "It's not childcare, and it's not the pay. What's the problem?"

"There's not a problem," Dre says. "Mav will take it."

What the—like hell I will.

Mr. Wyatt fold his arms. "He's got a mouth, Andre. I wanna hear from him. Maverick, do you want the job?"

Hell no.

On the other hand . . . I *do* need something now that Dre made me stop slinging. I can't leave all them bills plus my son on Ma.

Goddamn. Guess I gotta man up. "Yeah. I'll take it."

"Good," Mr. Wyatt says. "You can start the same day that school starts. Four hours after school, all day on Saturdays, and off on Sundays. Jamal handles things then. Some days you'll work here in the store. Other days, in my garden. I don't tolerate foolishness, and I don't tolerate gang drama."

Mr. Wyatt know we claim King Lords. It's pretty normal around here, messed up as that is.

Dre drape his arm around my shoulder. "He won't bring any foolishness or drama, Mr. Wyatt."

I shake his traitor ass off. "I'm gon' go get my stuff," I mumble.

Mrs. Wyatt offer to watch my son while I shop. I grab a cart and give it a shove down the aisle as hard as I wanna shove Dre. He come up behind me, talking 'bout, "You a'ight?"

"Hell nah," I hiss, and turn on him. We far enough that the Wyatts won't hear. "You know what you got me into?"

"Dawg, it's a job! A job that your ass *needs*. Long as you do what you supposed to do, you'll be a'ight. Besides, Mr. Wyatt ain't that bad."

"Says who?"

"It could be worse. You could be working for Mr. Lewis."

True that. Mr. Lewis the barber next door, and that man

the definition of pain in the ass.

"You said you wanna help Auntie Faye out," Dre go on. "This a good way to do it. Men do what they gotta do, and it's time to man up, remember?"

I hate when this fool right. "Yeah. A'ight."

He hold his palm out, and I slap it. "C'mon, let's get these groceries, starting with some toothpaste," Dre says. "'Cause your breath is kicking!"

I give him a middle finger. He go off down the aisle, cracking up.

I get everything on Ma's list. It take all the money I have left after buying Lisa's necklace. I ask Mr. Wyatt for an employee discount. He look at me like I spoke another language. I don't get a discount.

Dre push the shopping cart toward the door, and I push my son's stroller. Li'l Man is knocked out after Mrs. Wyatt worked her magic. I almost wanna beg her to put him to bed tonight.

Before Dre can open the door, somebody on the other side do it for him. I freeze.

It's Tammy, Lisa's best friend.

Tammy's momma, Ms. Rosalie, is right behind her. She give us a bright smile. "Hey, Maverick and Dre! How are y'all—"

She notice the stroller and the baby sleeping inside of it, and her eyes get big. Tammy's eyes already wide.

Dre said it would bite me in the ass if I didn't tell Lisa. This feel like my ass getting put on the platter.

I clear my throat. "We good, Ms. Rosalie. How y'all doing?"

They exchange looks, and I swear they talking without talking. "We're fine, baby," Ms. Rosalie says. "Came to pick up a couple of things."

Tammy eye me like a damn detective. "Whose baby?"

Aw, shit.

"Uh, we gotta bounce." Dre come through with the save. "Y'all have a good one."

"You too," says Ms. Rosalie.

Tammy make this sound like she sucking something from between her teeth. I ain't gotta say the baby is mine. She know.

I follow Dre out the door, heart pounding in my ears. I wonder if that's really a ticking bomb I hear. It ain't a matter of if Tammy gon' tell Lisa, it's *when*. And when she do . . .

Shit gon' blow up.

I gotta talk to Lisa. Now.

SIX

Dre agree to drop me off at Lisa's house. He gon' drive around with Li'l Man for a bit 'cause car rides apparently help babies sleep. The time it take my son to nap is around the time it'll take for me to break Lisa's heart.

We pull up at a peach-colored house with a fence around it. Lisa live in one of the nicest houses on the west side. Her momma keep the yard on point. Step on her grass, she'll cuss you out. That's probably why she put the fence up. Let her tell it, she got it to keep "mannish boys" out. She said it while looking at me.

Her car ain't in the driveway. Carlos's hooptie is, unfortunately. Don't matter, I gotta do this. I go up the walkway, onto the porch, and I ring the doorbell.

Carlos answer, and lean against the doorway. He got some

height on me and bigger, like he lift weights on the regular. He used to be on the Saint Mary's wrestling team. That don't scare me. I'll take him down if I have to.

He fold his arms. "May I help you?" he asks dryly.

Here we go. "Is Lisa here?"

"Maybe."

"Can you let her know I'm here?"

"Maybe."

This dude get on my nerves. "Look, Carlton," I say, 'cause aside from the height and the muscles, his corny ass is Carlton from *The Fresh Prince*. "Go get Lisa."

"Oh, somebody's got jokes," he says. "Here's one for you: kiss my—"

"Car-los!" Lisa whine, and shove him aside. She pull me into the house. "You're always instigating!"

"Excuse me, where are you taking him?" Carlos asks.

"To my room."

"Like hell you are."

Lisa whirl on him. "I'm sorry, I didn't know you were my father."

"I'm—"

"Going back to your movie and staying outta my business," she says. "All right? Mmmkay."

I smirk at him as she pull me down the hall. Their house smell like potpourri and look like it with all the flowered wallpaper Lisa's momma got up. Lisa take me to her room and close the door, like she dare Carlos to say something.

I laugh. "He getting on your nerves?"

"That's always."

I hold her hips. It's hard to see them in the FUBU football jersey she got on—it's too big and covers them li'l shorts she wearing. She stand on her tiptoes and kiss me, and I forget what I'm here to tell her.

Till I start thinking 'bout Tammy. I pull back from Lisa.

Her eyebrows meet. "What's wrong?"

"Your brother might be listening in. Can't have him hearing us."

"You're probably right." Lisa lay across her bed. "So, you're not grounded anymore?"

I move this stuffed Hello Kitty she got and sit beside her. Lisa love that cat. It's all over her room, along with posters of Usher and Ginuwine, her "boos." She need to take them shits down, for real. "Yeah. My bad that we couldn't hang out."

"It's okay. Tammy came over and redid my braids. My schedule's gonna be nuts, and I don't wanna deal with getting my hair done every week."

I lie beside her. I know I gotta talk to her, but right now I wanna hear 'bout normal stuff in her normal life. "Why your schedule gon' be nuts?"

"Besides basketball I have both school paper and the yearbook committee. Momma thinks it'll look good on my college applications to show that I'm more than an athlete. Going to college means finally getting outta this house, so I am totally on board. Hope I actually get some acceptance letters."

"Don't worry. All them schools gon' love you like I do." I kiss her cheek.

"You always know what to say." She trail her fingers along my cornrows. That one little move got me thinking of things we could do if Carlos wasn't here. I miss what she say.

"Huh?"

"I said you should join some clubs at your school," Lisa says. "It would look good on your applications."

"Um . . . college may not be for me, Lisa."

"I told you, you don't need perfect grades for college, Mav. Plenty of people get in with Bs and Cs. I can see you now, joining a fraternity and repping it as hard as you rep King Lords."

It trips me out how she see this version of me that most people don't. She can actually imagine me at college. Sometimes it's hard for me to imagine that. Especially now.

I sit up.

"What's wrong?" Lisa asks.

I'm imagining a life for her. She gon' be one of the most popular girls on her college campus and gon' go to all the parties. Somehow she'll keep her grades in check as she work toward becoming a pediatrician. Some college boy will scoop her up. She'll marry him and live in a big-ass mansion with a couple of kids. I'll be a memory from when she was a kid.

She sit up. "Maverick, for real, what's wrong?"

I need a little more time with her. I kiss her neck and make my way to her lips.

She pull away. "Maverick."

I get up and fold my hands on top of my head. Shit, I gotta tell her. "I want you to remember that I love you, a'ight? When I did what I did, I wasn't thinking that way."

"O . . . kay," Lisa says slowly. "What did you do?"

"Remember when me and you broke up after Carlos thought he saw me with a girl?"

"Yeah?"

"Well, I was stressed out. I went over to King's crib to clear my head, and . . . he hooked me up with Iesha one time."

"Hooked you . . . ?" Her eyes get big. "You had sex with her?"

"Lisa—" I try to take her hand. She move to the other side of the room. "It was only one time. Me and you weren't together."

"We only broke up for two weeks! What the hell, Maverick?"

"I know, I know. I'm sorry, a'ight? I haven't messed with her or anybody else since."

Lisa hug herself real tight. When she do that, it's like she tryna keep the world away. "Why are you telling me this now?" Her voice so soft it hurt.

I gotta do this. "Iesha had a baby three months ago."

"You gotta be kidding me."

"We . . . we got a DNA test done—"

"Oh my God." She holds her forehead. "Oh my freaking God—"

"He mine."

"Oh my God." Lisa sink to the floor. She look up at me. "You have a baby?"

Man up, I tell myself. "Yeah. I got a son."

"You lied to me," she says.

"I didn't lie—"

"Yes, you did! For weeks, I've asked you what's wrong! You said nothing. You went and got a freaking DNA test done on a baby, and that's nothing?"

"I didn't wanna stress you out! I thought he was King's baby."

"Oh my God. This explains sooooo much. Whenever I run into Iesha and her friends, they laugh at me. Tammy told me I was imagining it. I was right, wasn't I? They were laughing 'cause you played me!"

"I didn't play you!"

"Everybody knew that you slept with another girl except for me!"

"Everybody didn't know," I say.

"Iesha knew! Her friends knew! King knew! I bet Dre knew, didn't he?"

I can't respond, 'cause they did.

"You know what?" Lisa murmurs. "Maybe my mom and my brother are right about you."

"What?"

Lisa look me dead in the eye. Hers are filled with tears. "Get out."

"Lisa—"

"Get out!" she yells.

The door fly open, and Carlos rush in. "She said leave!"

"Man, mind your goddamn business!"

"She *is* my business!"

"Carlos, stop," Lisa says softly. "He's not worth it."

It hit like a gunshot. That's the worst thing she ever said 'bout me.

Carlos eye me, and he smirk. He finally got what he wanted.

"You heard her," he says. "Go."

Lisa wipe tears from her cheeks. I wish I could wipe them away myself. More than that, I wish I could kick my own ass for making her cry.

Instead, I do what she asked. I leave.

SEVEN

Two days go by, and Lisa won't talk to me.

Three days.

A week.

Two whole weeks, and I don't exist to her.

This time different. Usually when Lisa mad, she hang up when I call. Nah, she done blocked my number. I went over one day, hoping she had cooled off. Her momma's car was gone and so was Carlos's. I heard the TV inside, and I know I caught a glimpse of Lisa in the window. No matter how many times I rang the doorbell she never answered.

This shit hurt, man. I'm talking listen-to-sad-R&B-songs-all-day kinda hurt. I done had my Boyz II Men CD on steady rotation. Lisa was my best friend. The one person who could always make me smile and who I wanted to make smile. Call me soft, I don't care. The thought of not having her in my life almost too much to handle.

Ma claim I walk around looking like a sad puppy. I can tell she feel bad for me. All she say is, "You made your bed, now you gotta lie in it."

If this a bed, it's made outta rocks—everything hard. Iesha ain't come and got our son yet. I talked to her twice, and both times she asked me to keep him a little longer. Never said how "long" that is.

In the meantime, Li'l Man got me beyond tired. He ain't cheap neither. I have to buy diapers, wipes, and formula all the time, and my money looking real funny now that I'm out the game. Ma asked the light company for an extension so we could afford a changing table. She talking 'bout working on weekends at the hotel to keep things from being so tight. Dre also a big help. Some days he'll come watch my son for like an hour so I can nap, and he buy clothes for him that I can't afford.

I really hope this job with Mr. Wyatt help. Today gon' be my first day of school and my first day of work. While I ain't really looking forward to work, I ain't been this excited for school since my elementary days. I'm finally getting out this house. On top of that, I get to be with my boys. I ain't seen none of them these past two weeks. They probably busy, I'm not tripping. Not like I got time to hang out. I'll only be with Rico and Junie today though. King got expelled from Garden High last year.

I should be resting up for my long day, but around 2:00 a.m. Li'l Man wake up, screaming his head off.

It scare the shit outta me. I check his diaper first, and it's clean. He can't be hungry, I fed him a little while ago. I run outta ideas real quick, so I take him to Ma's room.

I'm surprised he didn't wake her up. Then again, I think Ma could sleep through a bomb. Her bonnet stick out from under all of her blankets. She keep the air on high in the summer only to sleep under a bunch of covers.

I shake her shoulder. "Ma, wake up."

"What, Maverick?" she mumbles.

"Li'l Man won't stop crying."

Ma pull back the covers and squint at us. My son cry and gnaw on his hand. Drool and tears run down his face.

"He's teething," she says.

"How you know?"

"Trust me, I know." She touch his forehead. "He doesn't have a fever. His gums are probably bothering him. Get him one of those teething rings I bought. He'll calm down."

"What if he don't? I got school in the morning, Ma. I'm tryna sleep."

The look she give me . . . man, she cuss me out with her eyes. "You should've thought of that before you had sex with that girl." She turn her back to us.

"Ma—"

"Take care of your son, Maverick."

Fine, then. I take him to my room and grab the teething ring.

"C'mon, man," I mutter as I put it to his mouth. "Gnaw on it, okay? It'll help you feel better."

He cry around it. I sit on my bed and rock him. I talk in them hushed tones like Ma do and tell him it's okay. Minutes and minutes and minutes pass, and that li'l brown face scrunched up with tears all over it, and that tiny mouth won't stop wailing.

"Please, man?" My voice crack. I only wanna sleep. "I'm tired. Please, calm down."

He cry louder.

"What's wrong with you?" I cry. "Just take the teething ring!"

I shouldn't snap, but I don't know.

I don't know.

I don't know.

I don't know what the hell I'm doing.

I can't make him stop crying.

I can't sleep.

I can't do this.

I set him in his crib as he scream at the top of his li'l lungs, and I walk out the room.

To the hallway.

Then the living room.

And out the front door.

I stop at the porch. It's so quiet and calm outside, unlike

in my room. I sit on the steps, and I bury my face in my hands.

What the hell is wrong with me? I can't get a teeny little baby to stop crying. Then I left him in there by himself when he need me the most.

He need so damn much. I don't wanna be needed no more. I'm tired. I wanna sleep. And now I'm sobbing like a baby as if I ain't got a baby sobbing for me.

I don't know how long I been sitting here when the front door squeak open.

Ma come up behind me, rubbing my shoulder.

I try to suck it up. "I'm sorry."

"All parents have moments," she says softly. "I got him settled and back to sleep. Go get some rest, baby."

Somehow I'm still her baby.

I drag myself back to my room. It feel like I just got back in my bed and closed my eyes when it's time for me to get up for school. My body ache, I'm so tired.

I check on Li'l Man in his crib. He sleep peacefully as he suck on his pacifier. I hope he don't realize I walked out on him. I love him, I swear I do, but it's a lot, man.

I lean in the crib and kiss his forehead. "I'm sorry."

While he sleep, I iron my clothes: Girbaud jeans and a red Polo shirt to go with my white-on-white Reeboks. I'm gon' have to throw a durag over my cornrows. Lisa would go in on me if she saw them all frizzy like this. Would say I better come to her house after school so she could redo them. I'd grin and tell her that's what I hoped for.

I'm all twisted up over her.

Li'l Man still asleep, so I can go eat. I pour a bowl of cereal and watch a little TV. Maybe these *Martin* reruns will help wake me up. Ma stand in the living room doorway, rubbing cocoa butter on her arms. She never leave the house ashy.

"I know you're probably exhausted, but you have to push through today, Maverick," she says. "The first day of school sets the tone for the rest of the year."

Then the rest of the year ain't looking good. I just tell her, "Yes, ma'am."

"Don't go to school with your pants sagging. Don't nobody wanna see your drawers. Hell, I clean them, and I don't wanna see them."

She always say that, and I always wait till she gone to let them sag. "Yes, ma'am."

"Don't be late on your first day of work. Mr. Wyatt was kind enough to give you this job, show him you appreciate it by being prompt."

"Ma, you ain't gotta lecture me, dang."

She set her hand on her hip and tilt her head. That mean *shut up.* I do.

"As I was saying, be prompt," she go on. "Whatever he tells you to do, you do it. Did you pack enough stuff for Mrs. Wyatt for Man-Man?"

I took Mrs. Wyatt up on her offer to watch him. It was

either her or this daycare nearby and they charge way more. "Yes, ma'am. I packed his diaper bag last night."

"Good," Ma says. "See if you can talk to Iesha at school. Some conversations are better held face-to-face, and you obviously need some help."

I watch my Froot Loops float in my milk. I know exactly what she getting at. "I'm sorry for last night, Ma."

"I told you, Maverick, all parents have moments. At least now you have a small idea of how Iesha felt. You've had him for two weeks. She took care of him by herself for three months."

I nod. I definitely understand why Iesha need a break.

"You two also need to discuss a new name for the baby, since you don't wanna keep 'King,'" Ma says. "We can't call him Man-Man and Li'l Man forever."

"I know. I think I got an idea for a name."

"Oh, really. What?"

"It's gon' sound stupid—"

"If you put thought into it, it's not stupid," she says. "Spill."

I've gone back and forth on this one. After talking to Dre 'bout the Tupac theory, I read up on the meaning of the number seven. Ay, when you awake feeding a baby at night, it's a good time to grab a book. It said that seven represents perfection and that people tend to hold it above all the rest. It gave me a wild idea. "I think I wanna name him Seven."

Ma frowns. "You wanna name him after a *number*?"

"See? You think it's stupid."

"I didn't say it's stupid, Maverick, calm down. I'd like some clarity behind the decision, that's all."

"Oh. Well, seven supposed to be holy and the number of perfection," I say. "I think I wanna make Maverick his middle name. Everybody say he look like me. Since that's the case, I want him to be the best version of me. The perfect Maverick Carter."

"That's not stupid at all," Ma says, with a small smile. "You still need to talk it out with Iesha first."

"I will."

Li'l Man start crying in my room.

"Somebody's awake," Ma says.

I sigh. It's always something. "He probably want his bottle." I got it ready. I also packed his diaper bag and laid his outfit out, including the Air Force 1s Dre bought him. Li'l Man gon' be as fresh as his daddy.

What ain't fresh is the smell that hit me, soon as I walk in my room. I cover my nose. "What the fuck?"

"Watch your mouth!" Ma yells from down the hall.

If she smelled what I smell, she'd be cussing too. I inch over to the crib, and Li'l Man all squirmy. That smell come straight from his diaper.

"Ma! C'mere!"

"What, Mav—" That smell hit her. She cover her nose. "Seems like you got a problem."

"You won't help?"

"You don't need me to help you with a diaper."

This not a regular diaper. "Ma—"

She go toward her room. "You can handle it, Maverick."

This "tough love" shit she do is whack.

I pick my son up, and I swear I almost drop him. What's in the diaper don't stay in the diaper. It end up on my Polo, my jeans, and my Reeboks.

"Shit, man!" I yell. "Shit!"

Li'l Man cry even more. I can't tell him it's a'ight when I wanna cry myself. "Ma!"

"Maverick, handle it! I gotta go to work!"

"I gotta go to school!"

"Then you better hurry up!"

Goddamn, man. I clean my son and bathe him. After what I see I never wanna change another diaper in my life. I change outta my outfit and throw on some wrinkled clothes. I put on my new Jordans so at least my shoes fly. Ma leave for work. I put Li'l Man in his car seat, throw on my backpack, grab the diaper bag, lock up the house, and rush next door.

Mrs. Wyatt waiting on the porch. She laugh at the sight of me. "Tough morning?"

I give her the diaper bag and the car seat. "Oh yeah. I think he teething. He had a bad accident a li'l while ago. I packed a bunch of diapers, baby wipes, and clothes. I didn't have a chance to give him his bottle—"

She set the car seat down and pick Li'l Man up. "I've got it, baby. You hurry on to school now."

I'm stuck. Ever since I got my son, we haven't been apart. I already feel bad as shit for walking out on him last night. What if he think I'm leaving him like his momma did?

"He'll be fine, Maverick," she says.

"A'ight," I tell her and myself. That boy got me tripping. I kiss his forehead. "Daddy love you, man. I'll see you later."

Mrs. Wyatt lift his hand to wave at me. By the time I get to the end of the block, they gone inside.

As hard as it was to leave him, this relieved feeling come over me. For the next few hours I ain't gotta change a diaper or fix a bottle. I ain't gotta try to figure out why a tiny baby crying for what seem like the hundredth time.

I'm free.

It take around fifteen minutes for me to get to school. I have to pass by Aunt 'Nita and Uncle Ray's house on the way there. Dre wash his ride in the driveway as his pit bull, Blu, lie in the grass and watch. Dre had that dog for a couple of years now. Some pit owners like to put them in fights around the neighborhood for money. Not Dre. He treat Blu like he treat Andreanna.

I got enough time to stop by for a quick minute. Blu notice me coming up the walkway before Dre do. He bark and try to break free from his chain. Once I'm close enough, he jump all over me.

"Whaddup, cuz?" I say to Dre.

He wipe his windows with a towel. "Whaddup? Ready for the first day of school?"

"I guess." Blu climb up my legs and sniff at my pockets.

"Chill, boy. I don't got snacks today."

Dre look at me. "Hold up. You showing up for the first day of school like *that*? I know crackheads who iron their clothes, Mav."

Nobody roast you like your own family. Nobody. "Forget you. I had a fresh outfit till Li'l Man shitted on me."

Dre bust out laughing. Fool sound like one of the hyenas from *The Lion King*. "He showing you who in charge, huh?"

"Who you telling?" I get quiet as I scratch behind Blu's ears. "I walked out on him last night, Dre."

"Who? Your son?"

I nod. "He wouldn't stop—I didn't know how to make him stop crying, man, and I was tired and—" I shake my head at myself. "I walked out the house and left him crying."

"Did you go back?"

I look up at him. "Of course I did."

"That's what matters," Dre says. "Parenting is hard, cuz. You gon' break sometimes. The most important thing is that you pull yourself together and go back, playboy."

"A'ight, Oprah," I say, and straighten up. "I better get outta here 'fore I'm late to school."

"Hold up." Dre come over to me. He slip his gold chain from his neck and drape it over mine, then he slide his gold watch off and clasp it on my wrist. The watch used to be our granddaddy's. He gave it to Dre before he died. "There. That'll make you a li'l bit fly. Bring my shit back tomorrow, I ain't playing."

I crack a smile. "I owe you."

"Focus on them grades, that's all you gotta do for me. You bet' not get in trouble either, or I'll roll through. Now get outta here."

"A'ight, a'ight," I say as he push me toward the sidewalk. "Holla at you later."

Garden High is really named Jefferson Davis High School, but people rarely call it that. I researched that man and nothing need to be named after him. He was a slave owner and the president of the Confederate states. Garden Heights always been mostly Black, and I figure whoever named the school after him did it as a middle finger to all of us, like they calling us slaves.

Fuck that, and fuck Jefferson Davis.

I climb the front stairs of the school. Since my first day freshman year, I've had one goal—graduate and get up outta here. I figure I been in school this long. It would be stupid to not walk away from it all with *something*. Just gotta pass my classes, stay outta trouble, and be done with it. Then I can focus on important stuff, like making money.

The hallways mad packed, and it's obvious it's the first day. Everybody else look like they came from the mall and from getting their hair done. Li'l Man got me looking like a bum.

People say, "Whaddup, Li'l Don," as I pass them in the halls. I guess I'm popular or whatever. This one dude mean-mug the shit outta me though. I think his name is Ant. That green bandana hanging from his back pocket tell everybody he a Garden Disciple. This the only high school in the neighborhood, so King Lords and GDs all go here, and stuff always pop off.

I don't know why this dude staring me down, and I really don't wanna get into nothing on the first day. I keep it moving till he call out, "Tell your bitch-ass cousin to watch his back."

I turn around. "What?"

Ant close in on me. His name make sense—he short as hell. It's always the short ones who instigate, on some Napoleon shit.

"I said tell your bitch-ass cousin to watch his back. He got some nerve coming to the east side with that racing shit and making money on our turf."

Dre love to race his car for money. Usually he only do it on the west side. Said the east too risky, being GD territory and all.

It ain't against the codes for him to race over there, and I ain't finna let nobody come at my cousin.

"He can race wherever the hell he wanna. We run the Garden, fool."

"Y'all don't run shit!"

"Ayooooo!" Junie come up behind me. We been cool since kindergarten, and he claim gray. "We got a problem here?"

Rico with him, and suddenly it's three King Lords versus one Garden Disciple. Ant outsized too. Junie almost seven feet tall—college basketball recruiters love that. Rico built like a linebacker; he always been the heaviest kid in class.

Ant back up, glaring me down. "Your cousin better watch his back."

"Can your short ass reach his back?" I ask.

Junie and Rico bust out laughing. Once he gone, we do our handshakes.

"'Preciate it, y'all."

"He really tried it on the first day," Rico says.

"Feet probably dangle from the sidewalk, and he wanna start shit," says Junie. "Them GDs been on one lately."

"Word?" I say.

"Oh yeah. Dawg, remember last weekend?" Rico say to Junie, and they both crack up. "They didn't see it coming!"

I look back and forth between them. "What happened last weekend?"

"You had to be there, Mav," Junie claims. "Some stuff can't be discussed in public, you know?"

"Oh."

"Don't sweat it, my G," says Rico. "You'll be back in the streets before you know it."

"The big homies not tripping 'cause I'm stuck at home, are they?"

"Nope, you good," Junie says. "Shawn and Dre got your back. Not like your ass ever get in trouble no way, *Li'l Don*."

Him and Rico laugh.

"Man, forget you," I say. Some people think I get special

treatment 'cause of my pops. I hate that shit.

"We playing, we playing," Rico says. "How daddy duty going?"

"Rough. This morning he pooped on me. I had to change my whole outfit."

"Hold up. They can poop on you? Was that mentioned in the parenting manual?" Junie asks.

He act like my son is a car. "What manual? I'm learning as I go. It's messed up."

"What's really messed up is these kicks!" Rico bend down to look at my Jordans.

"I know you ain't come to school in these, Mav."

"What's wrong with them?" I ask.

"They fake."

"Nah. I just got these."

"From where?"

"Red." He a hustler who sell stuff out the trunk of his car. I ran into him while I went to get Li'l Man some diapers last week. I agreed to swap some of my video games in exchange for these since I don't got money for kicks. "He hooked me up with them."

"He hooked you up with some fakes," says Rico. "Your Jumpman got a booty crack."

"What?" I yell, as Junie laugh. "You lying!"

I look at them closer, and he right. The Jumpman do got a booty crack.

"Yoooooo," Junie says into his fist. "Mav got ass-crack Jordans!"

"He got them booty-crack Elevens!" Rico says.

They run around in a circle, howling laughing.

I'm gon' whoop Red's ass. "Shut up!"

"A'ight, a'ight, chill, Rico." Junie drape his arm around my shoulder. I shrug him off. "Mav got enough problems. Cut him some slack."

"Yeah, a'ight." Rico hold his fist to me. "We cool?"

I push his hand away. "Hell nah!"

"Dawg, I ain't sell you them shoes. Be mad at Red."

"Trust, I'm gon' take care of him."

The bell ring, and everybody head for class. We take our time going to ours. It's good to be back with my boys, for real. Got me feeling normal again.

"I hate my schedule this year," Junie says. "I got Phillips for homeroom."

"I got him too," I say. Mr. Phillips the history teacher. He at least seventy-five. He yell all the time and get mad over the stupidest stuff.

"Ol' ET-looking ass." Junie throw back some sunflower seeds. "He oughta phone home."

"You know damn well they'd send him back," I say.

Rico brush his hair. Gotta keep his waves on point. "Goddamn! I wanna go home already."

These girls pass us, looking fine as hell in their new 'fits and hairdos. Rico and Junie watch them walk away.

"Forget that, I'm staying," Junie says, and Rico give him dap.

"I'm with you on that," I lie easily. Fine as them girls are, they ain't Lisa. I'm a sucker, for real.

Rico go on his way, and me and Junie go to history class. Mr. Phillips write on the chalkboard as everybody file into the room. It's hot as hell today, and this man in a wool blazer. He real weird, yo.

Iesha's best friend, Lala, run her mouth while sucking her thumb. She got an overbite from always doing that. Usually wherever Lala is, so is Iesha, but I haven't seen Iesha since I got here.

I tap Lala's shoulder. "Ay."

She turn around and roll her eyes. Her blue contacts match her blue weave and her blue outfit. Girl overmatching. "What you want?"

"Is Iesha at school? I need to talk to her."

"Do I look like I'm her babysitter?"

"Why you copping an attitude? I only asked—"

"Mr. Carter!" Phillips shouts. "This is not a social gathering. Take a seat!"

I ain't even said much to that girl.

Whatever. It ain't worth getting into it with him on the first day. I head to the back of the room and take a seat.

* * *

Halfway through the day, I'm dragging myself around.

I fell asleep in US history. It was boring anyway. I'm tired of hearing 'bout all these fucked-up white people who did fucked-up stuff, yet people wanna call them heroes. Phillips talked 'bout how Columbus discovered America, and all I could think was how the hell can you "discover" a place where people already lived?

Funny how that work.

World lit kept me awake. I like books, and we got a long list we'll be reading this year. Mrs. Turner said we'll cover Shakespeare first. His stories the bomb. *Romeo and Juliet* was basically on some gang shit. You could say she was a Queen Lord, and he was a GD. They went out on their own terms like some straight-up Gs.

That one dope class wasn't enough to energize me. I could crash, for real. I go to the library during free period, grab a book, and sit in one of them beanbag chairs in the back. I hold the book in front of my face to hide the fact I'm taking a nap.

The class bell wake me up, and I head to my Spanish class. No sign of Iesha yet. Honestly, she one of them students who only make "guest appearances" at school. It's not a big shocker that she not here.

My pager vibrate in my back pocket. I take it out, and King's number pop up on the screen, followed by three digits—227. That's our code for *Yo, I'm outside.*

When King was a student, the two of us used to sneak off on the first day. It ain't like nothing important happens—teachers spend most of the time telling us what we gon' do the rest of the year. We'd hit up the mall for a couple of hours.

Guess he wanna keep the tradition going even though he expelled. Forget the mall, I wanna sleep. I could crash at King's crib for a while, and maybe that'll energize me enough for work later. That sound way better than going to class.

Getting outta here might be tricky. Ms. Brown the school secretary always watch the doors like a hawk. Today she distracted as Mr. Clark the security guard talk to her. They can't stop smiling. I don't know what that's about and don't care. Long as they don't notice me, I'm good, and they don't. At first.

"Hey!" Clark yells.

I run for it. Clark's feet thump behind me. Everybody know he slow as hell.

I shove the doors open. King sit on the hood of his silver Crown Victoria in front of the school. He see me, and then he see Clark.

"Oh shit!" he says.

King jump in the car, turn the engine on, and throw open the passenger door. I haul tail across the schoolyard. Clark huff and puff behind me.

"Got me sweating like this on the first day," Clark says. "Get your butt back here!"

The second I'm close to the car, I throw myself in. "Go, go, go!"

King peel off. I look back, and Clark bent over on the sidewalk, gasping for air. I think he throw me a middle finger. I don't care. I'm outta there.

EIGHT

At Garden High, King is a legend. If he walked in the building right now, people would act like he Jesus.

Unfortunately, he can't walk into the school. He not allowed on the grounds.

See, King used to be on the football team. He was probably the best defensive end that Garden High ever saw. Problem was he hated his coach. To be honest, everybody hated Coach Stevens. Dude was a straight-up redneck. He didn't throw around the N-word, nah. It was other stuff, like having a Confederate flag on his truck, calling it "heritage." Heritage my ass.

One day last year he told King to wash his car before practice. King told Coach Stevens he wasn't his slave. Coach looked him dead in the face and said, "You are whatever the hell I say you are, boy."

King beat the mess outta him.

I swear I ain't seen nothing like it. King threw blows like Tyson. He got expelled and sent to juvie. Coach Stevens never came back, and now none of us have to deal with his redneck ass. King forever a hero for that.

He crack up as he drive farther from the school. "Clark still can't catch nobody, huh?"

"Hell nah, never. What's up? I haven't seen you in a minute."

"You know how it is," King says. "These streets keep me busy. Had to scoop you up so we chill like we usually do on the first day of school."

"Straight up? I just wanna crash at your crib, dawg. I'm tired as hell."

"What? You trippin'! We gotta hit the mall. You know how we do."

"I don't got it in me, King. I need to rest up before I go to work in a couple of hours."

"*Work?* What kinda work *you* doing?"

"Dre convinced me to take a job with Mr. Wyatt," I say. "I'll be helping him in his store and with his garden."

"Hold on. You walked away from our side hustle to go make pennies for that old man? You may as well work for the police!"

The Wyatts were King's last foster family right before he went to juvie. He always said they were too strict with him.

I shrug. "It's Mr. Wyatt or Mickey D's. I gotta provide for my son somehow."

The car get real quiet. The only sound is the DJ on the radio.

"Everything good with the side hustle?" I ask.

"Yep."

"No problems from Shawn and them?"

"Nah," King says.

Neither of us say anything else for a while. Some Master P joint start on the radio. King's speakers thump it hard.

"You got them new subwoofers installed?" I ask.

"Yep."

"Damn. They sound real nice."

"Fa'sho."

These short answers, the sudden vibe in the car . . . this not us at all. We were cool till I mentioned my son. "We good, man? If the baby stuff bothers you—"

"Goddamn, Mav! How many times I gotta tell you it's all good? Trust me, I'm glad I don't gotta change diapers no more." He laughs. "How Li'l King doing anyway?"

"He fine except he won't let me rest. I'm tryna figure out a new name for him."

King look over at me. "What for?"

"You really gotta ask? It don't make sense for him to have your name when he my son."

"I'm your boy. He can be named after me."

"C'mon, man. Considering the situation, don't you think that would be weird?"

King don't respond.

I sigh. "I don't mean nothing by it—"

"He your kid now, Mav. Do whatever you want," King says as his beeper go off. He take it out and peek at it. "White Boy Aaron want me to hit him up."

White Boy Aaron is this stoner kid who go to Saint Mary's Catholic School. King met him once at a football game, and now he one of King's regulars. When it comes to making money in this drug shit, rich white kids are where it's at.

Only one thing on my mind now: Lisa. That's her school. I could holla at her real quick. What do I say? *I'm sorry?* A million of them mugs wouldn't be enough.

I gotta try, even if it take a million and one apologies. She worth them all.

Saint Mary's is downtown, and a bunch of students in uniforms crowd the sidewalks as they head for the restaurants nearby. Saint Mary's let them leave campus for lunch. Garden High ever do that, half of us might not come back.

King turn into the school parking lot and pull into a spot near the back. I open my door. "Ay, I'm gon' go look for Lisa."

"What? I don't got time for that, Mav."

"Give me ten minutes, King. That's it. I won't go far, I swear."

King stare at something across the parking lot. "You definitely won't. Ain't that your girl right there?"

I follow his eyes. Lisa lean against a car, talking to a blond-haired white boy. He all up on her and got her giggling.

Hold on. I been to'e up, listening to Boyz II Men all day every day, and here she is smiling in some white boy's face?

I go straight over there. "Ay!"

They both look up. "Oh my God," Lisa groans. "What the hell are you doing, Maverick?"

That's what I wanna ask her. But that's a sure way to get cussed out. "We need to talk."

"*Talk?* There's nothing to talk about. Don't you have a son to take care of?"

"Wait, *this* is the asshole who had a baby with another girl?" the blond boy asks.

First off, who the hell is he? Second, why she telling him my business? Third, who the fuck he think he talking to? I step toward him. "Who you calling a asshole?"

He ball his fists like he wanna square up. Man, I'll beat the mess outta this fool.

Lisa put a hand on his chest. "Connor, it's okay. I can handle this."

Connor? She went from me to a white boy named *Connor?* What kinda plain-ass name is that?

"Long as you're sure," Connor says to her while eyeing me. He leave us alone.

Lisa turn to me, and her stank eye is lethal. "Go home, Maverick."

"Nah, man! What you doing all up on him? We *just* broke up."

"Oh, don't even! At least I haven't slept with him and made a baby because I'm stressed."

That hit hard. "I'm sorry, Lisa."

"You're right, you are sorry," she says. "A sorry excuse of a boyfriend. And I was stupid to fall in love with you."

Her voice crack like there's a sob down in her, tryna get out.

Knowing she wanna cry tear me up inside, but ain't nothing worse than hearing she regret loving me. "I'm sorry, Lisa. I swear to God I am. Let me fix this."

"You have a baby with another girl! How do you fix that?"

"I don't know—"

"Leave, Maverick," she says.

"Lisa, please? I promise, I—"

"Leave!"

"Hey!" a deep voice yell out. This tall, dark-skinned dude in a security uniform hurry over. He come up, talking 'bout, "Young man, you're trespassing onto school property."

I try to catch Lisa's eyes for a sign that we got a shot. Something, *anything.*

She won't look at me.

"Fine," I say to her more than the guard. "I'm gone."

I walk away from her, and it honestly feel like I'm walking away from us.

King drive us back to the Garden.

Lisa really done with me. It used to trip me out that a girl like her had feelings for me. Now here I go, doing something stupid and losing her.

"Chin up, Mav," King says. "Don't be letting no female get you like this."

I straighten up. "I'm good. It is what it is."

"No doubt. Keep it moving. Don't give her another thought."

That would be easy if she wasn't the main thing in my head.

We cruise down Magnolia Ave. There's a couple of cars at the old Cedar Lane shopping center. There used to be a grocery store there, but it shut down years ago. Today there's tables set up in the parking lot with clothes, electronics, CDs, and tapes on them. The trunk of an Impala is opened up, revealing even more stuff for sale.

That's Red, the hustler who gave me these booty-crack Jordans.

"Turn around," I tell King.

"What for?"

"I gotta talk to Red. He gave me some fake sneakers in exchange for some of my video games."

"What?" King says. "Aww hell nah. He need to give you your stuff back."

"He better or we gon' have a problem."

King turn into the shopping center parking lot. "Holla at me if you need me. You know I'm always down for whatever."

That's one reason he my boy. "'Preciate it, but I got this."

I hop out the car. Red smile all in this one lady's face as he show her a purse. Bet it's fake. He probably using some weak pickup line to convince her it's real. Red one of them dudes who claim he "pretty" 'cause he got light skin with green eyes and wavy hair. The girls at Garden High love that. Red don't go there; he around twenty-four, twenty-five. He the type that hang around the school and pick up young girls.

"Red!" I call as I cross the parking lot. "Let me holla at you!"

Don't think I miss that "Shit" he hiss. He force a smile, flashing that one gold tooth he got in the front. "Mav! My main man. You good?"

"Hell nah! You gave me some fake Jordans."

That lady he was talking to go, "Fake? Oh, hell no," and walk off.

"Wait, baby! This a misunderstanding," Red call after her. He turn to me and stomp his foot. "Maverick! That ain't the kinda shit you announce! You tryna ruin me?"

"You lucky that's all I'm doing. The Jumpman on these Jordans got a booty crack, Red!"

He put his hands up. "Hey, not my fault. You should've checked them first."

"Dawg, you told me they were real!"

"And?"

This nig . . . "You know what? I done had a bad day and I ain't in the mood. Give me my games back, and we'll keep it moving."

Red look me up and down like I dissed his momma. "All

trades are final, partna. I sold them games already."

"Then give me the money you made off of them."

"I'm not giving you a damn thing! What I look like, a pawn-shop?"

"Give me my money!"

King make his way over. "We got a problem here?"

"King, get your boy," Red says. "I told him all trades are final."

"And I told him he better give me my money!"

"Ay, ay, calm down, Mav," King says with a hand on my chest. "It's all good."

What the— "No it ain't!"

"Red told you trades are final," King says. "Respect that man's policy."

Red smile wide. "Thank you, King! I knew you were a good dude."

What kinda twilight-zone shit is this? "King, what the hell—"

King get this real sneaky grin. "It's okay," he says. "Since Red don't wanna give you no money, we'll make sure he can't make no money."

King flip one of the tables, tossing Red's merchandise to the ground.

"What the hell!" Red yells.

You know what? Fuck it. I grab the other table and do the same thing. CDs, DVDs, and tapes crash onto the concrete. Red cuss like crazy. We run to the car, laughing our asses off.

* * *

I'm fifteen minutes late for my first day of work.

Me and King went to his crib, and I took a nap on his couch. Man, I didn't realize how much I love sleep. One of the best things God ever created. When I woke up, a couple of hours had passed.

King drop me off at the Wyatts' house. Mr. Wyatt told me his nephew would handle the store and I'd be working in the Wyatts' garden today. A wood fence surround the backyard, and Mr. Wyatt tall enough that I spot him over it.

Hope he not mad that I'm late. "Hey, Mr. Wyatt."

"The gate is open," he says.

The Wyatts' backyard is a garden. Flowers, fruits, and vegetables everywhere. There's bird feeders and li'l fountains all around. A stone pathway lead to a gazebo in the middle. Hard to believe something this pretty in our neighborhood.

Mr. Wyatt water some flowers. Mrs. Wyatt bounce Li'l Man on her knee in the gazebo. He laugh with his fist in his mouth as drool run down his arm.

I smile. "Hey, man. How was he, Mrs. Wyatt?"

"Perfectly fine. This boy knows he has a big appetite. He'll be ready for baby food soon."

"Dang. I better work, then, huh?"

She laugh with me. "You got that right."

Mr. Wyatt clear his throat real loud. Mrs. Wyatt stand up. "It's time for this sweetie pie's nap," she says. "Let me get him inside."

She leave me alone with her husband. I think it's on purpose.

"Come here, son," he says.

His tone say more than he do. I make my way over. "Sorry I'm late. I had to stay at school and—"

He spray water over his tomato plants. "Don't let the rest of that lie come outta your mouth. I saw who dropped you off. I know what he's into, and I doubt he only gave you a ride home. What were you doing with him?"

Play it cool, I tell myself. I only took a nap at King's crib, but I left school early. Mr. Wyatt won't be okay with that. "He my friend, Mr. Wyatt. We only hung out."

"I told you I don't tolerate that gang—"

"It wasn't gang related, I promise."

"Why did you lie if that's all y'all were doing?"

"I figured you'd be cool if I said it was a school thing. He picked me up and we hung out. That's it."

Mr. Wyatt nods. "Okay. However, this is your first strike. Three strikes, and you're fired."

See, this what I'm talking 'bout. He so hard on me. "C'mon, Mr. Wyatt. It was only fifteen minutes. You act like I was an hour late."

"It wasn't a life-or-death situation. You were hanging out with your friend and showed up late *on your first day of work*. Then you tried to lie about it."

"I'll make up for it. I'll stay an extra fifteen minutes and—"

"No, you'll stay an extra hour."

I almost cuss. *"An hour?"*

"Yep. For every fifteen minutes you're late, you gotta work an extra hour without the extra pay."

"That ain't fair, man!"

"Who said anything about fair? It's the rules, son, and I make the rules. You've got a problem with it, you're more than welcome to quit."

Shit, I'm tempted to.

Then I think of the light bill Ma couldn't pay and the extra hours she thinking of working to help provide for my son.

Quitting ain't an option. "What you need me to do, Mr. Wyatt?"

"Roll up your sleeves," he says. "We're planting roses today."

The sun go down, and I'm still working in the garden. You'd think once it's dark it wouldn't be so hot, but dang. I'm sweating bullets. I catch a whiff of myself, and I know what Ma mean when she say I "smell like outside."

I dug up plots for the roses. Mr. Wyatt got these big bags of garden soil, and we poured them out. Soil got this almost sweet scent to it. It remind me of when the sun come out after a rainy day, and everything smell fresh, like the whole world took a shower.

We taking a break now as Mr. Wyatt go to get us some water. Mrs. Wyatt came out a little while ago and told me she getting Li'l Man ready for bed. Said he'll be knocked out when I take him home. I appreciate it 'cause I can't imagine dealing with that boy now.

Mr. Wyatt hand me a glass of ice water. "Don't drink fast. Might make you sick."

"Yes, sir," I say, and try to take small sips. I'm thirsty as hell.

He sip his water and wipe his forehead with his arm. "Make sure you put them gloves on before you pick up them rosebushes. Otherwise the thorns will get you."

Bushes? Them things look like twigs. "You only putting roses in this bed?"

"That's the plan. Roses need space to grow. Why you ask?"

He got greens, green beans, tomatoes, strawberries, blueberries—all kinds of fruits and vegetables out here. "Seem like a lot of space to give something you can't eat."

"You might be right," he admits. "I like to be reminded that beauty can come from much of nothing. To me that's the whole point of flowers."

I smack my arm. These mosquitoes ain't playing. "Summer gon' be over soon. You ain't worried they'll die?"

Mr. Wyatt slip on some gardening gloves. "No. We're planting them well before the first frost. That'll give them time to grow some roots before they go dormant. There's a small chance they'll die. Roses, they're fascinating li'l things. Can handle more than folks think. I've had roses in full bloom during an ice storm. They could easily survive without any help. We want them to *thrive*. We'll have to prune them, things like that."

He may as well speak French. "What pruning mean?"

He grunt as he get down on his knees. I'll know I'm old when I start grunting. He set a rosebush in a hole and pack dirt around it. "Pruning means getting rid of what they don't need. Thin canes, dead canes, damaged canes. If it doesn't help them grow—" He does his fingers like they're scissors. "Snip it off. Hand me another bush."

I slip on the gloves and grab one. "Why you call them bushes? They look like twigs."

Mr. Wyatt chuckles. "I suppose it's like the Word says: 'Calleth those things that be not as though they were.' Romans 4:17. Hmm!" His shoulders shiver like he caught a chill. "That's a good one."

Mr. Wyatt is a deacon at Christ Temple Church. He'll throw a scripture into a conversation in a minute. Hope he don't go into one of his mini sermons. We'll be here all night.

He grunt again as he straighten up. "These knees can't handle a lot more of that. Plant the rest of them for me."

I do like he did—set a bush in the hole and pack dirt around it. Then another.

Mr. Wyatt watch me. "Looks like you've got the hang of it. Here I was, thinking you would give me some lip about messing up your clothes."

"Nah. This nothing compared to what I dealt with earlier with my son. He pooped on me before school."

Mr. Wyatt laughs. "Sounds like you had a rough morning."

"Rough day more like it."

"Wanna talk about it?"

I look up at him. Nobody ever really asked me that. "I'm a'ight, Mr. Wyatt."

"I didn't ask if you were. I asked do you wanna talk. I can tell something on your mind."

I been tryna shake Lisa outta my head for hours, and I can't. Like I'll get caught up in something else, then I remember that crack in her voice, and it's all I can think about.

"I saw Lisa earlier," I say. "She refuse to give me another chance."

"Well, this isn't exactly the kinda situation a young lady gets over," Mr. Wyatt says. "Frankly, that's a lot to ask of her."

"I ain't asking her to get over it, Mr. Wyatt. I just want another shot."

"Which would require her getting over it, son," he says. "Have you considered how she feels about all of this?"

"I know she hurt—"

"No, have you really *considered* how she feels? What if the shoe was on the other foot and she had a baby with some other boy? Would you be willing to give her another chance?"

Just imagining it make me a little tight. I'd be pissed, fa'sho. And hurt . . .

The same way she is.

I can't say that to Mr. Wyatt.

I don't have to. "You can't ask her for anything right now, son," he says. "You gotta love people enough to let them go, especially when *you're* the reason they're gone."

I can't say nothing to that either.

He pat my shoulder. "Go 'head and get those other bushes planted. I'm gonna check on my collards."

Mr. Wyatt leave me alone with the twigs. It seem as impossible for them to turn into rosebushes as it is for me and Lisa to get back together.

I grab one and plant it. Unlike me, the roses deserve a chance.

NINE

This job is no joke.

I been working for Mr. Wyatt for a month now. The days I'm in the store are the easiest, 'cause that garden is a lot. I haul bags of fertilizer and pour them out. I get on my hands and knees and yank weeds. I pull fruits and vegetables when they ripe. Saturdays, I cut the Wyatts' grass along with Ma's, and on Sundays I rest up to do it all over again.

So yeah, no joke. The pay, on the other hand, that's a joke.

Maaaan, that first check? Pissed me all the way off. After social security and some mess called FICA, I only had enough to help Ma with the light bill and buy diapers and formula. All that hard work for practically nothing. Ma says it's still a big help, and that's the only reason I ain't quit.

Plus, I gotta admit I like working in the garden. Flowers and plants a trip though. One day everything can be cool with them. You could water them, feed them, and do everything right. The next day, them shits look half dead. I mean goddamn. They switch up on you worse than girls. It's cool when they grow like they should.

They remind me a lot of my son, honestly. See, with plants and babies it's all about survival. Nobody flat-out say that when it comes to babies, but it's the truth. I gotta make sure the plants get everything they need to grow like I gotta do with Seven.

Far as I'm concerned, that's my son's name. I know I'm supposed to talk to Iesha, but she basically MIA. At first, she kept saying she needed a break; straight-up begged me to keep him a little while longer. Then like two weeks ago when I called, her momma said she had moved in with a friend.

"She got tired of my rules and decided she was grown enough to live on her own," Ms. Robinson said. "Fine by me. I have enough to deal with."

I don't got words for that lady right there.

She didn't know who Iesha moved in with. My first thought was King, but nah, he said she wasn't with him. I asked Lala the next day at school. She said it was none of my business. Made me think Iesha told her to keep quiet.

Ma want me to talk to Cousin Gary regarding legal stuff. Nah, man. One day Iesha gon' show up and we'll figure this out.

I hope. 'Cause I don't know how much longer I can do this.

Between work, school, and Seven . . . I'm barely making it. Li'l Man still don't sleep through the night, meaning I don't sleep through the night. Sometimes I drop him off with Mrs. Wyatt, sneak back home, and sleep until it's time to go to work. Ain't no way my first report card gon' be good with all the skipping and sleeping in class I do.

Straight up, school the last thing on my mind lately. Tonight a real good example of that. It's Friday, and instead of tackling my pile of homework, I'm dealing with this pile of laundry my son made. His clothes stay dirty from when he pee, poop, or puke. *My* clothes stay dirty from when he pee, poop, or puke. Boy won't give me a break.

I sort through his stuff on the couch. Ma took extra hours at the hotel this weekend, so it's only me and Li'l Man. He lying in this bouncy seat thing Dre bought. Bugs Bunny got Elmer Fudd looking like a damn fool. Seven real into it, cooing and kicking.

"You going to bed soon, man," I tell him. "You not staying up all night."

I don't talk to him like he a baby. Nah, I talk to him like I talk to anybody else. He understand it, that's why he whining now.

The phone ring on the coffee table. "Stop talking back," I tell Seven as I pick it up. "Hello?"

"Whaddup, fool?" King says. Goodie Mob blast in the background. "What you getting into tonight?"

"All I'm getting into is some laundry, homie."

"Aw nah, Mav. I'm finna hit Magnolia with Junie and Rico. You oughta roll with us and get out that house."

On Friday nights it's like an outdoor nightclub on Magnolia as folks cruise up and down the street, showing off their rims, their paint jobs, and their sound systems. I used to hang with the homies in some parking lot until gunshots sent everybody running.

I miss it. Except the gunshot part, of course. I don't get to chill with my friends no more. Dre the only one who come over. The rest of them not tryna watch me take care of a baby, and I'm too busy to go out. Got me feeling less and less like a King Lord.

I guess this my life now. "I wish I could, King. Ma at work, and I gotta be here with Seven."

"Goddamn! I don't know why I keep asking. Can't you hire a babysitter? You got Mrs. Wyatt right next door."

"She keep him during the week, King. I can't afford to have her keep him no more than that."

"Maybe if you didn't let Dre punk you outta making money, you could," he says.

"I told you, I—"

"Do you, Mav," he says. "You wanna waste away in that house, fine. Holla at you later."

He hang up.

I set the phone down and put my face in my hands. He act

like I don't hang out with him and the homies on purpose. I didn't choose none of this. Trust, I'd give anything to get out this house.

Seven watch me instead of the TV, almost as if he sense something not right. Now I feel guilty as hell.

"Daddy a'ight, man," I say, and pick him up. I could use a break from laundry, and he need tummy time. It's basically where I lay him on his stomach on a blanket. The more he lift his head, the more strength he'll get in his neck. This parenting book said that's real important.

I put Seven on the blanket and get on my hands and knees. "Hey, man." I smile. "Hey."

Seven roll over onto his back, laughing. It don't take much to entertain him. Pops claim I was the same way.

We haven't had a chance to take Seven to meet him yet. It's a three-hour drive one way, and that's a lot with a baby. I mailed Pops some pictures, and he called a day or two later, talking 'bout how much Li'l Man look like me.

I play with Seven on the floor for a while. Eventually he whine and rub his eyes. That's that sleepiness kicking in. Soon as I pick him up, he start crying. He know I'm taking him to bed.

"Ay, stop that," I say. "Sleep a good thing. Trust, I wish I could go to sleep now."

He not hearing me. He cry into my shoulder. He cry the whole time I put him in his pajamas. I stick his pacifier in his mouth; he stop.

I put him in the crib and turn on his mobile. It's got planets and stars on it. "Fussing for nothing." I kiss his forehead. "Night, man. I love you."

I can't be in here when he tryna fall asleep. He'll watch me and stay awake. I take a shower and change for bed. When I peek back in, Seven looking at his mobile all wide-eyed.

This boy. I don't know why he fighting sleep. I go to the living room and plop down on the couch. The pile of laundry and my homework wait for me on the coffee table.

Shit, man. Never thought I'd be spending my Fridays this way. Nights like this used to be the perfect time to invite Lisa over. We'd watch some movies—a'ight, we fool around while some movies played—and eventually head to my room to do the damn thing.

I definitely miss that. I handle things myself, but it's hard, no pun intended. Considering how sex put me in this predicament, I probably need a break.

Still. If me and Lisa were together . . .

I can't think on that. I gotta get this laundry done. I put Seven in his last clean outfit, but damn if my bed ain't calling me.

"C'mon, Mav," I mumble. "Push through."

Just when I make myself pick up one of Seven's onesies, the doorbell ring.

"Shit!" I hiss. Last thing I need is for somebody to disturb Seven. Who the hell coming over this time of night anyway? I peek out the front window.

Dre's car out front. He not.

I open the door. "Dre?"

Nothing. There's a Super Soaker on the porch, one of the bigger ones that you gotta pump water into. Dre love collecting them things.

I go down the steps. "Dre, where you at?"

Nothing.

I pick up the Super Soaker. It's full of water. "Why would he—"

Water blast me in my face.

"Say hello to my little friend!" Dre says, like he Scarface.

He got a big-ass Super Soaker, the kind with the water tank you wear on your back. He spray the hell outta me. Got my shorts and my tank top soaking wet.

"What the hell, dawg?" I yell. "You play too much!"

"Ain't nobody playing, cuz! This is war!"

He spray me again. He never should've left this Super Soaker for me. I spray him dead in his face. We soon got a full-out water-gun war in my front yard. My Super Soaker don't hold nearly as much as his. I end up grabbing the hose.

Dre put his hands up. "A'ight! A'ight! I surrender!"

"You what?" I spray his face again.

He try to block it with his hands. "I surrender! Stop!"

"Drop your shit first!"

"A'ight, a'ight!" He toss his water gun.

I turn off the hose. "Goddamn," I say, looking at my clothes.

I'm soaked from head to toe. "I just got out the shower."

"Now you real clean," Dre says. "Probably need to wash them dusty cornrows anyway."

I wring water outta my shirt. "Forget you."

Dre bend down and pick up something glistening in the grass. His watch fell off at some point. "Damn, got my shit scratched up."

I look at it. There's a little scrape on the glass of the face. "That's what you get, asshole. Why you not over on Magnolia?"

"Aw, I can go over there any Friday. I figured I'd chill with you and itty-bitty cuz."

"Damn, man. I can't tonight. I got laundry and homework."

"Can't you do that this weekend? I got us a pizza from Sal's, and I got that new Lawless CD that drop next week."

"Yooo!" I say, into my fist. "How you get that?"

Lawless this rapper from the east side. He raw as hell. Can hit you with some real shit and give you them club bangers. Word is he roll with Garden Disciples, as most dudes on the east do. A lot of King Lords don't mess with him 'cause of that. Ay, if you the bomb, you the bomb. Me and Dre will listen to you.

"I put a new sound system in his ride," Dre says. "He paid me and gave me his new shit early. So you down or what?"

I do need a break.

Separating light onesies from dark onesies or that new Lawless?

History report or pizza?

Laundry and homework can wait. That pizza can't. "Hell yeah, I'm down."

We use some of Ma's good towels to dry off. She gon' kill us, but that's all I could find that was clean.

I check on Seven real quick. He finally knocked out. I take the baby monitor with me in case he wake up.

Me and Dre hop in his Beamer and let the windows down. Dre put the Lawless CD in. When that first track hit, I nod along.

"Goddamn! This tight."

"Yep," Dre says. "Law on the come up for real."

Dre set the pizza box on the dashboard. I ate not long ago—Mrs. Wyatt sent me home with gumbo—but I can never turn down pizza. I pop the box open. It's got ham, cheese, and—

"Pineapple? What the hell?"

Dre pick up a slice. "It's called Hawaiian pizza. This shit the bomb, I'm telling you."

I pick the pineapples off mine. "Fruit don't belong on pizza, Dre. Can you eat anything normal?"

I swear, he always eating weird stuff. Ketchup on popcorn, potato chips on peanut butter sandwiches. Just nasty.

"Not my fault you got simple taste buds," he says. "I got Keisha to eat it, and her picky ass love it."

"Keisha not that picky. She marrying you, ain't she?"

He push the side of my head. "Whoever get your behind ain't got no taste at all."

"Man, I doubt I'll get a girl anytime soon. You see how I did Lisa." All these weeks later, and that one still sting. "I messed up, Dre."

He squeeze my shoulder. "You'll be a'ight. Learn from it and do better next time. Focus on Seven and on school for now."

"I don't got much choice. Lisa won't have shit to do with me; King, Junie, and Rico don't come around. When I ain't at school or work, I'm stuck at home. Shit is whack, Dre. Feel like I ain't me no more."

"*That's* what defined you?" Dre ask.

"I didn't mean it like that. I just miss the way it used to—"

"What y'all doing?" somebody shout.

Me and Dre jump.

"Tony, what the hell?" Dre yell.

Bus Stop Tony lean in through Dre's window with a toothless grin. "I scare y'all?"

"You can't be sneaking up on folks!" I say.

"If your heart racing, it's working!" he says.

Tony a crackhead, ain't no getting around it. He sleep at a bus stop near Magnolia, so we call him Bus Stop Tony. Anybody sit there and he'll raise hell. Don't nobody wanna sit there no way. It smell like piss.

"What y'all doing?" He stretch his neck, looking all in the car. "That's some Hawaiian pizza? I love me some Hawaiian pizza. Pineapples make it good!"

Dre got the same tastes as a crackhead.

"You ate today?" Dre ask.

"Nope! You hear my stomach growling, don't you?"

Dre laughs. "Nah, I guessed. Here." He hand Tony the box. "You can have the rest."

"Bless ya, brotha! You got some drink to wash this down?"

I know damn well . . . "Hold up. He was nice enough to give you the pizza. How you gon' ask him for a drink, Tony?"

"Close mouth don't get fed and thirst don't get quenched!"

Dre shake his head. "Go on, Tony."

Tony huff off down the street, talking 'bout, "Stingy asses!"

"That fool," I mumble. Suddenly, Seven cry on the baby monitor. "Shit! He probably need his diaper changed."

"Hope he don't poop on you this time," Dre says.

"You not the only one. Ay, let me whoop that butt on *Mortal Kombat* a couple of times."

Dre turn off his ignition. "Fool, you wish. I'll be there in a minute. I need to call Keisha and tell her good night."

Tell her good night? What? "Dawg. You whipped."

He take out his Nokia and dial her number. Dre one of the only people I know with a cell phone. "Says the person who lovesick over Lisa."

"You still whipped."

Dre wave me off and put the phone to his ear. "Hey, baby."

"Ay, Keisha! You got him in check, don't you?" I holler. "Bet he gotta get permission for everything."

Dre flip me off. I laugh all the way into the house.

All the squirming Seven doing in his crib, yep, he got a dirty diaper. Thank God I don't smell this one when I walk in the room.

"A'ight, a'ight," I say, and pick him up. "It's okay, man. I got you."

I'm a pro at diapers now. The key is to distract him while I'm changing him by rapping or singing. I can't sing worth a damn. Seven don't care.

I lay him on the changing table and unbutton his onesie. "Any requests for Daddy radio? What if I take it old-school?"

I hit him with that "Cool It Now" by New Edition, using the baby powder as my microphone. My voice off-key, my dance moves stupid, and if Dre see this I'll never hear the end of it, but Seven smile and kick, and that's all I care 'bout.

Can't lie, I get into the song. Once I'm at the rap, I'm buttoning Seven's onesie back up.

I lay him in his crib and lean on the railing. "See? I told you Daddy got you. I always got you. Now go back to sl—"

Pow! Pow!

I jump. I'm used to gunshots. They as normal as birds chirping around here. Those sounded close.

Dre.

Tires screech outside. I push the front door open. "Dre!"

He don't respond. I run as fast as I can, but it's like time, space, and everything working against me. Wisps of smoke rise into the air near Dre's door.

"Dre!" I scream.

His silence the worst sound. I run around to the driver's side. Halfway there I stop.

My cousin is slumped against his steering wheel. There's a bloody hole in his head.

I yank his door open. "Dre! Dre, wake up!"

He not moving, not breathing. Blood drip from his mouth like drool. His phone near his feet like it fell from his hand. Keisha scream on the other end.

I gotta do something. CPR, first aid, something. I unlock his seat belt and try to pull him out, but he too heavy. He dead-weight. Nah, man. Nah, nah, nah.

I use all my strength to pull him out, but my legs give up on me. We end up on the ground. I sit up with Dre's head in my lap. His eyes wide open, but he see nothing at all.

"Help!" I scream till my throat hurt. "Somebody help!"

It's quiet and still. Gunshots make people disappear.

I pat Dre's face. "Dre, wake up! C'mon, man! Wake up!"

He don't move.

He don't answer me.

He'll never answer me again.

TEN

A week ago, I sat in the street with Dre as he stared at nothing at all.

The Wyatts rushed outside first. Mrs. Wyatt called 911. Mr. Wyatt tried to get me to let Dre go. I wouldn't—*couldn't*. I held him until the ambulance came.

The paramedics didn't try to save him. It's like they took one look at him and gave up. I cussed them out. Swore I'd kick their asses if they didn't do their job. See, they don't know my cousin like I do. He a fighter, man. I don't give a damn that a bullet was in his head, he would've come back. He would've.

They put a white sheet over him and left him in the street. He wasn't a person no more. He was a crime scene.

The cops found Bus Stop Tony in the area and questioned him. They don't think he did it. Tony not the type to rob or kill no way. Keisha said she heard a guy tell Dre to hand over his shit. Dre's wallet, his watch, and his drug stash all missing. We only know the drugs gone 'cause the cops definitely would've mentioned if they found them in his car. They think it was a random robbery.

I don't. When a King Lord gets killed, chances are it was a GD. I remember the one who told me my cousin better watch his back.

Now Ant got a target on his. I swear if he did this, I'm gon' kill him.

What, I'm supposed to let this slide? Dre was my family. My *blood*. Whoever killed him is asking for it.

The world got some nerve going on without him. People laughing and dreaming when Dre can't. That make me not wanna. I didn't go to school or work this week. Ma didn't make me go, and Mr. Wyatt told me to take as many days as I need. My thing is, what's the point of any of that now? One of the most important people in my life getting lowered into a grave today. A fucking grave in the cemetery near the interstate like he wasn't somebody's son, somebody's daddy. Fiancé. Nephew. Cousin. Big brother. *My* big brother.

Pops told me the other day that grief something we all gotta carry. I never understood that till now. Feel like I got a boulder on my back. It weigh down my whole body, and I be wanting to cry out to make the pain go away.

Men ain't supposed to cry. We supposed to be strong enough

to carry our boulders and everybody else's. What I look like crying when Aunt 'Nita cry all the time? I gotta wipe her tears. Ma cry almost as much, and I gotta be there for her. Uncle Ray always snapping on folks, and I take whatever he dish out. Keisha walk around, looking like a zombie. I make sure she eat. Andreanna ask for her daddy all the time. She don't get that he gone. I fly her around like an airplane like he used to do. I can never get her to laugh like he could.

I'm taking care of all them plus my son. Ain't got time to grieve.

Today I gotta be real strong for the fam. Dre's funeral in a couple of hours. Mrs. Wyatt came earlier and took Seven next door. Funerals not good for babies, and babies not good for funerals.

Ma peek in my room as I button up my dress shirt. She got on her black dress and some house shoes. She always wait to put on her heels. "You ready, baby? The limo will be at your aunt's soon, and I want us to ride with the family."

"Almost. Gotta put on my tie."

She come in my room. "Let me do it. You've gotten so grown I don't get to do much for you these days."

"You more than welcome to change Seven's diapers."

Ma chuckles. "I'll gladly leave those to you." She stand on her tiptoes and drape my tie around my neck. I've towered over Ma for a while now, yet I always feel like a little boy when she in front of me. "Grandmas handle hugs, kisses, and cuddles. I spoil him, you clean him up. That's the deal."

I smile a little. "You got the spoiling part down pat."

"Hey, your granny was the same way with you. Would spoil you now if I let her. She used to get you the cutest little outfits. My Stinka Butt was always sharp."

"Maaa," I groan as she laugh. "You gotta drop that nickname, for real."

She brush her fingers through my 'fro. I took my cornrows down the other day and let my hair do whatever it want. "It doesn't matter how old you get. You'll always be my Stinka Butt." Her lips start to tremble, breaking her smile, and tears build in her eyes. "I . . . I keep thinking of that night. We could be burying you today."

Mrs. Wyatt paged Ma after she called 911, and Ma rushed straight home. Cops and people crowded our street, and she had to park a few blocks away. Ma ran toward our house, screaming my name. She hugged me like she'd never let go.

I wipe her cheeks. Ma's tears the worst things to ever exist. "It's okay, Ma. I'm a'ight."

"No, you're not. You haven't cried since it happened, baby."

The boulder feel heavier. I straighten up. "Don't worry 'bout me."

"All I do is worry about you."

We stand here for a moment, and she won't let my eyes look at nothing but hers. That boulder ain't tryna break me—Ma is.

I can't break, man. I can't. I kiss the top of her head. "I'm okay, Ma."

"Maverick—"

"C'mon." I take her hand. "We gotta go if we wanna ride with the family."

I was at Dre's funeral, but I wasn't.

I zoned out for most of it. Only remember bits and pieces. Dre lay in the coffin in a suit he should've gotten married in. Aunt 'Nita wailed so loud she screamed. Ma and Granny tried to calm her down, but they were crying too. Keisha almost passed out. Somebody took Andreanna outside so she wouldn't have to see it all.

The whole set was posted up in the back of the church. King Lords stand during funerals so the family can have the seats—that's the rules. Everybody had on their gray and black or T-shirts with Dre on them. King nodded at me as the family marched in, his way of telling me to keep my head up. He checked on me a lot this week.

Shawn got choked up as he spoke at the funeral. Folks in the pews told him, "It's okay, baby" and "Take your time," and that helped him finish. Then the pastor did the eulogy, I think. That's what happen at funerals, right? After that, all I remember is the coffin lowering into the ground, taking Dre with it.

We in the church basement now for the repast. There's fried chicken and side dishes lined up on a table, buffet-style. Granny fixed me a plate. She say I don't got enough meat on my bones. But I'm just sitting here, pushing the green beans around in the mashed potatoes.

The whole family down here, including all my great-aunts and -uncles and cousins. Granny come from a big family. Ma over in a corner, talking to some of them. Moe right beside her, holding her hand for support. Aunt 'Nita and Uncle Ray sit with the pastor. Andreanna laugh and play with some of our little cousins, like they ain't at a repast for her daddy's funeral. Kids lucky that way.

I rest my head back and close my eyes. We supposed to be spending time together as a family. Meanwhile Dre in the ground by himself.

"Hey."

I look up as Moe sit beside me. Granny call her that "big-boned brown gal." She a nurse at some doctor's office downtown. When I met her, she brought me a Tupac CD. We been cool ever since.

"How are you holding up, baby boy?"

"I'm a'ight. Is Ma okay?"

"She's holding up. I'm just trying to be there for her."

"I'm glad she got you for a friend." I mean that. Ma could be stressed over bills or something with Pops. Once she and Moe hang out she all good again.

Moe give me a small smile. "I'm glad I can be there for her. You too, if you want. Y'all are a package deal."

"I'm good long as Ma good." I loosen my collar. Either I'm hot or this room cramped as hell. "I'll be better once this repast over."

Moe glance back at Ma then look at me. "I tell you what, why don't you get outta here for a bit? I'll let Faye know."

I sit up. "For real?"

"Yeah. Not like you're doing anything besides making a mountain out of those mashed potatoes." Moe smirks. "Faye will understand. I'm sure Dre would, too."

My throat tighten. "Yeah. A'ight."

Moe squeeze my shoulder. I push away from the table and head upstairs.

The weather shouldn't be as nice as it is today. The air got the kinda coolness that mean the state fair coming. Me and Dre would always hit up Midnight Madness. It's the first Saturday of the fair, and from nine until closing you can get on as many rides as you want for fifteen dollars. They'd basically have to kick us out.

Almost everything make me think of him.

A bunch of big homies stand around Shawn's silver Benz in the church parking lot. They helped a lot this week. Paid for the funeral, brought food for the family, checked on us constantly. They also bought my suit and shoes so I'd have something nice to wear to the funeral. After being so busy with work and my son, it felt good to know I'm still one of them.

Shawn on the hood of his car with a forty-ounce in hand.

Dark shades hide his eyes. He hold his palm out to me. I slap it and let him pull me into a hug. Then he give me the forty-ounce. I pour out a little liquor for Dre and take a swig myself.

Shawn take the bottle back. "You too young for more than that. Dre would've got on me for letting you take that li'l sip."

I almost smile. "He was a pain in the ass."

"The biggest pain." Shawn bow his head. "They really eulogized our brother today, Mav."

"It was a beautiful service though," P-Nut says. "Had me on some introspectalness, know what I'm saying?"

Hell nah, I don't know. I doubt this fool ever picked up a dictionary in his life.

"Beautiful or not, this shit shouldn't have gone down," Shawn says. "I'm telling you, Mav, when I find out who did this, they as good as dead."

I'm with him one thousand percent on that. "You know anything yet?"

"We pretty sure it was the GDs. Hard to say which one, since Dre ain't have beef with none of them."

That's not true. "Dre did have beef with one."

All the homies seem to be listening now.

Shawn sit forward. "What? With who?"

"This dude named Ant." I see his short ass real clear.

"Ant." Shawn say it, as if he tryna place it. "He a li'l light-skinned kid?"

"Yeah. He go to my school. He stepped to me on first day and said Dre better stop coming to the east to race for money. Now a few weeks later Dre dead? That ain't no coincidence, Shawn."

"It could be though," Shawn says. "We'll look into it before we make a move. Whoever did it, I'll handle them myself. You got my word." He hold his palm out for me.

Fact is, the fam won't ever ask the police to solve Dre's murder. Not like the cops care no way. Ma, Aunt 'Nita, and Uncle Ray will never say this out loud 'cause it ain't something you wanna admit and street shit shouldn't be discussed no way, but our family been King Lord–connected enough to know this one for the set to handle.

That's where they wrong. "Nah. *I* need to handle this."

Shawn lower his hand. "Whoa, hold up Li'l—"

"Nah, man! Dre was my *blood*. I can't let nobody get away with killing my family!"

"Look, I'm mad as hell that Dre gone too," Shawn says. "But I ain't letting my homie's li'l cousin get caught up. This don't concern you no more."

"Like hell it don't!"

"I'm not making a suggestion, Li'l Don."

All eyes on us, and I swear a couple of the big homies smirk.

My nostrils flare. If I was anybody else, it would be no question that I should handle my cousin's killer. But I'm *Li'l Don*, the dude who weak compared to his pops. "You don't think I can do it, do you?"

Shawn lift his shades, revealing two teardrops tatted under

127

his eye for two people he killed. "You ever shot somebody, Li'l Don?"

I feel myself shrink. Fact is, I never even pulled a trigger. "No."

"You got a gun?"

"I can get one—"

"I said do you got a gun?"

I clench my jaw. "No."

Shawn pull his shades back down. "I thought so. We'll handle it."

"Weak," P-Nut says, behind a fake cough. The big homies smirk. I'm nothing but a joke to them.

I storm toward the church. I found Dre with bullets in his head. The least Shawn could do is let me handle the dude who killed him.

But nah. I'm just a li'l kid who can't live up to his pops's name.

I'm gon' prove all them fools wrong one day. Believe that.

I barely watch where I'm going, and I almost walk dead into somebody. "My bad."

"Mav?"

It's the sweetest voice I know.

Lisa got her braids in a bun and wearing a black dress. After what I did to her, she still came to my cousin's funeral and repast.

"I was looking for you," she says. "Moe told me you came

outside and—are you okay?"

"Yeah. I'm straight."

Lisa study me real hard. I got a feeling she ain't buying that. "You wanna go for a walk?"

I nod.

Lisa take my hand into hers, and I let her lead me away from the church.

ELEVEN

Me and Lisa walk around the neighborhood for a while. She don't talk, and I never feel like I gotta. We eventually end up at her house.

I sink onto her couch, and Lisa sit cross-legged beside me. "Saying I'm sorry isn't enough, but I am sorry, Maverick," she says.

I clear my throat. "Thanks for coming to the funeral. You ain't have to do that."

"Of course I did. I loved Dre like family . . . except when he was a nuisance at my games."

I fight a smile. Dre would go with me to Lisa's basketball games all the time. He became a fan of hers quick and would trash-talk the other teams. Nearly got us put out a few times.

"He was a loudmouth, huh?"

"The definition of a loudmouth. You remember when I met him?"

"Yeah. At that away game you had outta town."

"Uh-huh. Which you tricked him into driving you two hours to." Lisa laughs. "He was sweet to me, but I could tell he was mad as hell at you."

I laugh. "He got over it. All it took was some gas money and a rib-tip plate from Reuben's, with peach cobbler *and* banana pudding."

"He was sooo greedy. Remember when we went to Sal's with him and Keisha and he—"

"Ordered an entire pizza for himself. Then put mustard all over it."

"Oh my God, he had the weirdest taste buds ever."

"Yo, you not lying. I was messing with him 'bout that the other week before—"

I lose the words. I see him slumped over his steering wheel.

"It's true, then," Lisa murmurs. "You found him."

I nod as I stare at my loafers. "He was already gone when I got out there."

Lisa suck in a breath, like it hurt her to hear that. "I'm sorry."

We get quiet again. It's honestly *too* quiet. I'm surprised Ms. Montgomery ain't come and cussed me out. "Your momma gone?"

"Yep. She's at rehearsals. Her theater department is doing *A*

Raisin in the Sun in a few weeks. It's kept her busy all month."

Ms. Montgomery is the theater teacher at Midtown School of the Arts. That explain why that woman dramatic as hell. "Oh, that's cool."

"Yeah. I'm glad it keeps her off my back."

"You know damn well that won't last long. At least you don't gotta deal with Carlos, right?"

"Thank God, he's back at college. Won't see him until Thanksgiving. I'm trying to convince him to bring his girlfriend so he'll be too distracted to get in my business."

"Whaaat? Carlton Banks got a girlfriend?"

Lisa push my head. "Stop calling him that!"

"Ay, he is like Carlton. Surprised he got enough game to get a girlfriend."

"Apparently he does. Her name is Pam, and she's premed. She's supersweet, although I don't know what she sees in my brother."

"Damn," I say. "Your corny brother actually got a girl-friend."

"Whatever, Maverick." She hop up from the couch. "I'm gonna get changed. Feel free to get something from the kitchen if you want."

She actually letting me stay. "Thank you."

Lisa give me the tiniest smile. "You're welcome."

She go off to her room, and I help myself to the kitchen. I'm thirsty as hell. Ms. Montgomery keep her cabinets and refrigerator stacked. I find all kinds of drinks and liquor. Lisa's momma know how to throw them back.

I pop open a Pepsi and wander down the hall. Lisa take her bun down at her bedroom mirror. I say she fine all the time (that ass looking right in that dress, goddamn), but this girl straight-up beautiful.

She catch me staring. "What?"

I lean against the doorway and sip my drink. "Nothing. Watching you."

"So you can learn how to do your hair? Because *clearly* you haven't combed that mess on your head."

"Why you hating?"

"Why do you hate yourself?" She put her comb in my hair, and it get stuck. I wince as she snatch it out. "Damn, Maverick. When was the last time you brushed your hair?"

"I got a 'fro now!"

"So? You need to brush it, comb it, take care of it. Bet you haven't washed it since I did those cornrows, have you?"

"I take showers!"

Lisa's mouth make a line. "That's not enough. You need shampoo, conditioner."

"That's girl shit."

"Tell that to your dirty hair. Go to the bathroom."

"Lisa—"

She point across the hall. "Go!"

Damn, she tripping. I go to the bathroom, take off my shirt

and tie, and kneel beside the bathtub.

Lisa sit on the side of it and grab the handheld showerhead. She turn the water on. "This doesn't make any sense, Maverick. Seriously."

"It ain't that ba— *Aaagh!*" She spray water in my face, strangling me. "Ay!"

"Oops, sorry," Lisa claims. "I'll warn you next time."

A lie. "You worse than my momma. She not tripping 'bout my hair."

"Mrs. Carter is grieving. She's probably not paying attention to your hair." Lisa massage the shampoo into my scalp. I can't front, that feel good. "I'm surprised Mr. Wyatt lets you come to work looking like this."

"You know I work for him?"

"My momma told me," Lisa says. "Said you bagged her groceries one day."

Oh yeah, I did. She gave me the dirtiest look. That's saying something, 'cause Ms. Montgomery done gave me plenty of dirty looks. "What she telling you for? You tryna keep up with your boy?"

"Nope!" Lisa spray my face again.

"Ay!" I scream as she laugh. "Stop playing, girl!"

"Sorry," she lie again. She massage more shampoo in. "Since you're working for Mr. Wyatt, does this mean you gave up drug dealing?"

"Yeah. I got a son to think 'bout now. Wanna be around for

him. Can't lie though, between that job and taking care of him, I'm tired as hell."

"Doesn't Iesha help take care of him?"

"Nah, she needed a break. I've had him since the day I found out he mine."

Lisa quietly rinse the shampoo outta my hair. "What's his name?"

"Who, my son? I named him Seven."

"*Seven?* You did not name that baby after a number, Maverick. Oh my God."

"It's the number of perfection!" I always gotta explain that. "He perfect. It make sense."

Smells like she pour something else into my hair. Conditioning or whatever that stuff is. "Okay, when you put it like that it's kinda sweet."

"Thank you. Plus, it's unique. Now, if I gave him a plain-ass name like Connor— *Agh!*"

Lisa sprayed my face again.

"That was on purpose," she says. "Not sorry."

"It is a plain-ass name! Can't believe you went from me to him."

"Um, you are not all that, sir. Calm down," she says. "Not that it's any of your business, but I'm not with Connor."

"Oh." My lips turn up a little. Yeah, she dissed me, but she not with Richie Rich. "He ain't got no game, huh?"

"That's none of your business as well."

I snort. "Your answer say it all. I knew he was whack—Ow!"

She popped me with the showerhead. "That was on purpose too."

I rub the back of my head. "You mad 'cause I'm right."

Lisa dry my hair off and take me to her room. I sit on her bed, and she kneel behind me to see over my head. She run the comb through hard.

I wince. "Damn, girl! Why you so rough?"

"Had you done this yourself, it wouldn't be this bad. Be still."

"I am still. You rough as hell," I say. She hold the comb at the edge of my scalp, near the middle of my forehead, then comb through my hair from there. She call that making a part. "You gon' cornrow it?"

"No, that'll take too long. I'm gonna put it in a ponytail."

"A'ight . . . Thank you for doing this."

She put my hair in a ponytail. "You're welcome. That'll be two hundred dollars."

"*Two hundred dollars?*" I say. "You strangled me and abused me!"

"Nobody abused you!"

"You hit me with the showerhead, and you snatched my hair!"

"I did not snatch your hair!" Lisa says. "You're tender-headed."

"I ain't tender-headed."

"Right, like you swear you're not ticklish," Lisa says.

"I ain't!"

She try to tickle my underarm. I hop off the bed.

"Ay, girl! Stop!"

Lisa smirk. "I thought you weren't ticklish."

"I ain't. But you are."

I pounce her on the bed and tickle the hell outta her. She laugh her ass off, and she got me laughing. Them pretty brown eyes meet mine, and we stop.

Nobody else exist.

I look at her lips, and I ain't never wanted to do anything more than I wanna kiss them right now. So shit, I go for it.

Lisa kiss me right back.

It's been a long time since we did this. We can't kiss fast enough, can't keep our hands off each other. It's like she hit me with jumper cables. My whole body on fire.

"Damn," I mumble, and look down. It's real obvious I'm into this.

Lisa look at it, too. Then she look me in the eye and unzip my pants.

It's on.

I help her get out that dress, and she help me get my pants off. We both down to nothing when we slide under her covers. I'm ready to put it down.

"Shit!" I hiss, and raise up. "I don't got a rubber."

Lisa sit up a little. "Seriously?"

"Yeah. I ain't have no reason to keep them on me. You on the pill, right?"

"No. Had no reason to be."

For a few seconds, our heavy breathing the only sound in the room.

The way she feel against me . . . it's driving me outta my mind. "I could be careful—"

"If you pull out before you—"

We spoke at the same time. Our eyes lock, and, goddamn, I want her bad.

"Do you wanna do this?" I ask.

Lisa bite her lip. "Yeah. Do you?"

I never wanted anything more in my life. "Yeah."

Lisa pull me back down and kiss my neck. "Then be careful."

That's all I need to hear.

PART 2

GROWTH

TWELVE

Damn. That was wild.

Me and Lisa lying in her bed, all sweaty and panting. We went at it for hours. A'ight, an hour. A'ight, a'ight, more like fifteen, twenty, ten minutes. Either way, I did the damn thing.

This was the first time we ever had sex without protection. I see what the homies mean, it do feel different. I was careful though, just like I said I'd be.

I brush Lisa's hair back and kiss her forehead. Your boy made her sweat them baby hairs out. Hell yeah. "Damn, I missed you."

She cuddle up against me. "I can't lie, I missed you too."

"I could tell, the way you were screaming."

Lisa smack my chest. "You play too much!"

I smirk. She can't deny the truth.

I close my eyes. Lying here with Lisa, there ain't no gun-shots. There ain't no dead cousins. There's only us.

Till a car hum into the driveway.

Lisa sit straight up. "Oh, shit! My momma!"

Shit!

We jump outta bed. Lisa throw on a T-shirt and shorts, and I throw on my pants. Damn, wait, my boxers. Gotta put on my boxers.

The front door open. "I'm home," Ms. Montgomery call out. "Come help me get these groceries out the car."

Shit, shit, shit.

Lisa shove me toward her window and push me halfway outta it. "Go!" she hiss, then holler, "Be there in a minute, Momma!"

"Wait," I say, straddling the ledge. "I love you. See you later this week?" I lean over to get a kiss.

Lisa step back, biting her bottom lip. "I . . . I'm sorry about Dre."

Hold up. Did she— Is she swerving me? "Lisa—"

She give me a slight nudge, and I hit the grass in her back-yard. Lisa close the window behind me and let her momma know she coming.

I glance around. I can't go out the front gate or Ms. Mont-gomery gon' see me. Can't go down the driveway, she'll see me. I climb over their fence and into the yard behind theirs. A Rott-weiler charge at me, and I almost piss myself. Thank God a chain hold it back. I go out the gate, hauling ass down the street.

* * *

It's the next day, and I don't understand what went down with Lisa.

I thought we was cool again. I mean damn, she let me hit. Told me she missed me. I tell her I love her and try to make plans, and she push me out the window? I tried to call her once I got home, but she still got my number blocked.

Girls confusing as hell, man. I almost called Dre to get his advice. He always know how to help me with Lisa.

Then I remembered.

Life without him won't ever be normal.

I'm working in Mr. Wyatt's store today. Usually I'm off on Sundays, but Mr. Wyatt's nephew, Jamal, couldn't come in today, and I told Mr. Wyatt I could. I gotta do something to keep Dre outta my head. Plus, let's be real, your boy need the money. I hate to think how my check gon' look after a week off from work.

Ma agreed to watch Seven for me. Said she'd love some time with her Man-Man. I bet she need a distraction, and babies good at helping you forget death. Probably 'cause they so new.

Mr. Wyatt got a long list to keep me busy. First I gotta mop the floors, and then he want me to restock the shelves. After that I'll put his sales posters in the windows. He running a special on pork chops and turnip greens. Once that's done, he say he got a whole 'nother list for me.

Meanwhile, he out on the sidewalk with Mr. Lewis and Mr. Reuben. Mr. Reuben own the barbecue joint across the street.

The three of them laughing and talking like they ain't got businesses to run. I guess that's how it go when you the boss. Other people do the hard work, and you hang with your homies. Shit, I'm tryna get like them.

I dip the mop into the bucket and slap it onto the floor. I mopped all the aisles, and now I'm in the back, near the office. Mr. Wyatt want the floors to shine so bright you can see your reflection.

The phone ring in the office. I put down the Wet Floor sign, so why I dash toward his office like I don't know it's slippery? Almost bust my ass.

And it's the wrong damn number. The lady catch an attitude when I tell her this ain't the Church's Chicken on Magnolia. Hope she get bubble guts. I start to put the phone down, but I stop.

I bet Lisa ain't blocked the number to the store.

I see the sidewalk real good from here. Mr. Wyatt busy running his mouth with his friends. He won't notice me using his office phone.

I quickly dial Lisa's number. Oh, hell yeah, the phone ring. She didn't block my work number. It ring again and again and then—

"Hello?"

Gah-lee. It's Ms. Montgomery.

When Lisa's momma met me, she gave me one hard glare and been giving me that same hard glare ever since. She think

I'm a no-good thug and done grounded Lisa plenty of times to keep us apart. Lisa would sneak out to see me anyway, and it only led to her momma hating me more.

I clear my throat. No matter how much Ms. Montgomery don't like me, Ma told me to show her respect regardless. "Hi, Ms. Montgomery. How you doing?"

"Well, look who it is," she says. "Mr. I-Get-Other-Girls-Pregnant. You got some nerve, calling my daughter after what you did."

Show respect, show respect. "I'm sorry, Ms. Montgomery. Is it okay if I speak to Lisa?"

"You don't have a damn thing to speak to her about. Lisa is done with you! Your li'l thuggish, ruggish, bonehead behind bet' not come near her or I've got something for you. Do I make myself clear?"

"Ms. Montgomery—"

She hang up. Goddamn, she just had to be the one to answer the phone.

The bell on the door ding up front. I hurry outta Mr. Wyatt's office as him and Mr. Lewis step into the store. I grab the mop and get back to work like I never stopped.

Mr. Lewis eye me suspiciously. "Boy, you ain't finished mopping yet? You slow as hell. Jamal would've finished by now. I don't know why you put up with this, Clarence."

I can't stand Mr. Lewis, for real. He always tripping. You come in his shop with your pants sagging, he make you leave.

You rep King Lords or Garden Disciples, don't come through the door. He wouldn't cut Pops's hair, and everybody love Pops. Mr. Lewis on some ol' bullshit.

"Since when did I ask for your opinion on *my* employee, Cletus?" Mr. Wyatt ask.

Cletus? This fool named Cletus?

"You need somebody's opinion," Mr. Lewis says. "Hurry up, boy! You oughta hop in my chair and let me cut that mess off your head."

"Somebody need to cut that mess off yours," I mumble, 'cause his Jheri-curl ass don't need to talk 'bout nobody's hair.

"What was that?" he ask.

"Nothing, Mr. Lewis."

He go, "Uh-huh," like he not convinced. "It's ridiculous that you done made Faye a grandma, as young as she is. Ri-damn-diculous. You know how to use a condom? I can give you some tips. I know they say them lambskin ones feel good but—"

Aww hell nah, I'm not having this conversation with him. Hell nah. "You want me to sweep the curb, Mr. Wyatt?"

Mr. Wyatt's lips twitch like he wanna laugh. "That would be nice."

I grab the broom out the storage room and walk outside so damn fast.

Marigold pretty calm on Sundays. Reuben's the busiest place on the block. Folks come in and out in dresses and suits, looking straight outta church. Me and Ma only go to church for funerals. Ma say she don't need a building to be close to God.

A couple of girls come outta Reuben's in clothes so tight, I doubt they went to church. One of them is Lala, Iesha's best friend. The other is Iesha.

I drop the broom and run across the street. "Yo, Iesha!"

She look dead at me, *dead at me*, and I swear she walk faster.

What the hell? I catch up with her and grab her arm. "Ay—"

She snatch away. "Get your hands off of me!"

"Oh hell no! Don't be grabbing my girl!" Lala shouts.

I put my hands up. Never get two Black girls riled up. Shit, don't get *one* riled up. "I ain't mean nothing by it, I swear. Iesha, where you been?"

She look at Lala. "Go on, girl. I'll catch up with you later."

"You sure?"

"Yeah, it's fine."

Lala give me a stank eye. She brush past me and go on her way.

Iesha hug herself tight. "How's my baby?"

"You gon' answer my question? Where you been? Your momma said you moved out."

"I did. She was getting on my nerves. I been staying with different friends. Being homeless ain't good for a baby. That's why I haven't come and got him."

Hold up. She standing up here with hair and nails freshly done, wearing new FILA sneakers and Tommy Hilfiger clothes.

"I'm really supposed to believe you homeless?"

"You can believe what you wanna believe, Maverick! I'm telling the truth!"

Fine. Besides, Ma says poor don't always look the same. "Okay then. You homeless. That don't explain why you haven't visited Seven."

"*Seven?*" she says. "What the hell is a Seven?"

"That's our son's new name."

"Hold up, how you gon' rename my baby without asking me?"

"It's obviously not official yet, since I need you for that, but it's the name he answer to now. He don't need to be named after King no way. He *my* son."

"So you named him after *a number?*"

Once again, I gotta explain. "Seven is the number of perfection. He perfect, ain't he?"

Iesha's eyes get dim. They drift down to concrete. "He too perfect for a momma who couldn't handle him."

This girl dipped on our son and I should be mad as hell, yet . . . I feel bad for her. "Iesha, you can't beat yourself up, a'ight? This parenting shit is hard. You don't have to deal with it by yourself no more. We can take care of him togeth—"

"I need to go."

"Iesha, hold up!"

She done ran off.

THIRTEEN

"Yo, Mav!" Rico wave in my face. "Where you at, dawg?"

My body in the school cafeteria having lunch with him and Junie, but part of me stuck on that conversation with Iesha yesterday.

She feel guilty that she couldn't handle taking care of our son, and it made me think of how much I struggle. Sometimes I wanna give up, man. Like that night I walked out on him and left him crying in my room. This stuff get real overwhelming.

So I get how Iesha feel. Man, do I get it. I just wish we could figure this out.

Lisa on my mind too. I can't call her since my number blocked, and I don't have time to go over there, so what the hell I'm supposed to do?

The biggest part of me keep thinking on Dre. This my first

day back at school since he died, and it's rough. It started this morning when I passed Aunt 'Nita's house and didn't see him or his ride in the driveway. I teared up. Once I got to school, seem like everybody said "Sorry 'bout your cousin" instead of the usual "whaddup." Condolences just constant reminders that Dre ain't here no more.

The coward who killed him is sitting across the cafeteria, laughing and talking with the rest of the GDs. Every class we got together I know where Ant sit. In the halls, I spot him. I don't know how I'm gon' kill him, but best believe I'm gon' kill him. Forget Shawn and his orders.

"Since Mav not paying attention, I'll help a brother with them fries." Junie try to pick one off my tray.

I smack his hand. "Man, if you don't take your greedy ass on—"

Rico almost spit out his Sunkist.

"I was making sure you here," Junie says.

"I'm here." Well, I'm tryna be. I finally notice everything around me, and damn, the cafeteria off the chain. A boom box play at one table, and a rap battle go down at another. The girls from the cheerleading squad do the U-G-L-Y chant at some dude who tried to holla at one of them. I feel bad for homeboy.

The cafeteria split up almost like the neighborhood. You got King Lords on one side and Garden Disciples on the other. People who don't claim sit in the middle. That mean it's a lot of people between me and Ant. I spot him like it's nothing.

"Dawg, what you keep staring at?" Rico turn around and look.

I can't tell him and Junie that Ant killed Dre. The whole school would know before the day over. "Nothing. Zoning out. You know how it is."

"I feel you," Junie says. "Probably got Dre on your mind, don't you?"

Rico let out a slow whistle. "That shit hard to shake, dawg. I be remembering what happened to my brother outta nowhere sometimes."

"Same with me and my auntie," says Junie.

When Rico was nine, his twin brother, Tay, was killed by a stray bullet while they slept in their bunk beds. Junie's aunt got stabbed at a block party freshman year. The Garden take somebody from everybody, and we still go hard for it. I guess it's 'cause it's all we know.

"Keep pushing, Mav," Rico says. "Tough situations don't last. Tough people do."

"Ooooohwee," Junie says into his fist. "That boy dropping knowledge on 'em."

Rico pop his collar. "On my Gandhi shit."

I crack up. I can always count on these two to make me laugh. "Y'all a trip."

"We got so much to catch you up on, Mav," Junie says. "Cortez got sent to juvie again. It wasn't for that big lick him and DeMario hit though. This was something else."

"What big lick?" I ask.

"You know, that suburb thing they had going," Rico says. "When they was hitting different houses every day?"

"Oh yeah. That," I front. I'm so lost.

"We got our own lick now though," Rico says.

"Yeeeeah." Junie rub his hands together. "King brought us in on his shit."

I look away from Ant. "What?"

"He told us you had to step away from it," says Rico. "He needed some help, and we needed some cash. We doing the damn thing."

This my first time hearing any of this. "How come none of y'all told me?"

Junie take a bite of his second burger. He eat a lot on days he got ball practice. "You not around, Mav. We figured stuff like that don't concern you no more."

That hit hard. Or I could be tripping 'cause I'm still pissed with how Shawn did me the other day. Speaking of . . . "Y'all ain't scared of Shawn and the big homies finding out?"

"Man, it's like King say: forget them," Rico claims. "They don't look out for us the way they should."

"Don't get it twisted, I ain't on their side or nothing, but they do watch our backs."

"My back ain't hurting. My pockets are," Junie says. "Them fools drive Benzes and Beamers. You see any li'l homies in Benzes or Beamers?"

"Nah," I gotta admit.

"Exactly. We out here hot-wiring hoopties and taking the bus," says Rico. "We gotta look out for ourselves. And if they come at one of us 'bout it, they gotta come at all of us."

"Damn." I sit back and glance between them. I never ever heard them talk this way. "This sound like some coup shit."

"Yeah, it's cool as hell."

This fool. "I said 'coup,' Rico. *C-o-u-p*. It mean a rebellion. That's what Napoleon did in France back in the day."

"Oh. Nah, we ain't rebelling. Just making money."

"Yep," Junie talk around a mouth full of fries. "You read too many books, Mav. Do something better with your time."

Man, whatever. It's the way King act toward Shawn and them sometimes that made me wonder. Now he got other li'l homies slinging on the side. If Shawn ever find out, I don't wanna know how that'll go down.

The bell ring, signaling that lunch period over. We take our trays to the trash bins. I watch Ant dump his. He head to the same world lit class that I go to.

I keep my eyes on him as we walk in the room. He take his seat in the middle. I start for mine but Mrs. Turner gently catch my arm.

"Hey, Maverick," she says. Mrs. Turner the sweetest teacher at the school and one of the youngest. She kinda fine, too. Got ass for days, good Lord. "I'm glad to see you back. How are you holding up?"

"I'm fine," I say, and glance at Ant. He watch us all amused.

"I'm so sorry about your cousin," Mrs. Turner go on. "Grief can be overwhelming. Mr. Clayton would like for you to come to his office this period and talk."

The whole class watching now. I'm not Li'l Don no more. I'm the dude who saw his cousin with a bullet in his head.

I sigh out my nose. "I told you I'm fine, Mrs. Turner. I don't need to talk to the counselor."

She hand me a hall pass. "Go, Maverick. I'll catch you up on the lessons tomorrow."

Ant snort. "Weak ass."

I start for him. "What?"

"You heard me! You as weak as your cousin. It was only a matter of time before his disrespectful ass got killed."

Mrs. Turner grab me before I can get to him. She strong as hell. She turn me toward the door. "Maverick, to the office now! Antwan, you can explain your abhorrent comments to me later in detention."

"Ooooh," echo around the classroom.

Mrs. Turner nudge me out the door and close it behind me as Ant try to plead his case.

I pace the hall for a second. I swear to God I could walk in that room and strangle that dude with my hands. Now I'm supposed to go discuss my "feelings" with Mr. Clayton? What good will that do? It won't bring my cousin back or take care of the dude who killed him.

Nah, forget that. Forget everything. The condolences, the stares, all of it.

I toss the hall pass in a trash bin, and I walk out the building.

The wind no joke today. It whip my hood right off my head. That explain why hardly anybody outside.

I'm a few blocks from school when a silver Mercedes-Benz pull up beside me; a '97 S500 on twenty-inch rims, to be exact. The dark tint keep you from seeing inside, but everybody in the Garden know that's Shawn.

He roll the passenger window down. "Whaddup, Li'l Don? Where you headed?"

I keep walking. He the last person I wanna see. "Don't worry 'bout it."

"I ain't worried, I only asked," he says as he drive alongside me. "You good?"

"Yep."

Shawn sighs. "You mad over the other day, ain't you? Let's talk man-to-man."

I stop and look at him. "That's gon' be hard when you treat me like a kid."

"That ain't the case, Mav," Shawn says. He reach over and push open the passenger door. "Hop in."

Shawn's Benz is banging. Leather interior, sunroof, TVs in the back. I used to tell Dre I'm gon' get a ride like this one day. He'd laugh and say, "Yeah, and you gon' wreck it. You can't drive worth a damn."

I miss him so much.

Shawn slurp a big slushy from the gas station. He one of them weird folks who stick to one flavor. He glance over at me. "Okay, Li'l Don! I see you with the Lakers Starter jacket and the Reeboks. Flossin' on 'em!"

Don't nobody give props like big homies. He can go on somewhere with that. "You said you wanna talk. Talk."

"A'ight, well, first off, I didn't call myself treating you like a kid but like a brother," Shawn says. "It wasn't that long ago that you was tryna follow me and Dre everywhere. You'll always be that li'l dude we ditched in the mall."

"Y'all were dirty as hell for that," I mumble, and Shawn bust out laughing. I was around eleven, Dre and Shawn were around sixteen. I wanted to go to the arcade, and they were tryna holla at girls in the food court. I was being a pain in the ass, for real. They gave me money to buy a milkshake. When I went back to the table, they were gone.

"We were tryna get some ass, and you were cock-blocking," Shawn says. "We thought we was gon' teach you a lesson. Shiiid, we find you, you up in Victoria's Secret. Got them fine-ass clerks all over you. Had them and them girls mad at us."

"Ay, I had game. I'm surprised y'all let me go anywhere after that."

"That was all Dre. He wanted to keep you close," Shawn says. "He'd tell me all the time, 'If Mav can't go, I can't go.'"

I pinch that space between my eyes. He should've said that 'bout dying. I couldn't go, so he shouldn't have gone.

"The point is, part of me gon' always see you like that, Mav," Shawn says. "Now that Dre gone, he'd want me to look out for you. He didn't want you selling weed. You think he'd want you to murder somebody, even for him?"

As pissed as I am . . . "No."

"Exactly. Instead, he'd want you to look out for your family, take care of your son, be on top of your school shit. Now do I think you could kill somebody? Fa'sho. Killing easy. It's living after the fact that's hard, *if* you live. Them GDs may come after you quick, and Mrs. Carter could be burying you next week. You wanna put your family through another funeral?"

The thought of Ma crying over me make me feel sick. "No."

"Then let me and the other big homies handle this one," Shawn says. "And real talk, what I look like passing this off to you when Dre was my best friend *and* I'm the crown? I need to take care of this one."

"Everybody in the set already think I'm soft, Shawn."

"So?" he says. "Forget what them fools think. You gotta live for you *and* Dre now, you feel me? You can do everything he didn't get a chance to do."

I never thought of that.

"Raise your son. Be the best father you can be," Shawn says. "That's how you honor Dre. A'ight?" He hold his fist over.

I bump it. "A'ight."

He take another sip of his slushy. "Good. Why the hell you not in school?"

"Me and Ant almost got into it," I say. "He said Dre deserved to die, Shawn. Now I *know* that fool did it. Y'all gotta get him ASAP."

"Any idiot can talk shit, Mav. This don't prove anything."

"I guess. The way he said it though—"

"He probably a li'l asshole," Shawn says. "We'll look into it. In the meantime, don't let him get under your skin. Stay your ass in school. How things going over there anyway? Rico, Junie, and them holding it down?"

I shift in my seat, remembering all the stuff they said at lunch. "Yeah, they fine."

"And your boy King? He good?"

"Yep. What you getting into?"

"I'm looking for Red. I paid him to get me a big-screen. I haven't seen that fool for over a week now."

"You may not get that TV. Red always scamming folks. He gave me some fake Jordans."

"He bet' not be stupid enough to scam me." Shawn reach past me and pop open his glove compartment. His gun inside along with a li'l something-something, rolled and ready.

Shawn light and smoke the blunt with one hand and drive with the other. That's some next-level multitasking. He take a hit.

"Goddamn! This that good shit," he says, all choked up. He

hold it toward me. "Sound like you need to chill out. Nothing wrong with a li'l weed."

I've only smoked weed like twice in my whole life. King used to clown me 'cause he'd get high and I wouldn't join in. I wanted to sell weed, not smoke it.

Shawn's blunt got me thinking of the couple of times I did get high. I would be so far gone that nothing bothered me. No stress, no worries, no pain. I ain't felt nothing but pain since Dre died.

I grab the blunt from Shawn, and I take a hit.

Time go by slow, but then it's fast. One second I'm in Shawn's Benz, watching the Garden pass by. The next, it's time for me to go to work. Time is funny, man. Life is funny. We all on this huge planet tryna figure shit out. What if the planet already got it figured out? What if the whole point is for us to not figure it out? What if God playing with us like . . . like dolls? Some diverse-ass Barbies.

Deep shit.

I'm good. I ain't smoke that much. I'm just chill as hell. A'ight, I'm a li'l blazed.

Shawn drop me off at Mr. Wyatt's house. He a good dude, yo. Real good dude. We rode around the neighborhood, searching for Red's scamming ass. That ain't a good dude. That's the opposite of a good dude. Not like Ant. Ant the worst kinda dude.

Mr. Wyatt got a list of stuff from me to do in the garden today. He won't be here till later. Told me I could get the list from his wife. I climb the porch steps—damn, it's a lot of steps—and ring the doorbell.

Mrs. Wyatt answer with Seven in her arms. My son. Yo, I got a son. Life is wild, man. A year from now he gon' be talking. Talking! My li'l big man. Or is it my big li'l man? Shit, I don't know.

"Hey, man!" I hold my hands out for him.

Mrs. Wyatt pull him closer. She looking at me funny. "Clarence is waiting for you in the back."

What the what? It's like three thirty. He should be at the store. Aw, hell. What if he realize I'm high? Play it cool, Mav. Play it cool.

"Oh, a'ight. I'm gon' go on back." I point my thumb behind me. "Wait, not that way. That way." I point behind her. "Yeah."

"All right," she says, kinda slow.

I go down all them steps—for real, why they got so many?—and go through the back gate. Mr. Wyatt over in the root-vegetable section, where he had me plant turnips and carrots not too long ago. I gotta play it cool, like a ice cube. Or Ice Cube the rapper. Even better. "Ayo, Mr. Wyatt!"

He turn around, frowning. "That's not exactly how you address your boss."

Okay, that was *too* cool. "My bad, my bad. I'm surprised you not at the store."

"Decided to let my nephew handle things there so I could come spend time with my bride."

The way his eyes twinkle, they spent time together a'ight. I hope Seven was asleep. Can't have my baby exposed to old folks' sex.

Why I say that? Wait, did I say it, or did I think it? Why my thoughts so damn loud? Did somebody put a microphone in my head? How they get it in there?

"Son!" Mr. Wyatt says.

"Huh?"

He fold his arms. "You been smoking that reefer?"

I snort. "Who the hell call it reefer, yo?"

I definitely said *that* out loud.

"The name is irrelevant," he says. "It's obvious you've been smoking. I smell it on you."

I sniff under my shirt. I don't smell nothing. "You tryna say I stank?"

His lips get real thin. "Boy. This is strike number two."

"Aww, Mr. Wyatt! C'mon! I ain't high."

"And I'm James Brown."

"You ain't got enough hair for that."

Shit, I said that out loud, too.

Mr. Wyatt pick up a hoe and hold it toward me. "Get to work. When I'm done with you, you'll wish you never looked at reefer."

* * *

Three hours later, Mr. Wyatt done almost killed me.

First, I unloaded big bags of mulch and garden soil from his truck. Around ten of each. I had to carry them heavy things one by one from the driveway to the backyard. Then he made me pull weeds in this new section he wanna start. Next, I used the hoe to break up the dirt and poured garden soil over that. He want me to start planting now. I'm tryna catch my breath.

He sip a lemonade on the stone bench. "Hurry up, son. That garlic won't put itself in the ground."

I could fall over, that's how tired I am. "Mr. Wyatt, just a few minutes, please?"

"No, sir. Time is money, money is time, and you wasting mine. Hey, that rhymed. Think I can be a rapper? A hip-hop, a hippity-hop—ain't that how y'all do it?"

If he don't take his Dr. Seuss behind on somewhere. "Can I have some water?"

Mr. Wyatt sip his lemonade. "Mm! Refreshing. What you need water for?"

"I'm thirsty!"

"No, you're not. That's the reefer talking."

"Man," I groan. Every few minutes, he find a way to bring it up. "I'm not high no more! I'm thirsty. I need a break."

"Nah now, apparently all you need is reefer. You were bold enough to show up to work high. You must've thought you needed it."

"I wanted to get Dre outta my head, a'ight!"

I ain't mean to snap, but it's enough to shut Mr. Wyatt up.

He set his glass down and pat the spot beside him. "Come here, son."

I drop the hoe and go over there. As hard as this concrete bench is, it feel like the best thing ever.

"You wanted to get your cousin off of your mind, and you thought drugs were the best way to do that?" Mr. Wyatt asks.

"Not drugs, Mr. Wyatt. Weed."

"Which is considered a drug, son," he says. "It may not be harmful like the others, but it's illegal, and you're only seventeen. You don't need to be getting high."

I fold my arms on top of my lap. "I told you, I was tryna get Dre outta my head."

"Why?"

I look at him. "Why would I wanna think 'bout that? That was my brother, and I saw him with a bullet—" I shake my head. "I can't think on that."

"Why?"

"You a therapist or something?"

"Why?" he repeats.

"'Cause I gotta keep it pushing! I can't sit around crying over Dre. I gotta be a man."

Mr. Wyatt don't say anything for a real long time.

He sighs. "Son, one of the biggest lies ever told is that Black men don't feel emotions. Guess it's easier to not see us as human when you think we're heartless. Fact of the matter is, we feel things. Hurt, pain, sadness, all of it. We got a right to show them feelings as much as anybody else."

I stare at the ground, legs shaking like they ready to bolt me outta here. It ain't possible to run from all the things swirling inside of me. I been trying to since the day Dre died, and I ain't got nowhere.

Mr. Wyatt grab the back of my neck, strong enough to tell me he got me but gentle enough to almost be a hug.

"Let it out," he says.

This sound come outta me, and I don't know if I'm screaming or crying. I pull my shirt over my mouth, but that don't muffle the sobs. It only catch my tears.

Mr. Wyatt wrap his arms around me. He hold me tight, as if he know I'm breaking and he tryna keep me together.

"It's okay, son," he says.

No, it ain't. As long as my cousin is dead, it never will be.

FOURTEEN

At Friday night football games, it don't matter if you rep gray or green. Only the school colors matter.

This morning Ma stopped in my doorway and said, "Why don't you go to the game tonight?" At first I was like, nah. She off from her second job today. I couldn't ask her to spend her free time watching my son.

"You're not asking; I'm offering," she said. "It would be good for you to get out and have some fun."

I'm not stupid. This more 'bout Dre than anything. She gave me money, too, so I know she feel bad for me. Ten dollars. That should be enough to cover my ticket and a snack. I'm broke till I get paid the day after tomorrow. This ten is like a hundred to me.

I follow King, Junie, and Rico into the stadium. It's cold

enough to see my breath. I don't care. This my first football game this year, and it's gon' be off the chain. Garden High taking on whack-ass Washington High, the school from Presidential Park. Our rivalry with them make King Lords versus GDs seem minor. We in their territory at their field, yet the entire Garden High here plus half our neighborhood.

It's hard as hell to find some seats. We stand at the fence along the sidelines, right near the fifty-yard line. At least we'll have a decent view.

King blow into his hands. "Them boys better whoop some washed-up Washington ass tonight."

"Word," Junie says, watching this girl pass by us. Shorty in a referee costume with her booty practically hanging out. "Ay, baby! You can blow my whistle any day."

She flip him off. The rest of us bust out laughing. Halloween tomorrow. You'd think it's tonight with all the costumes out here. Me, Ma, and Aunt 'Nita taking Andreanna and Seven trick-or-treating in Cousin Gary's neighborhood tomorrow afternoon. A'ight, I'll trick-or-treat; Seven gon' chill in his stroller. Last year, folks acted funny if I asked for candy. This year I'll lie and say it's for the baby. People can't say no to a cute baby.

"Can't believe Mav finally out," King teases. "You act like you on house arrest."

Junie and Rico laugh. They know all about house arrest.

"Shut up," I say. "My momma watching Li'l Man. That's the only reason I'm here."

Rico brush his waves. He keep a hairbrush at all times. "Iesha never take care of him?"

"She going through some stuff." I look at King. "You seen her lately?"

"Man, forget that girl," he says. "The game finna start."

Whistles go off, and the Garden High band start an old Temptations song. They march into the stadium, led by the drum majors and majorettes and followed by the football team. Our side explode in cheers. Boos ring out across the field from the Washington High folks. Shit, we only get louder. Oh yeah, it's going down tonight.

The majorettes out there, looking fine as hell in their leotards or whatever them things is. Maybe I'll holla at one of them.

Yeah right. I ain't hollering at nobody. I miss Lisa too much. I walk by her house every day on my way to work and leave notes for her in the mailbox. Her or her momma must get them—they disappear by the next day—but I ain't got a response yet. I'm running outta options and ideas.

"The football team ain't the same without you, King," Junie says. "If you was out there tonight—"

"I wouldn't let them fools get a touchdown," King says. "I'm that n-i-double-g-a. They better recognize!"

We crack up. "You stupid, man," I say.

"Real talk, dawg, they oughta let you back on the team," Rico says. "You did everybody a favor by beating Coach's racist ass."

King watch the team do their pregame chant on the

sidelines. "I miss it, can't front. Would do almost anything to get back out there."

I think getting kicked off the team was worse to him than getting kicked outta school.

King do a double take back at the bleachers. "Why that fool staring so hard?"

We all turn around. Ant and some Garden Disciples sit a couple of rows back, and Ant mean-mugging me real hard. He do that at school. I never say anything to him 'cause I don't wanna risk us getting into it. Then I'd be breaking my promise to Shawn.

"He still mad that he got detention for talking shit to me last week," I say. "Mrs. Turner went in on him."

King hold his arms out like, *What it is, then?*

Ant wave him off and look somewhere else.

"Punk ass," King says. "He try something tonight, we got you, Mav."

"No doubt," Rico says, and Junie go, "Fa'sho."

That's the thing 'bout your homeboys—when they got your back, *they got your back.* I might've lost Dre, but I still got brothers.

Going to a football game is kinda like getting hypnotized. I mean damn, we freezing our butts off and our feet probably gon' be numb when this all over. We only care that our team up by ten at halftime.

For the first time in months, I feel like me again. Just me and my boys, cheering for our team and goofing off. I done had a kid for so long that I forgot that I'm still one.

The teams clear out, and the bands make their way onto the field. Battle of the bands can get as hype as the game. Most folks staying in their seats to see it. The line at the concession stand probably ain't long then.

"I'm gon' go get some nachos," I say. "Y'all want something?"

"A burger and a Sprite," Rico says.

"A Sprite sound damn good," Junie says. "Get me a chili cheese dog and a Frito pie, too."

"Ooh, a Frito pie." Rico point at him. "I forgot they do them. Ay, get me one of them, Mav. Thanks, homie."

"Yeah, you a real one for buying our food," Junie add.

What the hell? Who said I was buying? And where they get off giving me grocery lists? "Y'all better take y'all lazy behinds to the concession stand and buy your own stuff."

"Fool, you asked!" says Rico.

King laugh. "It's cool, Mav. I'll help out. C'mon."

Junie shake his head. "Trifling."

I give him his second middle finger of the night and follow King.

I was wrong—the line to the concession stand long as hell. Only two or three people working in the booth, and folks in line already complaining.

King blow into his hands and rub them together. "We bet' not have to wait all night."

"Man, this a hood stadium. Of course we gon' be waiting all night." I stretch my neck to look at the sale signs. "Shit! That's how much nachos cost? That'll be all my money."

"You *that* broke?" King asks.

"Basically. I haven't got paid yet. Ma gave me ten dollars for tonight."

"Ten dollars? C'mon, man, seriously? Look." King pull a fat roll of money outta his pocket. "This what I'm working with. All hundreds."

"Damn. You stepped your game up?"

"Fa'sho. Gotta give these fiends what they want. No disrespect, but Dre gone. Nothing keeping you from getting back in it. You could be making this kinda dough yourself."

Some lady huff outta line, saying these slowpokes not gon' make her miss her baby's performance. We move up a spot.

I scratch through my hair. "I don't know if I wanna get caught up again, King."

"Fool, you only got ten dollars! My bad, you don't got that after buying your ticket."

Believe me, I know. "I'm tryna stay outta trouble."

King shake his head. "You bugging. You at least gon' go after whoever killed Dre? Please tell me you not backing out on that."

"Shawn ordered me to let him and the big homies handle it," I say.

"What? You supposed to be a man do whatever for your family. Goddamn, you soft!"

I look him up and down. "What?"

"First you back out on our operation"—King count it out on his fingers—"then you stay at home all the damn time like a housewife. Now you won't get revenge for somebody you called your brother. That's some punk shit, Mav. I shouldn't be surprised."

"What the hell that supposed to mean?"

"Exactly what I said. Everybody know you—"

Loud voices cut him off, and we turn around. Fists fly in the parking lot as some dudes go at it. Four of them wear yellow bandanas—Latin Royals. Presidential Park known as their home. The other three are Garden Disciples. I ain't surprised one of them Ant. He always into something. The line really moving now, 'cause mostly everybody getting the hell outta here.

I pat King's arm. "Yo, we should bounce."

"Hell nah! This better than the game. Ay, who you think gon' win?"

That's the thing. Fights like this ain't won by fists. They usually won by—

Pow!

Pow!

Pow!

I flinch. People scream and run around the parking lot.

Tires screech. The band stop playing, and folks rush outta the stadium.

Only one person not moving.

Ant lie on the concrete, dead in a pool of blood.

FIFTEEN

The person who killed my cousin got killed.

It's been a weird three weeks since it happened. 'Cause Ant was shot at a school function it was all over the news. His parents cried on TV, and I realized he had parents. Like Dre. Some kids at school were really tore up over his death, and I realized he had friends. Like Dre. At the stadium, he got a memorial in the parking lot with flowers and balloons. Like Dre.

Everybody get mourned by somebody, I guess. Even murderers.

I don't know how to feel 'bout it. I'm not happy, and I ain't sad. I'm not relieved, not satisfied. I'm just . . . I don't know.

Shawn the same way. Based on stuff he heard in the streets, he think Ant did kill Dre. "I wanted to take him out myself," he said. "At least the coward got what he deserved. This could be

Dre's way of keeping dude's blood off my hands."

That's something he'd do fa'sho.

I'm doing my best to live like he wanted. I go to school, go to work, and take care of my son. That's it. Straight up, my grades probably not what he'd want them to be. Seven and work keep me busy, and school be the best place to take a nap.

I may not need to do that soon. Seven finally started sleeping through the night a week ago. At first I couldn't believe it. I kept waking up expecting him to wake me up. But last night? Man! I slept for four hours straight. Four! I counted them suckers. Can't tell me miracles don't happen.

It's Sunday, my day off. Ma gone out with Moe, so I'm home alone with Li'l Man. I lie on the floor and "fly" him around like Superman as *Space Jam* play on the VCR. We can only watch tapes and local channels since we got rid of cable. Seven eat baby food now, and that cost more than formula. Something had to go. I had to get rid of my Sega Genesis too. Li'l Man outgrew his old clothes, and the money the pawnshop gave me helped me get him some stuff from the swap meet.

I'm starting to think being a parent mean you don't get to have much yourself. All my energy, my money, and my time go to him.

Space Jam at my favorite part. It's that scene where Mike showing the Looney Tunes that he still the greatest as that "Fly Like an Eagle" joint play in the background. I sit Seven on my stomach. He gotta see this.

"Look, man, that right there? That's the greatest basketball player of all time, Michael Jordan," I say. "Six-time NBA champion, five-time MVP. Everybody wanna be like Mike. I'll buy you some of his shoes soon. Don't get it twisted, we Lakers fans. We got this guy named Kobe, and I think he gon' get us some championships."

Seven coo like, *Word?* A'ight, it could be gas. I'm gon' say he saying *Word.*

He yawn and lay down on me. Naptime creeping up on him. I stay this way a minute. I like listening to him breathe and feeling his chest rise against mine. He don't know that I'm tired all the time or that I'm technically a kid. He just know that I got him.

When we like this, I ain't gotta know a whole lot either. I just know that I love him. I kiss his temple so he'll know it.

The doorbell ring. Seven raise up and look toward the door.

"What? You gon' answer it?" I tease. I set him in the playpen that I sold my stereo to buy, and I peek out front.

What the hell? It's Lisa. I ain't seen her or talked to her since she pushed me out the window.

I open the door. "Hey?"

She in an oversized hoodie and some sweatpants. A baseball cap hide some of her hair. "Hey," she says, real soft. "Can I come in?"

I step aside and let her in. Lisa hug herself real tight, the way she do when she tryna keep the world away.

"You a'ight?" I ask.

"Um, yeah. Is this a bad time?"

"Kinda. I gotta put Seven down for his nap. If you cool with waiting a li'l bit—it won't take me long."

"Yeah. That's fine."

"A'ight," I say. Something not right, but I gotta get this boy to bed. I pick him up. "Seven, say hey to Lisa."

Lisa get this tiny smile that get bigger the longer she look at him. "Hi, Seven. Wow, what have you been feeding him, Maverick?" She laughs.

"Ay, don't hate. He just got more to love."

"Chunky babies *are* the best babies," she admit, and come closer. She take Seven's hand, and he give her a drooly grin. "Hi, Punkin. Hi."

"Punkin?"

"Yeah. He's a fat little pumpkin. He looks a lot like you." Her smile fade a bit. "I also see Iesha."

As much as I love my son, I hate that sadness in Lisa's eyes. I try to get rid of it. "Hold up. You said he look like a pumpkin and he look like me. You saying I look like a pumpkin?"

"You wish. He's cute. You a'ight."

"Dang, you a hater!" I laugh. It's as if the last few weeks never happened. "You wanna help me get him ready for his nap?"

Lisa make faces at Seven, and he giggle. She real good with babies. "Depends on what I gotta do. I'm not changing a diaper. No, sir, I'm not," she says, in her baby voice.

I chuckle. "I'll change him. You just help me get him to sleep. I want him on schedule. The parenting book said that's important."

"Parenting book?"

"Fa'sho. I got a couple of them. I wanna do this right."

Lisa's smile don't reach her eyes. "Wow. That's . . . that's great."

I tilt my head. "You sure you okay?"

"Um, yeah. Let's get this cutie pie down for his nap."

She lying, but she obviously not ready to talk. We go to my room, and I swear Seven realize I'm finna put him down. He start crying.

"Ay, stop acting like that in front of company," I say as I put him on the changing table. "You got this beautiful girl here, and you catching an attitude. That ain't cool, man."

Lisa look around my room. It's real different from the last time she was here. Seven's stuff took it over. "Wow, you finally took down those hoochie-momma posters."

I snicker as I undress Seven. She mean all them girls from *Playboy* that I had on my walls. Lisa hated them. "Yeah. Couldn't expose him to all of that."

I pull Seven's shirt over his head. He whine like, *Hurry up!*

"A'ight, a'ight!" I say. "Since we got a special guest with us today, I'm gon' do one of her favorite songs for Daddy radio."

I beatbox "Baby-Baby-Baby," by TLC. That's Lisa's favorite group and one of her favorite songs. I hold the baby powder like it's a mic and do a li'l dance.

She laugh. "Oh my God, what are you doing?"

I motion her over to the changing table. She join me. I sing, and she pass me the baby wipes and a clean diaper. Soon she singing too.

It take no time to get him changed. I pick him up, and we dance with him around the room and sing to him. We make him laugh more than I ever have by myself.

Ain't nothing felt this good.

Seven really like Lisa. So much that he reach for her. He don't do that with everybody. Ma say he antisocial.

Lisa take him. He yawn and rub his eyes. "Did we wear you out?" Lisa ask, kissing his cheek. He rest his head against her.

I brush his hair. "We better put him down before he fall asleep on you."

Lisa lay him in his crib. I turn on his mobile and kiss his forehead. "Sweet dreams, man."

This one time I don't think he gon' fight sleep. His eyes barely open. I motion Lisa to follow me to the hall, and I gently close the door. "Damn. It's never that easy to put him to bed."

"Really?"

"Yeah. You must got that magic touch. I need you to help out every night." I'm joking, but Lisa don't laugh. "My bad. I ain't mean nothing by—"

"It's cool. He's a sweetheart. You're a great dad, Maverick."

"Thank you. I'm trying. It's scary sometimes."

Lisa hug herself tight. "Can we talk now?"

"Yeah. What's up?"

She look me in the eye, and I know something real wrong. "We should sit down."

Damn, did somebody die? "Yeah, a'ight."

I lead her to the kitchen. It smell like the Fabuloso Ma made me mop with last night. The fam coming over for Thanksgiving later this week. Ma want the house spotless, and she expect me to make it happen.

"You want something to drink?" I ask Lisa as she sit at the table.

"No, thanks."

I sit across from her. "A'ight. What's up, then?"

"Maverick, I . . ." Lisa's voice crack, and she start crying.

I got this sinking feeling in my stomach. I get up and hug her. "Ay, it's a'ight. Whatever it is, I got you, okay?"

Lisa wet my shirt with her tears. "Maverick . . . I'm late."

I think I heard her right, she kinda muffled, but I'm confused. "Late for what?"

Lisa pull back, and her teary eyes lock with mine. "I'm *late*."

My heart pound hard. She gotta mean something else. "What—what you mean?"

Teardrops fall down Lisa's cheeks, and she say four words that stop time.

"I think I'm pregnant."

SIXTEEN

Pregnant?

What?

I gotta sit, and the floor closer than any chair. I sink onto the tiles.

How the hell? We only did it once without protection, and I was careful. Ain't no way unless . . .

I look up at her. "Is it mine?"

Her tears dry up quick, and Lisa get this murderous look.

"Is it yours?" she repeat, and stand. "Is it yours?"

In seconds, she beating the crap outta me. Hitting me, kicking me, punching me.

I ball up in the fetal position. "Ay, ay! Chill!"

"Is it yours?" She punch my arm. "Are you freaking kidding me?"

"I'm sorry! I didn't know!"

"You should know! I haven't been with anybody else, Maverick! This is all your fault!"

"How the hell is it my fault?" I yell.

"You should've been careful!"

"I was!"

"Obviously not enough! Ooooh!" She punch my arm again. "I was supposed to be done with you! I was supposed . . . oh God . . ." She gasp for air. "Oh God, oh God—"

I get up and hug her. She hit me at first, but she crying too much to put up a good fight.

"I can't be pregnant, Maverick." She sob into my chest. "I can't."

I'm so freaked out I can't calm her down. "You sure you are?"

Lisa wipe her eyes. "I haven't taken a test, but I'm late, and I'm never late. Then this morning I threw up. Luckily Momma wasn't home or—oh God. What am I gonna do?"

"Ay, chill." I help her sit down. "You might not be pregnant. We need to go buy a test."

"I can't. What if somebody sees me and tells my momma? You know how she is."

Ms. Montgomery one of them strict, churchgoing types even though she cuss like a sailor and drink like one. Lisa definitely can't be spotted buying a test. Her momma would kill her whether she pregnant or not.

"I'll go buy one then," I say.

"What if somebody sees you?"

"We gotta know, Lisa. This the only way."

"Is it bad that I almost don't wanna know?"

I stare at her stomach, too. It's hard to imagine a baby might be in there. "Nah. I'm right there with you."

We get quiet. One li'l test might change our whole lives.

Lisa close her eyes. "What if I am pregnant, Maverick? What are we gonna do?"

"We'll figure it out," I say.

She sniffle. "*We?*"

"Yeah." I brush her tears from her cheek. "We in this together."

Lisa wrap her arms around my neck and cry into my shoulder. I hold her and tell her it'll be okay, but that feel like a lie.

I kiss her forehead and go to my room. Seven knocked out with a smile. He must be dreaming something good. He don't know I'm living a nightmare.

I throw on my Starter jacket. My best bet is to go to Wal-Mart on the east side. It's a twenty-minute walk one way, but that's nothing compared to being seen buying a pregnancy test. I look through my wallet, and my stomach knot up.

I only got two dollars. Pregnancy tests cost way more than that. I'd have to steal to get one from Wal-Mart. There's only one store where I can get it now and pay for it later.

I gotta go to Mr. Wyatt's.

* * *

I walk around the corner with my head down. I don't know what I'm gon' say to Mr. Wyatt. He gon' wanna know why I need a pregnancy test. I should tell him it's for a friend. Yeah, that's it. It's kinda true too—Lisa *is* a friend.

Who I'm kidding? He won't buy that. He gon' lay into me. Only thing worse would be—

Shit, Ma. When I told her Iesha's baby might be mine, she was so disappointed. There I was, doing exactly what the world expect from Black kids—making a baby while I'm a baby. If I got another one on the way already . . .

God, please let this test come back negative.

I nod at Mr. Wyatt's nephew Jamal as he sweep the curb in front of the store. He a quiet, nerdy, stocky dude with dreadlocks. I don't know if he ever said five words to me. The door to the store feel heavier than usual. The bell ring to let Mr. Wyatt know he got a customer. He at the cash register, talking to Mr. Lewis. Damn, do that man ever cut hair?

"Hey, son," Mr. Wyatt says to me. "You okay?"

Hope he don't see my legs shaking. "Yeah. I gotta grab something real quick."

"Bet' not expect to get it for free," Mr. Lewis butts in. "Just 'cause you work for Clarence don't mean you get freebies."

"Hold on now, Cletus. Don't come up in my store tryna run things."

While they fuss, I go look for the test. Problem is, I don't know where pregnancy tests would be. Near the bathroom tissue? That make sense. Lisa gotta pee on it. I go to that aisle but nah, they not there. Near the baby diapers? That make sense. You checking to see if you having a baby. Nah, they not there. I go near the lady stuff. Pads, tampons, that kinda shit. Ma send me in here sometimes to buy her tampons. It's embarrassing as hell.

That's exactly where the pregnancy tests at. Mr. Wyatt got two kind. I can't tell a difference, and I ain't taking a chance. I grab one of each.

Time to face Mr. Wyatt. My steps sound loud as hell to me, and the cash register farther away than usual.

Mr. Wyatt and Mr. Lewis watch me approach. Mr. Wyatt's eyes drift down to what's in my hands. His forehead wrinkle, as if he not sure of what he see.

I make it clear for him. I set the pregnancy tests on the counter.

"Aw, hell. You don't need condoms," Mr. Lewis says. "You need a damn vasectomy." He limp out the store, going, "Ri-damn-diculous!"

Mr. Wyatt pinch the space between his eyes. "Son. Please tell me these are not for you."

I stare at the floor. "They not. They for a friend."

"Look at me and say it."

I can't. I couldn't look at myself in a mirror right now and say it.

"Good God, boy. When the Lord said replenish the earth, he didn't expect you to do it yourself. Do you know how to use a condom?"

"I usually wear protection, Mr. Wyatt. It was only this one time."

"Obviously not. You got Seven. Son, you gotta be smarter than this. You can't go around just making babies. How are you gonna provide for them? Take care of them?"

I don't know. All I can do is stare at my kicks.

Mr. Wyatt come from behind the counter and clasp the back of my neck like he did that day in the garden. He sighs. "Who is the young lady?"

"Lisa," I mutter. "She waiting at my house now."

"Don't keep her waiting, then."

I swallow. "I don't have the money. Can I—"

"I'll take it out your paycheck," he says.

I mumble a "thank you," stuff the tests under my jacket, and go home.

Lisa pace around my kitchen. There's three empty soda cans on the kitchen table, and she sip from a fourth.

I set the boxes on the table. "What you doing?"

"I'll need to pee to take the tests," she says. "So I'm trying to fill my bladder."

"Oh. I got two tests. I couldn't tell the difference, so I grabbed them both."

"Good. The more, the better. You know, I bet I'm not pregnant. It's probably a coincidence that I'm late and that I threw up. I know my body. I would know if a freaking embryo was in my uterus, right?"

I don't know nothing. "Maybe?"

"I would know." Lisa grab the boxes. "They're gonna be negative."

She mutter that the whole way to the bathroom. I follow her and wait in the hall.

"They're gonna be negative," she says on the other side of the door. "They're—shit!"

Oh, damn. "What it say?"

"Nothing! I peed on my freaking hand!"

I'd laugh if this were another situation. "You need more pee?"

"What, are you gonna pee for me?"

"Dag, I was only asking!"

"Whatever," she mumbles.

I shut up and wait. After a while, the toilet flush, and Lisa open the door. "Both tests will take five minutes."

Five minutes never seemed so long. "A'ight."

I set a timer on my watch, and we sit on the bathroom floor. It's hard not to stare up at them li'l sticks that could change our lives.

"Thank you," Lisa says. "For getting the tests, for being so supportive. Although, that's what you should do in the first place, so, frankly, I shouldn't thank you."

I smirk. "You right. This what I should do. I told you, we in this together. No matter what." Even though the "no matter what" scary as hell.

She must think that too, 'cause she don't say nothing.

I glance at my watch. "Three minutes."

Lisa nod. She rest her cheek on her knee and look at me. "Have you been washing your hair?"

I've kept my hair in an Afro puff ever since she washed it. I put shampoo in it sometimes in the shower. Conditioner still for girls. "Yeah. This 'fro shit a lot to keep up. I think I wanna cut it and get a fade."

"That would look good. How's school?"

"A'ight, I guess. Tryna get through it. You?"

"Busy, but fine," she says. "There's basketball, college applications, yearbook, school paper. Prom."

"Prom? That ain't till spring."

"I know, but Momma wants me to get a dress now. She says they're cheaper. We're gonna get my measurements this week." Lisa glance down at her stomach. "May not matter now."

My watch beep, and both of us jump. Time's up.

"Okay," Lisa says. "One line means no baby; two lines, baby."

"Got it."

We stand together. Lisa close her eyes and inch her hand toward the counter. She pick the tests up.

"Please, God. Please?" she prays.

Lisa open one eye and then the other. Her face fall. My stomach drop.

"No," she says. "No, no, no!"

She toss the tests onto the counter.

Both of them got two lines.

Lisa pregnant.

For the past hour, the words been on repeat in my head like the worst song I can't forget.

Lisa pregnant.

She ain't stopped crying since we found out. I hold her on the couch, and I wanna cry along with her.

Lisa pregnant.

We waiting on Ma to come home so we can break the news. I'm so damn dead.

And Lisa pregnant.

She straighten up, wiping her eyes. "What are we gonna do?"

"I don't know," I mumble. *Lisa pregnant.* The words pound my skull. I hold my forehead. "I mean, you got options. What you wanna do?"

Yeah, it's gon' affect me, but I ain't pregnant—Lisa is. This her decision.

Lisa bite her thumbnail. "I don't know. There's an abortion clinic downtown. I heard it's expensive."

Goddamn, I'm always needing money. "I'd find a way to get it."

"I don't want you selling drugs again, Mav. I could call my dad. He'd pay for it."

Lisa don't mention her dad much. I know he married and it ain't to her momma. He got a whole 'nother family across town. He give Ms. Montgomery money and scoop her up sometimes. That ain't my business though.

"There's also adoption," Lisa go on, "but I don't know." She put her face in her hands. "I don't know, I don't know, I don't know."

Seeing her cry got a way of cutting me deep. I wrap my arms around her. "Whatever you decide I'm on board, a'ight?"

She look up at me. "You mean that?"

"Fa'sho." I kiss her hair. "You got my word."

Lisa bury her face in my shirt and cry her eyes out. I already know what she gon' do. It's the only option that make sense. I'll be right by her side when she do it.

An engine hum into the driveway.

Lisa gasp. "Oh God."

The engine fade off, and the car door creak open and shut. Ma's feet thump against the walkway. Her keys jingle on the porch and the front door open.

"I'm back! Brought you some—" She notice us on the couch. "Dinner. Lisa, baby, what are you doing here?"

Lisa's chin tremble. "We're sorry, Mrs. Carter."

Ma set down the Red Lobster bag. That's one of her and Moe's favorite spots. "Sorry? For what? What happened?"

"We . . ." My heart pound so loud I can hardly hear myself. "We . . ."

Lisa cover her mouth. She hop up and rush down the hall.

"What in the world?" Ma says, and we hurry after her. We find Lisa bent over the toilet, puking her guts out.

"I'm so sor—" She can't talk for throwing up. "We didn't mean—"

Ma hold Lisa's ponytail back. "Baby, what are you talking about? Sorry for what?"

It's easier to look at Ma's hair than to look her in her eyes. I see them couple of grays she say I gave her, and I feel like shit knowing I'm 'bout to give her more.

I swallow. "Lisa pregnant, Ma."

Ma don't respond. Her face don't even react. She just rub Lisa's back.

Maybe I didn't get the words out like I thought. "Ma, I said Lisa—"

"I heard you," she says, and her voice almost a whisper. "Go get her a ginger ale."

I go to the kitchen and grab a cold one outta the refrigerator. When I get back, Lisa sitting in front of the toilet. Ma wipe around her mouth with a washcloth.

I pass Ma the soda. She pop it open and give it to Lisa. "This will help settle your stomach."

Lisa nod and take little sips.

Ma sit on the side of the tub and close her eyes. She take a deep breath. "Haven't we discussed this stuff, Maverick?"

Ma never told me 'bout the birds and the bees—nah, she told me exactly how babies are made without any dumb metaphors. She bought my first condoms when I was fifteen, when she realized me and Lisa were together a whole lot. That wasn't her way of saying, "Go have sex." She made it clear she only want me prepared.

Now I gotta admit I wasn't. "Yes, ma'am. We discussed it."

"And you had unprotected sex anyway," she says.

"Yes, ma'am. It was an accident."

"An accident is dropping a plate on the floor. Y'all were dumb."

We can't argue against that.

Seven wake up, crying. Ma push up from the tub. "I'll go check on the baby."

She step over Lisa and walk out. She ain't looked at me yet.

Tears fill Lisa's eyes. "What have we done?"

I sit on the floor beside her and wrap my arms around her. Eventually, I help Lisa to the living room sofa so she can lie down a bit. All that crying can't be good for her, and she can't go home like this right now. I go to my room to grab a pillow and a blanket.

I find Ma hunched over Seven's crib, so still she look frozen.

I inch toward her. "Is he a'ight, Ma?"

She wipe her face, and that's when I realize she crying. "Have I failed you, Maverick?"

Her soft voice hit me as hard as a brick. I swallow the lump in my throat. "No, ma'am."

"You're sure? Because it feels like it. I've tried my hardest, God knows I have, and yet here we are. Two babies before you're eighteen. It's bad enough your father convinced me to let you join a *gang* for protection." She shake her head. "Some mother I am. Loving you isn't enough. Being hard on you isn't enough. *I* haven't been enough."

I wanna hug her, but I don't got the right. "Yeah, you have, Ma. I made some bad decisions, that's all. I'll do better, I promise."

She whirl around, and her eyes finally meet mine. They wet with tears. "How, Maverick? What are your plans? What are you gonna do?"

I open my mouth, but . . .

I don't know.

I think that hurt her the most.

She wipe her face again. "You know what? We've been putting this off, but it's clear that it's time we take a trip."

Huh? "A trip? To where?"

"To the person you need the most," Ma says. "We're going to see your father."

SEVENTEEN

It's the day before Thanksgiving, and instead of baking desserts like she usually do, Ma gon' make the three-hour drive to Evergreen Prison.

It's a miracle we going. There was all this paperwork that had to be done so Seven could go. I'm not legally his daddy yet—we need Iesha to make that happen, and I don't know where she at—so we technically couldn't do the paperwork for him. Cousin Gary had to call in some favors. It's stupid that people have to get approved to see their loved ones in prison in the first place.

I pack Seven's diaper bag on my bed and hold the phone with my shoulder. I wanna check on Lisa real quick. She ain't told her momma she pregnant yet. She waiting for Carlos to get home. She say he can keep Ms. Montgomery from going too overboard. He supposed to arrive today.

Lisa haven't told me what she wanna do 'bout her pregnancy. I think she scared to admit she want an abortion. I keep telling her I'm fine with whatever she decide, hoping she'll go on and admit it.

The phone only ring once before she go, "Hey, Mav."

I forget her momma got caller ID. "Hey, how you feeling?" I ask. Baby girl dealing with morning, noon, and night sickness. She got her momma thinking it's a stomach bug.

"I'm okay," she says, kinda low. "Carlos got here a few minutes ago."

"Oh. Cool." That explain why she keeping her voice down. I wanna ask if this mean she gon' tell them, but I'm trying not to push her, you know? "What you got planned today?"

Lisa snort. "If that's your way of asking if I'm telling them, nicely done."

I smile. She know me too good. "Ay, you said it, not me."

"Mmm-hmm. Well, I'm not telling them today. I wanna wait until after Thanksgiving in case there's a bunch of drama."

"Ay, don't worry. They probably gon' be mad, but we'll get through this. It'll all be over before you know it."

"Um . . . about that." She take a long pause. Then, "I wanna have the baby, Mav."

It's like an elephant plop down on my chest. "You . . . you do?"

"Yeah. Some girls would make a different choice, and that's

cool. That's their choice to make. But I wanna be a mom."

"You wanna keep it, too?"

"Yeah."

I thought—I figured—she got so many plans, like college and basketball. A baby don't fit in that. Messed up as this gon' sound, thinking she was gon' have an abortion was the only thing that kept me from balling up in a corner somewhere. It ain't been a baby. It's been a pregnancy.

Now it's a baby—*my* baby—that I gotta take care of and provide for.

"Mav? You there?"

I clear my throat. "Yeah. What, um . . . what made you decide to keep it?"

"I think—I *know* I can handle it. My momma and Carlos will be upset at first, but they'll help out. I'm sure my dad will, too."

My head throbbing, man. "What 'bout college? You wanted a basketball scholarship."

"I have the grades to get academic scholarships," Lisa says. "I'm still gonna go to college. Keisha did. This baby won't mean my life is over."

I never met anybody with the kinda determination Lisa got. She act like if she say something, it's settled. No question. She say her life ain't over, then her life ain't over.

Feel like mine is. Being Seven's daddy is hard enough. Another baby mean more crying, more diapers, more bottles, more money. More, more, more. I don't got more. I don't know what to do. I don't even know what to say, and now the phone so quiet it's awkward.

"Wooow," Lisa says. "So much for being on board with whatever I decide."

She throw my promise back in my face, and it hit like ice water. "Lisa, hold up—"

"I should go. Hope you have a good visit with your dad."

I'm met with the dial tone.

Me and Ma get ready to hit the road.

I try to get Seven situated in his car seat, but the straps real snug on him. I tug at them, hoping that'll help.

Ma notice me struggling. "He needs a new car seat. He's outgrowing that one."

I look at her. "What? I thought these things fit all babies."

"No. That's an infant seat. You have to get something a little bigger."

And it's gon' cost money that I don't got. Story of my life.

Ma speed down the highway, doing eighty. Granny say she got "a heavy foot." She might cut this three-hour drive into two. Seven babble in his snug car seat like he tryna make up for the talking me and Ma not doing.

Before we left, I told Ma that Lisa keeping the baby. She got that same blank look she had when we told her Lisa pregnant and went, "Okay." That's it.

I watch woods pass by my window, and I almost wanna jump out and run into them. Lisa think she can handle this baby, but can I? Seven need me for everything already, and most days I ain't sure I'm doing that right.

I screwed up. Ma used to tell me, "Don't grow up too fast. You'll miss being a kid." I thought she was bugging, but I get it now. 'Cause suddenly, I got kids, and I wish more than anything that I could be a kid. Then wouldn't nobody depend on me.

Tears fill my eyes. My life really over, man. I'm never gon' sleep no more. I'm never gon' have enough money. I'll never be able to hang out with my friends. I'll never go to college. I'm gon' be bagging groceries for the rest of my fucking life.

I pull my shirt over my mouth and turn toward my window. Ma shouldn't have to see me cry when she the one with the broken heart.

Evergreen Prison's in a small town that's only got a general store and a diner. Me and Ma went in that diner once. It was nothing but white people in there, and they gave us dirty looks soon as we walked in. We walked right back out.

It's *that* kinda town. Don't help that it feel like we driving up to a plantation. The prison is surrounded by miles of fields. Sometimes they have the inmates out working in them. When I was a kid, I thought the prison was like a castle—a mountain of concrete surrounded by a tall, razor-wire fence. I came up with this whole story in my head, that it had been taken over by bad guys who kidnapped Pops, and he'd find a way out. He can't find a way outta forty to life.

They not doing car searches today, so Ma park and we go right in. Holidays popular for prison visits, and that mean the lines longer. We go through metal detectors and pat-downs before we ever get to the visiting area. I could only bring in one pacifier, one bottle, one diaper, one toy, and one change of clothes for Seven. I carry him through the metal detector, and they pat him down to make sure we not hiding something in his diaper.

I hate this shit.

The visiting area look like a school cafeteria but with guards standing around it. They got these dull yellow tables and chairs that's bolted to the floor. The walls light yellow cinder block, and the floors are white and yellow. Guess they tryna make up for the sunlight since no windows in here.

We get a table and wait. Ma brought some money for the vending machine. That's all she could bring besides her car key. She buy every snack they got and lay them out on the table. Our own version of a family Thanksgiving.

It probably look like I'm bouncing Seven on my knee, but I can't keep my legs still. I don't know why I'm nervous, this my pops. He never come down on me.

A loud buzz go off, a door open, and one by one inmates in orange jumpsuits come in and reunite with their folks. Seem like every visitor here get their inmate, and I start to wonder if Pops gon' come out.

At the very end, there he is.

This man got my whole face. I mean, I got his. Ma say we identical. She'll bring it up at the most random times. I could be staring at my homework to the point my eyebrows almost touch, and Ma will go, "You look so much like your father."

She say we walk alike, too. Pops walk like the world was made for him. He bald now—back in the day, he had a Jheri curl like Eazy-E. He used to be skinny, but ain't much to do in prison besides lift weights. They got him jacked up.

He catch sight of us, and his smile take over his face.

Ma hurry into his arms. This hug the only time they can touch during the visit. Prison rules. They kiss, and I glance away like a li'l kid.

Pops look at me. These days we eye to eye, but I feel like a ant standing in front of a mountain—he always seem bigger than life to me. Don't know if that's 'cause folks in the Garden act like he a god or if it's just 'cause he my pops.

Ma take Seven, and Pops wrap his arms around me. It's one of them big, tight hugs that seem to get all of me.

"I missed you, boy," he says, all rough. "I missed you."

"I missed you too, Pops."

He hold me in front of him. "Damn, man. You . . ." He clear his throat. "You keep growing, huh? What you been eating?"

"Everything," Ma says.

Pops chuckle. "I can tell." He clasp the back of my head. "My main man."

That feel like a hug, too.

Pops turn to Ma, and Seven all he see. His eyes light up. "There go that baby."

He hold his hands out for Seven. Li'l Man grip Ma's shirt and whimper.

"It's okay, Man-Man," Ma coos. "That's your grandpa."

I brush his hair to tell him the same. Long as we good, he good—he let Pops take him without much of a fuss. As chubby as he is, he super tiny in Pops's gigantic hands.

"Seven Maverick Carter," Pops says it like he testing it out. "Can you say 'Grandpa'? Say 'Grandpa.'"

Ma chuckles. "Adonis, that baby's too young to talk."

"I don't know. Smart as you say he is, he'll be talking soon. I'm ready to hear whatever he gotta say." Pops kiss his cheek.

Me and Ma sit on one side of the table, and Pops sit on the other with Seven in his lap. He allowed to hold Li'l Man the entire visit, but he can't touch us again until the end. The guards watch to make sure he don't.

Seven babble, and Pops go, "Yeah. Yeah, I know," like they having a conversation.

"How was the drive?" he asks us.

"Fine," Ma says. "Traffic was a little heavy because of the holiday, but that's expected. You're doing okay?"

Pops pretend to eat Seven's hand. Seven squeal and laugh. Pops smile wide. "I'm surviving. Finally got that job in the kitchen that I wanted. Y'all looking at the newest prep cook at Evergreen Prison."

"Yo, word?" I say.

"Adonis, that's wonderful!" Ma adds.

"Oh yeah. I ain't a field nigga no more. Massa moved me into the big house."

He and Ma crack up. I get why, but this not cool.

"Hopefully I'll be able to use some of my recipes instead of that mess they got us cooking," Pops says. "I convinced Chef to order some seasonings. Food need more than salt and pepper."

"Hopefully he'll listen. I'm making your yams tomorrow," Ma says. "They won't taste the same though."

"Hear that, Mav Man? You cook right, a woman got no choice but to miss you." He wink.

I can't crack a smile. He should be home, cooking for us.

Seven babble real loud, and Pops go, "I know, buddy. I'm right there with you. How everything at home, y'all?"

Ma turn all the way toward me, and the mood change. Mommas, boy. They can murder you with a look.

"Your son has something to tell you, Adonis," she says.

His son. Ma act like I lose her DNA when I screw up.

Pops look up from Seven. "What he got to tell me?"

My legs shaking real bad now. Man, I'm tripping. Pops gon' have my back.

I look at the table anyway. "Umm . . . my umm . . ."

"My eyes not down there, and my name not 'Um,'" Pops

says. "Fix that shit. And straighten up."

Pops never let me talk to anybody without looking them in the eye, and he never let me stumble on my words. I better say what I mean, no hesitation.

I sit up like he taught me, shoulders straight, chest up, my eyes locked with his. "Lisa, she pregnant."

"What the hell?" Pops sit back in a daze. He look at Ma. "Ain't you taught him 'bout condoms?"

"Hold on one damn minute. Don't you dare blame me, Adonis."

"I'm just tryna figure out why this boy making babies like this?"

"I'm sure if his father was home to teach him better, he'd do better."

"Here you go," Pops groan. "I don't wanna hear this today, Faye."

"Then don't blame me," Ma says. "I'm doing the best I can."

"Are you? Maybe if you wasn't with *Moe* all the damn time—"

"Excuse you?" Ma says. "Keep her out of this."

"I didn't bring her in it. I call home to talk to my wife, and you running around with her. No wonder our son out there impregnating these girls."

"I'm sorry for finding time to live my life!"

Pops suck his teeth. "Living your life, that's what you call it?"

"You're damn right. Living my life however I wanna live it.

The world hasn't stopped because you're in here."

I wanna disappear, man. I hate when they argue. I don't get why Pops got such a problem with Moe. Ma oughta be able to hang out with her friend without worrying 'bout me.

"Pops, this ain't on Ma. This my fault, a'ight?"

"You got some nerve, coming at me," Ma says, like I didn't say a word. "When was the last time you actually parented our son, Adonis?"

"What you want me to do, Faye? Huh?" Pops ask. "What the hell you expect me to do?"

"I don't know, but you better figure it out. Fast."

Ma hop up. She take Seven from Pops and go to the other side of the room.

Pops rub his face. "Maverick, what the hell, man?"

"Pops, it was an accident. I didn't mean—"

"It don't matter what you 'meant.' This some irresponsible shit, man."

"I know. I'm sorry, okay?"

"That ain't enough!" he barks. "This not a bad report card or a fight at school. You making babies, Mav. Where the hell was your head at, huh?"

Why he acting like this? "I wasn't thinking, that's all."

"Wasn't thinking," he says with a mean laugh. "Wow, you wasn't thinking. What do your name mean, Maverick?"

"Pops, c'mon."

"Answer me. What do your name mean?"

I feel like I'm in first grade again. My teacher, Mrs. Stanley, was this middle-aged white lady who wore red lipstick. First day of class, she called roll and when she got to me she went, "Maverick? Huh. That's an odd name."

The other kids snickered. It felt like Mrs. Stanley punched me. I went home and told Pops what happened.

"You know what your name mean," he said. "Bet her name don't mean shit. Tomorrow ask her what it is and what it mean."

I did. She said her name was Ann and she didn't think it had meaning. It was "just a normal name."

I told her exactly what Pops told me to say next. "Maverick means 'independent thinker.' Your momma and daddy wasn't mavericks, naming you that."

She sent me home with a note. Pops balled it up and threw it away. After that, he'd make me tell him what my name meant every day, so I'd know who I'm supposed to be.

I look at Pops now and tell him what my name mean like I used to do.

"So why the hell you wasn't thinking?" he ask.

"That was the day of Dre's funeral."

Pops go quiet, the way people do when they remember I lost my brother. He let out a slow sigh. "Grief a hell of a burden, Mav Man. A hell of a burden. However, it ain't an excuse."

I look up. "What?"

"Dre wasn't on your mind when you was with that girl," he says. "We both know what was. You let that thing in your pants make decisions for you. Don't use Dre as a cover-up."

"I'm not using him as a cover-up!"

Pops slap the table. "Take that bass out your goddamn voice!"

"Pops, chill."

"Chill? You expect me to be cool with the fact my son doing stupid shit?"

Hold up. He in the orange jumpsuit. "That's not as stupid as hiding cocaine in the house where your wife and son live."

He may seem like a mountain, but I'm starting to feel like one myself.

"Oh, okay," Pops says, stroking his chin. "This is Attack Adonis Day, huh? Say what you want, but I was being a man and taking care of my family."

"You damn sure ain't being one now."

Pops's nostrils flare. "Watch it."

"Or what?" I'm feeling bold as hell, and things I've been scared to say suddenly not so scary. "You left us. Got Ma busting her ass to take care of me and put money on your books. I had to join a gang 'cause of you. You can't come at either of us."

"What I did ain't got *shit* to do with the fact you keep knocking girls up."

"Yeah, a'ight, I made some bad decisions," I admit. "I'm gon' be there for my kids. Unlike you."

He can't say nothing, like I thought.

I push away from the table. "Man, I'm outta here."

"Maverick, we not done talking—"

"Yeah, we are. First you wanna blame Ma, and now you wanna come at me? What you doing besides bumping your gums? I'm more of a man than you. I'm taking care of mine."

"Son—"

"'Son,' nothing. I ain't had a father since I was eight."

The way Pops shrink, I hit him hard. Good. I grab Ma's key and head for the door. Ma call after me, but I don't stop till I'm at the car.

That man got some nerve, for real.

I get in the car and pop open the glove compartment. Had to leave my beeper in here. I got a couple of pages while I was inside, all from a number I don't recognize.

There's a pay phone here in the parking lot. I jog over to it and put in a quarter. This bet' not be a wrong number, as many times as they blew my beeper up. That was my last quarter.

"Hello?" some girl answer.

"Ay, this Maverick. I got a page from this number."

"Hold on, Mav," she says, and I realize it's Tammy. There's a muffled sound, as if the phone being handed to someone else.

"Mav?" Lisa says.

I straighten up. She sound like she been crying. "Lisa, hey. You a'ight?"

"My momma knows I'm pregnant," Lisa cries. "She kicked me out, Mav."

* * *

Ma come outside around an hour later.

It's obvious she pissed at me for how I talked to Pops. That ain't new, she was pissed when we got here. We get Seven situated in the car, and I tell her everything Lisa told me.

Not long after we got off the phone this morning, Lisa threw up again. Ms. Montgomery asked if she was sure this was a stomach virus or something else. Lisa had a feeling her momma knew the truth. She admitted that she was pregnant with my baby.

Ms. Montgomery went off. Lisa wouldn't tell me what all was said, but it must've been real bad. It ended with Ms. Montgomery telling Lisa to get the hell outta her house. Lisa didn't know where to go, so she walked to Tammy's. That's where we headed now.

Ma give me the silent treatment the whole three hours there. Cool with me. She only took me to see Pops so he could "parent" me. She can't be mad that I called him out when she did the same thing.

She pull up at Ms. Rosalie's, mumble that she gon' take Seven home, and drive off.

Ms. Rosalie the neighborhood Candy Lady. It's nothing to see kids coming outta her front door with Skittles and Doritos. She make the best freeze cups. I think that woman put a whole bag of sugar in the Kool-Aid when she make them. She recently started selling nachos, and them things good as hell. She'll throw jalapeños and chili on there for an extra dollar. Add a hot pickle and a Sprite on the side, and that's a whole meal for me. I done spent a hell of a lot of money at this house. Ms. Rosalie might pull in more dollars than some dope boys.

I ring the doorbell, and Ms. Rosalie answer with a warm smile. Don't let that fool you. Word is she pack heat. "Hey, Maverick baby. How you doing?"

"I'm good. Is Lisa here?"

Ms. Rosalie hold the door open. "She back in Tammy's room."

There's plastic on Ms. Rosalie's living room furniture. Granny do that to keep her stuff like new. In the dining room area, the table covered with boxes of candy and chips and jars of pickles. There's a couple of Crock-Pots for the nacho cheese and chili and a deep freezer for the freeze cups.

I go down the hall, and I hear Lisa and Tammy talking hushed-like. When they see me in the doorway, they stop.

"Hey, Mav," Tammy says. She cross-legged on the floor while Lisa sitting on her bed.

"Hey, Tam. I didn't mean to disturb y'all."

"It's okay. I'll leave y'all alone." Tammy get up and close the door on her way out.

Lisa's eyes all puffy and red. I hate that she been crying. "How did the visit with your dad go?"

I sit beside her. "That ain't important. You a'ight?"

She hug her backpack to her chest. It's overstuffed, probably with her clothes. "Not really. I keep thinking of what Momma said—" Lisa get a catch in her voice. "Carlos stood there and let her say all those awful things, Maverick. He never defended me."

Of course his coward ass did. They lucky I wasn't there. "I'm sorry you had to go through that. They foul, man, for real."

Lisa sniff. "I knew Momma would be upset, but I didn't expect her to put me out."

"Don't worry, a'ight? You can stay at my house. My momma would be cool with it." I think. Real talk, some days I wonder if she cool with *me* being there.

"Your mom has enough on her, Mav. Ms. Rosalie offered me Brenda's old room. She moved outta town with her boyfriend. I told Ms. Rosalie I'd take it."

"You ain't gotta do that. I'm telling you, my momma would be cool with it. You my girl, you having my baby, you oughta be with—"

"Wait a second . . . Mav. This baby doesn't mean we're a couple. You know that, right?"

"My bad. I said it outta habit." Kinda. Talk about looking stupid. "Still, we having a baby together. It would make sense that you stay with us."

"I appreciate the offer, but I need some space, and I can't have that at your house."

She act like Ms. Rosalie live in a mansion. "We'll make it work. I'll sleep on the couch and you can have—"

"I don't mean that kinda space."

The way she look at me, it's obvious what she really mean. "You don't wanna be around me, do you?"

"Maverick—"

"I thought we was in this together."

Lisa scoff. "Yeah, that was real clear this morning."

I should've known that would come up. "I was shocked, a'ight? I got a lot on me with Seven; you gotta understand that."

"Then you shouldn't have told me you were down with whatever I choose to do! I thought—" She close her eyes. "You know what? It doesn't matter anymore. Now that my mom and my brother won't be helping me out, I need to figure out what's best for me and my baby."

"You tryna say I ain't best for y'all?"

"Honestly, I don't know if you are."

I stand up. "What's that supposed to mean?"

"Oh my God, you know exactly what it means. You're a King Lord, Maverick. You think I want my baby to have a gang-banger for a father?"

"You was a'ight with having one for a boyfriend!"

"This is way different! I don't want my child around that stuff. To make it worse, you're a drug dealer."

"I stopped slinging! I been busting my butt, working for Mr. Wyatt!"

"Great. What are your plans beyond that?"

"I'll figure it out!"

"I can't depend on you to 'figure it out,'" Lisa says. "I can't even depend on you to not screw other girls! You think that's enough for my baby?"

I thought it was bad that time she told Carlos I wasn't worth the fight. This is worse. "You think I ain't shit like your momma and your brother do."

"I didn't say that. However, you do make stupid decisions."

"I told you, I'm done with the street stuff," I say.

"Oh, you're no longer a King Lord? Great."

"You don't get it."

"What's there to get?" she asks.

"A lot! You don't know how it is in the streets! Sitting in your house without a clue."

"Wooow."

"I'm just saying we from two different worlds, that's all."

Lisa nod. "Yep. We're obviously two different people. I'm just the bougie Catholic-school girl, right? Well this bougie Catholic-school girl and her baby deserve better than you."

She could've slapped me, and it would've felt better. "It's like that?"

"It's whatever you think it is."

Here I was, thinking we in this together. This girl got me looking like a damn fool. She worse than her momma and her brother. They tell me outright I'm not shit. Lisa made me think she actually loved me.

I see how it is now. Real clear. "A'ight," I say, nodding. "Do you, Lisa."

I give her all the space she need. I leave.

EIGHTEEN

Thanksgiving used to be my favorite holiday. Then Dre died.

The fam's taken over our house. Besides Aunt 'Nita, Uncle Ray, there's Granny; Granny's brother Billy; Uncle Billy's wife, Hattie; their kids, grandkids, and the one great-grandbaby; Granny's older sister, Letha, and her husband, Joe, and their son, Joe Jr. Keisha bringing Andreanna later. They're with Keisha's parents right now. Granny's younger sister, Cora, will come after visiting with her son, Gary the lawyer. She says his wife can't cook and she gotta stop by here to get some real food.

Our house magically feel bigger on the holidays when it should feel smaller with all these people here. Somehow today it feel empty. Dre ain't here to sneak into the kitchen with me and taste-test the food. By now, he would've started a football game

ANGIE THOMAS

in the backyard. The second his team lost he'd claim somebody cheated.

This shit the worst. The fam ain't as loud and ain't laughing as much. It's like they're having Thanksgiving 'cause it's what they're supposed to do. This probably foul, but seeing how much Ant hurt them, he got what he deserved.

Lisa not helping my mood. All that stuff she said yesterday play on repeat in my mind. She think I'm a good-for-nothing thug. A lot of people probably think that, can't lie, but it hurt worse coming from her.

Uncle Ray, Uncle Billy, and them yell at a football game on the TV in the living room. All the kids run around in the backyard. Aunt Letha taking a nap in my room. She said she got a headache, but Granny think that's a cop-out 'cause she don't like to cook. Aunt Hattie can't cook, so Granny won't let her in the kitchen.

I carry Seven in there. I don't know if it's all these people or what, but he real clingy today. I tried to put him in his playpen with Uncle Billy's great-grandson, and he threw a fit. I ain't been able to put him down yet.

There's foil-covered aluminum pans all over the kitchen. Aunt 'Nita stir a big pot of greens on the stove. Ma and Granny take pans out the oven. It's smelling good up in here. The turkey ready—Uncle Billy fried it this morning. Last I checked, we waiting on the ham.

Seven fuss in my arms. He gotta be hungry, acting like this.

I grab a bottle outta the fridge and hold it up to his mouth. I guess I ain't fast enough. He hold it and feed himself.

"Don't let him drink too much, Maverick," Ma says. "Give him some mashed sweet potatoes later, see if he likes those."

Oh, she talking to me now? I keep that to myself. "Yes, ma'am."

"Give him some of that corn bread and pot liquor, too," Granny says, poking his belly. "Get that baby some good country cooking. Formula ain't worth nothing."

I love my granny, man. She a short, round force of nature with a voice that seem bigger than her. When she talk, you listen. When she mad, you run. She claim her shotgun ain't ever missed. She love me, no matter what, unlike Ma and Lisa. I don't know which one of them two get on my nerves more.

"Mav baby, I brought something for you," Granny says. "Look in them pans over there."

I peek under the foil of the ones she point at. I find two pans of Granny's mac and cheese, two corn bread dressings, and—oh, snap, some more corn bread dressing. "You made three pans of dressing?"

"I sho did," she says, smiling. Granny got her dentures in today. She hate wearing them things. "I know my Mav baby love my corn bread dressing."

I grin, but Ma go, "He's not a baby. He makes babies."

"Aw, hush, Faye," says Granny. "He ain't the first person to have a child as a teenager. Me and your daddy did. One baby don't mean the end of the world."

"It's not one baby," Ma says. "Lisa's pregnant. He's going to have two."

Aunt 'Nita turn around. "Whaaaat—aw, hell!"

She drop the spoon in the pot.

I wanna disappear, man. I know my situation bad, yet it sound worse hearing it. It transform me from Maverick into the dumbass seventeen-year-old who screwed up and made two kids.

I may as well accept that that's what I am, a dumbass.

"Lisa that short, high-yella gal he was dating?" Granny asks.

Ma nods. "That one."

"Whew, chile! You fertile!" Granny says to me. "You look at a girl, and she get pregnant. Lord hammercy."

My cheeks burning. I'd be a'ight with the floor eating me alive. "It wasn't like that, Granny."

"It never is. No wonder that one there holding his bottle. He getting out the way for the other one. Mm!" She shake her head. "Mm, mm, mm!"

The doorbell ring. God saving me, for real. "I got it."

I have to step over folks in the living room to get to the front door. It's probably Shawn or King. Shawn practically family, and he always come get a plate. Ma invite King every year so he won't be by himself. I open the door, and it is King. I'm shocked as hell to see who with him.

Iesha draped all over King, like a girlfriend do a boyfriend except that can't be right. My best friend would've told me that he was in a relationship with my son's mama.

"What y'all doing here?" I ask.

Iesha's face light up at the sight of Seven. "There go my big boy! Hey boo-boo!"

She reach for him, but I step back. "I said, what y'all doing here?"

"Who is it, Mav?" Ma asks, coming up the hall. "King! You made it. And—" Ma's voice drop. "You brought Iesha?"

"Sorry we late, Mrs. Carter," King says. He always real polite with Ma. "I appreciate the invitation."

Ma look at me, and I swear I hear her go, *What the hell?* "Of course, baby," she says out loud. "You're like family. I didn't know you were bringing somebody."

"Oh, my bad," King says. "I figured it was a'ight since Iesha is baby boy's momma."

Iesha hug up on him. "Mmm-hmm. I wanted to cook for my man at home, but he said we could come over here." She lean up and kiss him all nasty.

Yoooooo, what the hell? My son's momma is now my best friend's girlfriend? This right off of one them "stories" Granny love to watch. Call this one *All My Hood Children.* Got my uncles and my cousins staring at us. We more interesting than the football game.

Ma purse her lips tight. "King, will you excuse us for a

moment? Iesha and Maverick, follow me."

It wasn't a question but a command. Ma march straight to her bedroom. I take Seven in there with me, and Iesha follow us. Ma tell me to close the door. I do, and I'm pretty sure I hear the TV volume go way down. My nosy family wanna hear this one.

Ma fold her arms and zero in on Iesha. "Where have you been?"

"I told Maverick my situation weeks ago, okay?"

"Moving around shouldn't stop you from checking on your child," Ma says. "Our number is in the phone book, and it's obvious you know where we live."

"I wasn't ready to deal with all that."

"What? Being a parent?" I ask. "I have to deal with it every day."

"Boy, please! I did it for three months by myself."

"I been doing it longer!"

"Hey!" Ma snaps. "We will not have that back-and-forth, one-upping mess. And don't make arguing in front of this child a habit. Cut it out now."

Ma take a deep breath. "Now look, postpartum is hard, Iesha. I get that. I wouldn't wish it on my worst enemy. However, you could've checked on your son. There is no excuse."

Iesha wrap her arms around herself and stare at the floor. "I felt bad for leaving him and not being able to handle it."

"That doesn't mean you disappear, baby," Ma says. "I'm sorry that your momma didn't support you like she should've and that you had to go through so much by yourself. But you have responsibilities now. Seven needs you as much as he needs Maverick."

"Not if I get in that bad space again, he don't," Iesha murmurs.

Here I go again, feeling bad for this girl after all she did. "Iesha, it'll be a'ight."

Ma rub her shoulder. "If it's not, you're not alone. It takes a village to raise a child. Seven has a big one. That means that you do too."

Iesha can't look at either of us.

Ma sighs. "Here's what we're gonna do. Iesha, you're going downtown this week to my cousin's law firm. You'll sign papers that will make Maverick Seven's legal father, change his name, and give Maverick custody."

Iesha's head snap up. "Oh, hell no! I ain't giving Maverick custody of my baby!"

"What you call leaving him with me for months?" I ask.

"You his daddy! You supposed to take care of him, stupid!"

"You're his momma, but here we are." Ma motion to the room. "Maverick needs custody in order to get assistance. Your momma gets food stamps and WIC for Seven, and he hasn't lived in her house in months. Now we can go about this the easy way, or we can go to court. That's completely up to you."

"I wanna be able to see my baby!"

"You will," Ma says. "Maverick, you'll tell Iesha a day that's good for her to come visit every week. Iesha, you show up when you're supposed to. As time goes on and as trust is built, y'all can add more days and discuss overnight visits. Understood?"

"Understood," I mumble, but we'll see when it come to them overnight visits.

"Fine," Iesha says. "Can I have my baby now?"

Ma nod at me. "Go on, Maverick."

I let Iesha take him outta my arms, and Seven start crying. He go limp like babies do when they don't want you holding them, as if they tryna make you drop them.

Iesha try to keep ahold of him. "It's okay, big boy. Momma's here."

He don't care. Seven reach for me.

Not only do he know me, but he don't want nobody but me. He been like that all day, but in this moment I can't explain how that feel.

I take him in my arms, and his fat li'l hands grip my shirt. I kiss his forehead. "It's a'ight, man. Daddy got you."

Iesha frown. "Why he acting like this?"

"He hasn't seen you in months, baby," Ma says. "Give him time."

"Dinner's ready!" Aunt 'Nita call out.

Ma motion her head toward the door. "C'mon, y'all."

We go to the kitchen with the rest of the family. We don't sit around a dining room table and eat like people do on TV. Nah, everybody fix a plate and sit wherever they want around the house. First, Granny gotta say grace. We hold hands around the kitchen and bow our heads. Granny do them long prayers, man. She act like God don't know what's going on and it's her job to fill him in.

"And Lord," she says, five minutes in, "please help these young mothers get their priorities straight. Nobody said it was easy, but they acting like they don't have responsibilities and expect other people to care for their children. Help them, Father!"

Ma must've told her all about Iesha.

"Help my grandson Maverick, too, Lord," Granny says. "Help him to stop making all these babies. Take all that fertileness and mannishness away from him, Lord! Make them spirits loose him!"

There's a couple of "Yes, Lord" and "Amens" from the fam. Aunt Letha put her hand on my forehead, talking about, "In Jesus name!"

This floor need to go ahead and eat me up, man.

Granny end her prayer by thanking God for the years we got with Dre. Hard to be thankful knowing we should've gotten more.

After ten minutes, Granny done, and everybody can fix their plates. Not me. I get Seven situated in his high chair. I can never eat and feed him at the same time.

Ma come touch my shoulder. "Baby, fix yourself some food."

"I will later. I gotta feed—"

"No. Iesha came here to eat our food, she can feed her son."

Ma said it loud enough for everybody to hear. Iesha got two plates in her hand—one for her, and one for King. Ma give her a glare that I know real good.

Iesha set down the plates. "I'll feed him."

"Thought so," Ma says. She kiss my temple. "Go eat, baby."

I smile. It's real nice when she on my side.

I stack a plate with ham and turkey, a big scoop of mac and cheese with the yams next to it 'cause ain't no other way to do it, and then some collard greens. I fix another plate just for dressing. I scoop some cranberry sauce on that joint, throw two rolls on top, grab a canned Sunkist out the cooler, and I'm good to go.

Finding somewhere to sit the only problem. The kitchen table full. The dining room table crowded, and so is the living room. Me and Dre would eat on the front porch, so that's where I head. I sit on the steps and set one of my plates where he used to sit. Kinda like having him here with me.

I pour out some Sunkist for him. That was his favorite. "Wish you were here, dawg."

I take a sip and dig in. Goddamn, Ma, Granny, and Aunt 'Nita threw down. I'm gon' need a couple more plates before the day over.

Wonder if Lisa able to eat or if her morning sickness been bad. I ain't called her today. She want space, fine, I'll give her space. Don't mean she not on my mind.

The front door swing open. "Dang, ain't nowhere to sit in there," King says.

He plop down on the steps beside me with two plates. He really gon' sit here like he ain't pulled some foul shit.

I set my plate down. "Yo, man, what's up with this?"

"What's up with what?" he ask, mouth full of corn bread dressing. "Man, your granny put her foot off in this."

"You know what I'm talking 'bout. You and Iesha together?"

He put mac and cheese and a yam on the fork. "I guess. You got a problem with that?"

"You brought her to my house, knowing that girl ain't around for our son."

"Then shouldn't you be happy I brought her?"

"Dawg, why didn't you tell me she staying with you? I asked you at the football game, and you switched the subject on me."

"She wasn't staying with me then," he says.

"Once she was, why you ain't hit me up?"

"Ain't like I see you, fool," King says. "You never come around me or the set."

"'Cause I'm busy taking care of my son, thanks to Iesha! You foul for—"

A loud, rusty Datsun screech to a stop in front of my house. The driver's door fly open and a muscular, light-skinned dude jump out.

"What the hell?" King says.

The driver rush toward us. Nah, toward *me*. Right as I realize it's Carlos, Lisa's brother—

Bam! His fist connect with my eye.

"You son of a bitch!" he screams.

I don't get a chance to say or do nothing. Carlos yank me off the steps and sling me into the yard. Soon as I hit the ground, his boots ram into my stomach, my chest, my legs, my back. I ball up to try to block the kicks.

Sound like the whole fam rush outside. Granny hollering, my little cousins hollering. Ma yell for somebody to stop Carlos. It take King plus three of Ma's cousins to get him off.

"He knocked up my little sister!" Carlos screams as they hold him back. "This son of a bitch knocked up my little sister!"

I get on my knees. I can't stand—everything spinning. Everything I can see, I mean. My right eye swelling shut from that sucker punch.

"Carlos," I say as blood drip around my teeth. My lip busted. "I'm sorry, a'ight?"

"You piece of shit!" he says. "You ruined her life!"

He snatch away from King and them. Just as fast as he came, he get in his car, slam the door shut, and drive off.

NINETEEN

It's two days before I can see out my eye good. Four days later, and it's still bruised.

This the first day back at school after Thanksgiving break, and my black eye getting me a lot of glances. I can't go down the hall without somebody staring or snickering. I find Rico and Junie at the spot under the staircase where us King Lords hang out, and they both go, "Daaaamn," when they see me.

"Who whooped your ass?" Rico asks.

"I hope they look as bad as you do," Junie says.

"Forget y'all."

"For real, what happened, dawg?" says Rico. "We'll get back at somebody if you want."

"It's nothing. I bust my ass going down some stairs."

Junie raise his eyebrows. "Them stairs got fists? That's a black eye, my dude."

"It was Mrs. Carter, wasn't it?" Rico says. "Your momma look like she can throw hands."

Junie nods. "Yep. She fine though."

What the hell? "That's my momma, fool!"

"And? She got *ass*." He motion his hand like it's going over her butt. "I'll gladly be your stepdaddy."

I punch the mess outta his arm.

"Ow! You need to be hitting whoever gave you that black eye!"

"Forget you. What's up with y'all? How everything in the streets?"

"Dawg, did you hear? Shawn got busted on Thanksgiving," Rico says.

"What?" I almost yell. "You lying!"

"I wish. He got pulled over during a traffic stop. You know they love to do them things during holidays. Cops found his piece and it wasn't registered. They took him downtown."

I wondered why he hadn't come over on Thanksgiving. "He can't get bailed out?"

Junie shake his head. "He a felon, and they take that shit real serious. Homie may be in there a minute."

"Damn." It don't seem like it was that long ago when I was riding around with Shawn. I swear, in the Garden you'll see a person one day, and the next they either locked up or dead. "Who running the set, then?"

"All the big homies wanna be in charge," Junie says. "I'm

glad we making money with King so I don't gotta deal with they bull."

"Word," says Rico. "With Shawn *and* Dre gone, it ain't the same. They were the only big homies who really cared 'bout us. We gotta look out for ourselves now."

"Damn." I don't know what else to say.

"Don't trip, Mav. It's all good," Junie says. "Long as we got each other's backs, we'll be a'ight in these streets."

"In the meantime," Rico jump in, "we tryna figure out how we gon' roll to this winter dance. You oughta come through."

Winter dance? Oh dang, I forgot that's next weekend. "I don't know, man."

"Why not?" says Junie. "You momma can watch your son like she did for the football game."

Not when I done got Lisa pregnant. I ain't ready to tell my boys that I got another baby on the way. I don't need the whole school in my business. "Nah, she probably won't watch him for that. I don't got a date no way."

"Who said shit 'bout a date? I'm rolling solo so I can get as much sloppy toppy as I want." Rico slap palms with a laughing Junie.

"We getting a limo," Junie adds. "Gon' roll through in some fly-ass tuxes, looking like the Mafia. You can't miss out on this one."

He talking limos and tuxes, and I'm thinking dollars. "How much that gon' cost?"

"You just have to put down a couple hundred," says Rico.

"Man, I gotta get my son a new car seat. I can't waste money on no dance."

"Is that why you rock them dusty kicks every day?" Rico asks, and Junie bust out laughing.

My sneakers them same Reeboks I bought this summer. By now I would've had a new pair.

Every now and then, I wonder how different things would be if I was still selling drugs. I'd have fresh kicks, fa'sho, and I could buy Seven everything he need.

I can't go there. Dre wouldn't want me to. I shrug at Rico. "I got more important things to deal with than shoes."

"We need to start calling you Old Man Carter," Rico says. "I take that back. My grandma get out more than you *and* she fresher than you."

"Whatever," I mumble.

The first bell ring for class. I follow Rico and Junie down the hall as they discuss the dance and their plans. It's like they speaking a language I ain't fluent in anymore. The words real familiar, but they done lost all meaning for me.

Me and Junie go to history class. Mr. Phillips write notes on the chalkboard as we fill into the room.

"Hope you're all prepared for today's exam," he says, with his back to us. "I trust that you studied properly over the break."

I stop dead and close my eyes.

I didn't study for nothing. I was too caught up in the fact I got another baby on the way.

This already ain't my day.

I end up having three exams, and I studied for none of them. Just what I need when my grades already rocky.

I rest my head back against this hard-ass seat. I'm riding the city bus downtown to meet Lisa at her doctor's. She called me Friday, told me she had an appointment today after school, and said I was welcome to come. That's it. Girl get on my nerves, man. Mr. Wyatt told me I can come to work whenever the appointment is over, but of course that I mean I'm gon' have to stay late. I can never catch a break.

Lisa's doctor's office is on the fifth floor of a skyscraper. People walk around the main lobby in suits with briefcases. I'm real outta place in my hoodie, jeans, and backpack. I get on the elevator with this white lady, and she pull her purse closer, like she scared I'm gon' snatch it. People way more scared of me than they oughta be.

I get off at the fifth floor and follow signs to the doctor's office. This definitely not the free clinic. Water streams down a fountain, and elevator music play from some speakers. Fancy paintings hang from the walls.

I let the receptionist know I'm here to meet up with somebody, and I scope out the waiting area. Lisa near the back in the navy blazer and plaid skirt she gotta wear to Saint Mary's. She made her uniform fresh by throwing on some Jordans. She fill out paperwork and ain't noticed that I'm here.

The person next to her has.

Carlos stare me down. One of his hands bandaged up, probably from the sucker punch he gave me.

I ignore that fool and sit on the other side of Lisa. "I'm not late, am I?"

"No, we just got—" She look up, and her mouth drop. "Oh my God, Maverick, is that a black eye?"

"It's nothing."

"That's not noth—" Lisa look at Carlos's hand. Then she look at me. She sighs. "Did you two get into a fight?"

Carlos rub his knuckles. "It wasn't a fight. I beat his ass."

This fool won once, now he talking shit. "Only 'cause I let you. Won't happen again."

"Oh, I'm more than happy to have a rematch."

"What it is, then?"

"Y'all! Please," Lisa says. "Don't start."

"Fine," Carlos says, through his teeth. "However, I have every right to be pissed that he ruined my little sister's life."

"He didn't ruin my life, and he didn't make this baby by himself," Lisa says. "I was a more-than-willing participant. Maverick told me he didn't have a condom, and I still wanted to have sex with—"

Carlos cringe. "I don't need to know more, thank you."

"Obviously, you do. If you're gonna be mad at him, be mad at me as well."

"Believe me, I am mad at you."

"Yeah," Lisa says softly. "You've made that pretty clear."

Hold the hell up, what he do to her? I swear, if he said some sideways shit to Lisa—

"Lisa Montgomery?" a nurse call out.

I know that voice. I look up, and sure enough, it's—

"Moe?"

Ma's best friend hold open the door that lead back to the examining rooms. She see me, and her eyes widen. "Mav, what are you doing here?"

Me and Carlos follow Lisa over to her. "Lisa got an appointment," I say.

Ma told her the deal by now. She give Lisa a tiny smile. "I thought that name looked familiar. How are you doing, sweetie?"

"Okay, I guess. Ready to get this appointment done."

"You're in the right hands." Moe look at Carlos and raise her eyebrows. "Only one person is allowed back with the patient."

"I know," Carlos says, eyeing me. "Just want to remind my sister that I'm out here if she needs me."

Nah, he wanna remind *me*.

Lisa mumble, "Thank you," and step around Moe.

I pat her brother's shoulder. "Enjoy the wait, *Carlton*."

Before he can respond, Moe close the door behind me.

She lead us to a room where she check Lisa's weight and her

blood pressure. Another nurse take some of Lisa's blood and have her go pee in a cup. After that, Moe lead us to an examining room and give Lisa a gown.

"You'll have to change into that," she says. "Now, don't be nervous. It's a simple exam. Dr. Byrd will ask more questions than anything."

Lisa take a deep breath. "Okay."

"We'll take good care of you. Faye would kill me otherwise. How's she doing, Mav?"

"She good. Recovering from Thanksgiving. I'm surprised you ain't stop by."

Moe's smile dim a bit. "I didn't wanna cause any problems. Dr. Byrd will be here shortly." She grab her clipboard and hurry outta the room.

I frown and point my thumb back. "What's up with that?"

"Maverick . . . nothing." Lisa shake her head. "Never mind. It's not my place to say."

"Huh? What's not your place to say?"

Lisa sighs. "You haven't figured it out yet, have you?"

I know my eyebrows practically touching. "Figured out what?"

Lisa smirk. "You're actually kinda cute when you're confused."

"Oh, word? I thought I wasn't shit."

"I never said that, Maverick. You assumed." She slip outta her blazer and, yo, this girl start to strip down right in front of me. I'm not complaining (I ain't a perv), but it catch me off guard.

"You gotta take everything off?" I ask.

"Yep." Her shirt go, and then her bra next, giving me a real good view. Man, I do love the sight of them things. I just be wanting to hold them sometimes. I ain't a perv, I swear.

Lisa give me the evil eye. "Stop looking at them."

I look at the wall. "You act like I ain't seen them before."

"You are more than welcome to go to the waiting room with Carlos."

"Okay, okay! I won't look."

"Good idea," she says, and I hear a zipper.

I pick up this weird-looking toy on the table. It's kinda shaped like an upside-down triangle but got two things sticking out on each side. Handles? I don't know. The middle part is red and pink. It tunnels down to an opening, like for a ball or something to go in.

"What kinda toy is this?" I ask Lisa.

"That's a uterus, Maverick."

I drop that thing so damn fast.

Lisa snort. "It's only a model, relax. You can look now."

Her clothes and sneakers in a small pile on the chair beside me, and she on the edge of the examining table in the gown. She swing her feet back and forth. "Carlos really messed you up, huh?"

That's what everybody say. Granny wanted to call the cops

and get him arrested for assault. Ma wouldn't let her. She said I earned it.

"A little," I say. I'll never give him that much credit. "I let him win. I deserve everything he had for me."

"Oh." Lisa look down. "Mav, I'm sorry for what I said the other day."

"You don't gotta apologize."

"Yeah, I do. I threw a couple of jabs that I shouldn't have."

"It must run in the family."

Lisa roll her eyes. "I'm glad you can joke about getting beat up."

"Ay, I'm just saying. Straight up? I'm sorry too."

"You weren't lying, there *is* a lot I don't know when it comes to the streets."

"Nothing wrong with that. Wish there was some stuff I didn't know myself. Anyway, how you feeling? Everything good at Ms. Rosalie's and at school?"

"Morning sickness sucks, obviously," Lisa says. "So does afternoon and night sickness. Yesterday was better, I only threw up in the morning. So far so good today. Ms. Rosalie's been fine. School's . . . interesting."

"How so?"

"Earlier, I had to tell Coach that I'm pregnant. Less than an hour later, I was called to the front office. One of the sisters and the chaplain waited for me."

"What they want?"

Lisa watch her feet swing. "They wanted to discuss my salvation. Told me that I committed a sin by having premarital sex and by breaking my purity pledge. They said I must seek forgiveness, and if I have an abortion, I'll get eternal damnation."

What the hell? There's a whole lot I don't know when it comes to God, but that sound like some bull. "You believe that?"

"I believe God is way more merciful than they are," Lisa says. "I told them I don't plan on having an abortion. They want me to put the baby up for adoption. Gave me info on a Catholic agency they've worked with in the past."

First off, why they in her business like that? Second, why the hell does a school work with an adoption agency? "Is that what you wanna do?"

"No. I wanna keep my baby. I told them the same thing. They went into this spiel, saying I must marry you so my baby isn't born out of wedlock."

"We can hit the courthouse. Ain't nothing but a thang."

Her face drop. "What?"

"I'm playing, Lisa, dang." But something else has been on my mind. "We can't at least be boyfriend and girlfriend though?"

Yeah, I wanna get back with her. I wanted that since we broke up.

"Mav, I told you this baby doesn't mean we're a couple."

"I ain't saying that's the reason we should get back together either, but why can't we?"

She push a strand of hair behind her ear. "I don't wanna be with a gangbanger, Mav."

"You used to hang with me and the homies. I don't see why it's a big deal now."

"That right there is the problem," she says softly. "You *don't* see a problem."

"Lisa—"

There's a knock on the door and this heavy-set Black lady with freckles come in. "Well, hello! I'm Dr. Byrd. How are you two today?"

Wait a minute. Black receptionist, Black nurse, Black doctor. Everybody who work here is Black. I didn't know that was . . . "possible" not the right word. I'll just say I didn't know.

Dr. Byrd confirm that Lisa is pregnant. She ask Lisa if she continuing with the pregnancy. Once Lisa tell her she is, Dr. Byrd get into her medical history and her family's medical history. She wanna know mine, too. I tell her that Ma got asthma and that Pops's baby sister had sickle cell. She died when she was fourteen. I also tell her Seven allergic to cats. We found out when Aunt 'Nita kept him and he sneezed every time her cat, Bubbles, got near him.

Dr. Byrd don't flinch at the fact that I already got a baby. She don't talk down to us or turn her nose up 'cause we're seventeen. She real sweet and understanding. She do what she call a pelvic exam, and damn, I didn't know ob-gyns do so much.

She get *in there*, if you know what I mean. Lisa talk to her 'bout school and stuff, as if this woman not all up in her . . . yeah.

After the exam, Dr. Byrd allow us to ask questions. Lisa came with a list. For real, she pull a notebook from her backpack. She ask everything from, "Do I need to change my diet?" to "Can I have sex while I'm pregnant?"

That one get my full attention. I'm surprised she asked, that's all. I'm real surprised when Dr. Byrd say yeah.

"Won't the baby see it?" I ask. "You know, the . . ." I wiggle my eyebrows.

Dr. Byrd chuckle. She know what I'm getting at. "The baby won't see anything. You have any other questions, young man? You've been so quiet, I almost forgot you were here."

"I'm good. This Lisa's appointment."

Dr. Byrd spin her chair toward me. "You're here, you obviously want to be involved. What would you like to know?"

"Umm . . ." I don't wanna sound dumb. "When we gon' know what we having? When you gon' do the video thing?"

"The ultrasound," Dr. Byrd says. "We won't be able to determine the sex of the baby this early in the pregnancy. However, we are doing an ultrasound today."

"We are?" Lisa ask.

"Mmm-hmm. It can help me figure out your due date. We may hear a heartbeat."

She set up some machine and help Lisa get situated on the examining table. This ain't like the ultrasounds on TV where they put gel on Lisa's stomach. Dr. Byrd puts some kinda wand up Lisa's . . . yeah. This ob-gyn stuff is wild.

"What if you see something's wrong?" Lisa asks.

"We'll focus on that *if* we get to that," Dr. Byrd says. "Relax for now."

I go to Lisa's side and take her hand. She actually let me hold it.

The ultrasound screen resemble a TV that lost a signal. Everything black and white and fuzzy. There's a part in the middle that look like a black hole, and in that there's a small white . . . blob?

"And there's our baby," Dr. Byrd says.

I squint. "That li'l blob thing?"

Lisa backhand my chest. "It's not a blob! It's a little peanut."

Dr. Byrd laughs. "I get why he called it a blob. Look closely and you can make out the head and the limb buds."

Part of it do look like a li'l round head, and li'l things stick out near the bottom. "I think I see them."

"I see them," Lisa whispers. "And that part that's thumping in the middle?"

"That's the heart," Dr. Byrd says. "Sometimes, you can't hear it this early so don't be alarmed. But let's see if we can—"

She twist a knob on the ultrasound machine, and a muffled *boomp-boomp-boomp* fill the room. I don't got words. Don't think any good enough.

Lisa's eyes glisten. "That's my baby. I mean, my embryo."

Dr. Byrd smiles. "That's your embryo."

She later tells us that Lisa's due date is around mid-July. So far everything look good. Dr. Byrd print out a sonogram picture for Lisa and one for me and write a prescription for prenatal vitamins. She wanna see Lisa in a month.

Lisa get dressed, and I lead her to the waiting room and toward the billing desk. Lisa too caught up in her sonogram to pay attention to where she going.

"My little peanut," she murmurs.

Her momma's insurance cover most of the visit. As mean as Ms. Montgomery is, I'm surprised she didn't take Lisa off. Lisa only got something called a co-pay that we gotta cover.

I slide my backpack off and search for my wallet. "How much is it?"

"Twenty dollars," the older Black lady at the desk says.

I only got a stick of gum. Mr. Wyatt paid me last week. I covered the light bill, the water bill, and bought some toys for Seven.

I gotta have more than this. I search my wallet and my backpack all over. Lisa watch, and the lady at the desk watch.

"My bad," I mumble. My cheeks burn. "I know I got a—"

"Mav, it's okay," Lisa says. "I can pay it."

"Nah, I got it. I just gotta find—"

"What's wrong?" Carlos ask.

He would bring his nosy butt over here. "Nothing. I got it."

"My co-pay is twenty dollars," Lisa explains. "Mav's trying to pay but—"

This dude push me aside. He take out his wallet and hand the lady the twenty. "Somebody here has too many kids to pay for."

Man, if we weren't in this doctor's office . . . "I only got one other kid, fool."

"Apparently one too many. Exactly how do you plan on taking care of my sister's child?"

My jaw tighten. "That ain't your concern."

"In other words, you don't know how. Figures. C'mon, Lisa," he says. "I'll take you out to eat, which is more than this thug can do. My niece or nephew is probably hungry."

I wait for Lisa to defend me. But she stare at the floor and push a braid behind her ear. "Talk to you later."

She follow her brother outta the doctor's office, and I'm left alone with a stick of gum.

Lisa depending on me, Seven depending on me, and so is my new baby. It's real clear that I can't do much for any of them with what Mr. Wyatt pay me. If I can't pay a twenty-dollar co-pay, I damn sure can't pay for diapers or food.

The way Dre wanted me to live just don't work.

I gotta get back in the drug game.

PART 3

DORMANCY

TWENTY

Bright green grass starting to grow on top of Dre's grave. It's a sure sign that spring almost here, and the worst reminder that life going on without him.

He buried far enough in the back of the cemetery that there's no noise from the cars on the freeway. Aunt 'Nita and Uncle Ray got him a real nice headstone. It's got his name, birth date, death date, and it call him a beloved son and father, which don't seem like enough. In cursive it say, "We loved him, but God loved him more." Hard to believe that.

I sit on the grass with my back to his headstone. It's one of them cold February days where the sun so bright it almost fool you into thinking you don't need a coat. Teddy bears, flowers, and cards decorate Dre's gravesite. I pick up a piece of pink construction paper shaped like a heart. There's some little figures drawn in crayon. I guess it's supposed to be Andreanna and her daddy.

It's enough to make me tear up. I wipe my eyes. "This ain't cool, Dre. I shouldn't be crying already. It's been a while since I rolled through, huh? My bad, dawg. Things been hectic. I bet you too busy hanging with 'Pac and Granddaddy to notice. Before you start, nah, I ain't skipping school today. We off. The teachers got some developmental shit going on. I figured I'd holla at you."

I rest my head back against his headstone. "The streets real rough, Dre. You know Shawn got busted a couple of months ago. Word is, the cops traced his gun to a murder. He may not ever get out. Now P-Nut calling himself the crown." I shake my head. "That dumbass don't know how to run anything. Him and some of the big homies beefing. It's so much drama and division, dawg. Me, King, Rico, and Junie decided we gotta look out for ourselves. We watch out for the youngins, too. I know that's what you'd want us to do.

"Yeah, we got our own drug thing on the low," I admit. "I refuse to work for that idiot P-Nut. This temporary for me, Dre, I swear. Once I get a regular job and get on my feet, I'm done slinging."

I imagine him twisting his mouth like, *Yeah right.*

"I mean it, man. I don't sell a lot no way. Only enough to make sure I ain't struggling. Too much money would make Ma suspicious. I can easily hide a couple extra hundred a week from her."

I run my hand along the grass. "This some damn good grass you got growing on top of you. Look like centipede grass. That shit real low maintenance. Mr. Wyatt call it 'mighty fine.' He talk 'bout plants like they women sometimes, man. I still work for him. It help keep Ma from knowing I sling. She on my back 'bout school enough as it is."

Knowing Dre, he'd be like, *Your grades* that *bad?*

"Yeah, I can't lie. It's hard to stay on top of them and everything else. I bet I'll have to do summer school. I dread it already.

"Let me not think on that. I gotta give you these updates. Your folks and Keisha doing okay. They taking it a day at a time. It's wild how fast Andreanna growing. She and Keisha came over the other week. Andreanna wanted to see her 'Sevy.' Ma say you were the same way with me."

My lips start to tremble, and my eyes burn. "Fuck." I pull my shirt over my mouth, but before I know it, I'm crying. "Fuck, fuck, fuck!"

Mr. Wyatt says grief hit you in waves. Sometimes it pull me out to sea and take me under. No wonder it's hard to breathe as I cry.

This the moment Dre would clasp the back of my neck and go, *It's all good, cuz.*

"No, it ain't," I say. "This ain't fair, Dre. Don't tell me that 'Life ain't fair' bullshit. It don't count with this."

Says who? he'd ask.

"I say so, fool." I laugh a little and wipe my face on my arm. "I miss you so much. I don't got nobody to talk to or hang with.

Seem like I'm on a different planet from Rico and Junie. Me and King, I guess you can call what we got a work relationship. Ever since he moved Iesha in and didn't tell me . . ." I shake my head. "We not cool like that no more. I oughta be used to losing people. Pops, you, Lisa, King. The list long as hell."

I try to laugh at my own joke. Can't.

I clear my throat. "A'ight, back to the fam. Let's see, Granny good. Nothing gon' ever slow that woman down. Ma good. Working all the time as usual. Pops a'ight, I guess. I haven't talked to him much after that stunt he pulled when we visited. He shouldn't have come at me sideways, Dre. He the last person who can parent anybody, you feel me?"

Nah, I don't, Dre would probably say.

"Whatever, man. I don't need a father. I *am* a father. I wish you could see Seven. He getting so big. Iesha visit him every Sunday, but the day-to-day stuff still on me, and it's still a lot. I'm scared to death 'bout having another one."

I pluck a blade of grass and run it between my fingers. "Lisa pregnancy going real good. We find out what she having soon. If it's a boy, we giving him your name, Andre Amar. He gon' know all about you, especially how I beat you at ball."

I can almost hear Dre laughing and saying, *Lying ass.*

"Don't worry, Lisa probably gon' set the record straight. Me and her just friends. She say we don't got a chance long as I'm into this street stuff. Yeah, a'ight, we'll see. I got a surprise planned this weekend for Valentine's that I think gon' change her mind. I'm taking her to Markham for a tour of the campus. She gotta give me a chance after I pull this one off, right?"

I glance at my watch. "Speaking of Lisa, I better bounce. She had school today, and I like to ride the bus back to the Garden with her. I'll holla at you later. Tell Granddaddy I said hey." I give Dre's headstone dap. "Love you, man."

Leaving him here, that be the hardest part. My life still going on and he just something for grass to grow on top of.

For some reason I stick that blade of grass in my pocket.

Students pour outta Saint Mary's and onto the sidewalks. I post up near a pay phone at the end of the block. It probably look like I'm waiting on Lisa, but my customers know the deal.

Forget what you heard; drug addicts don't only live in the hood. I mostly sell to people who ain't in the Garden—white college students who pull up 'cause they wanna try something new, businessmen from downtown who want a "wild" weekend, these rich kids at Saint Mary's who will spend their entire allowance to get high. I got this one customer, Jack, who got two kids, a wife, and going to law school. *Law school.* Meaning he know more than anybody that weed illegal. Yet he come to the Garden every other week for some green. Had his li'l boy, Simon, with him one time, asleep in his car seat in the back of the minivan. Not the kinda dude people expect to buy weed.

It kinda peeve me how life set up. Here I am, tryna make money to keep my momma's lights on. Meanwhile, some rich brat might hit me up tomorrow, offering to spend a couple hundred for an "experience." He never think what that money mean to somebody like me. Then who gotta watch out for the cops? Not him. Nah, I'm the one who gotta glance over my shoulder 24-7.

I learned to be real slick with my shit so I won't get busted. For instance, these two Puerto Rican dudes from Lisa's school come over to me. We slap palms, and that's when they slide me the money. We talk a minute or so, in case anybody watching. I slap palms with them again and pass them the weed baggies, their usual. They go their way, and that's that.

White Boy Aaron head my way. He got stringy brown hair that almost cover his eyes. Look straight outta a boy band. Ay, for the record, I only know what them fools look like 'cause Lisa love her some *NSYNC. She around these private-school kids too much.

He wipe his nose, a signal that he want some powder. Then he slap my palm, putting money in my hands. "Mav, my man."

I pretend to scratch my forehead so I can see what's in my palm. Yep, that's enough. I slip my hand in my front pocket and feel around for a baggie. "What's good with you, A?"

"Chilling like a villain. Nice kicks, bro!"

"Thanks. I copped these joints at the mall."

"No, bro, thank *you* for hooking up my party last weekend," he says. "It was off the chain!"

I don't know what it is with white kids and cocaine. Ay, if

they buying, I'm selling. "Man, no problem at all. You always come through with big dough."

"It pays to have rich grandparents. That was 'just because' money."

"Shiiid, can they adopt me?" I ask.

"They're racist assholes. You wouldn't want that, and they wouldn't want you."

Damn. At least he honest.

"Catch you later, my man," he says, and hold his palm out. I slap it, sliding his cocaine to him. Easy money.

He walk off as Lisa come out the school doors. I smile . . . till I see she laughing and talking with Plain-Ass Connor.

What the hell? They real buddy-buddy like. She got her arm hooked through his as he carry her backpack. I swear they practically in their own li'l world.

Lisa slide on her backpack with his help. "Connor, you remember my friend Maverick. Maverick, this is Connor."

I'm her friend. He simply "Connor." She can't be checking for this dude. She can't.

He do a quick chin lift. "'S'up?"

Wait, this white boy know the nod? "Whaddup?" I say, with a nod back.

"Anyway," Lisa says, like I was an interruption, and she turn to him. "You promise you'll get that TLC CD the day it comes out? I know it's gonna be the bomb."

"Of course. As long as we can declare that I'm not a scrub."

Lisa giggles. "You definitely aren't."

Connor smile at her, and she grin back. I'm not even here.

"Oh! I almost forgot." Connor slide his backpack off and dig around. He take out a little brown teddy bear and hold it toward Lisa. "I got it for your baby."

"Awwww!" Lisa hug it to her chest. "It's so cute. Thank you, Connor."

"You bought a toy for *our* baby?" I stress that "our" part. "Ain't it early for that?"

"What can I say? I like babies." Connor look dead at me. "I'm good with them, too."

Yoooo, this fool basically just told me he tryna raise my kid.

He kiss Lisa's cheek. "Catch you later."

"Later," she says. She watch him walk away with a smile.

I point back at him. "Don't tell me you dating that corn-ball?"

"Wow, I'm doing fine, although your child had me nause-ated all day. Thank you for asking. How are you?"

"C'mon, Lisa. You can't really be into that dude. What you see in him?"

"For one, he's not a gangbanger," she says. "Two, he's doing things with his life. Three—"

"He corny as shit."

Lisa's lips thin. "That's your opinion. It's none of your business anyway. You and I are only friends, remember?"

"I know," I say, tryna play it cool. I can't let her think I'm tripping over this. "But I oughta know who might be around my baby, right?" I touch her stomach. Her puffy coat hide her bump. "How he doing today anyway?"

"*She* is fine."

"Nah, *he*. Bet you it's a boy."

"I bet you ten dollars and a rib plate from Reuben's that it's a girl," Lisa says.

"A rib plate?"

"Yep! With fries and extra sauce on the side."

"You so damn greedy. Fine. It's a bet." I hold my palm out.

Lisa slap it. "You may as well get me that rib plate now, homie."

I smirk as we start for the bus stop. "You hungry, ain't you?"

"Duh. They gave us some nasty steak fingers and mashed potatoes for lunch. Okay yeah, I ate them, but your baby wanted barbecue."

"*My* baby? Ain't he ours?"

"When *she's* like this, *she's* yours," Lisa says.

I shake my head. "You bad as my momma. I mess up, I'm Adonis's son. It's a trip."

Lisa grip her backpack straps. "You know . . . you really should talk to your dad."

I groan. "Drop that, Lisa."

"No. You love your father, he loves you. You know what I'd give to have my momma call and check on me?"

We sit on the bench at the bus stop. "He called me stupid

for getting you pregnant."

"Having unprotected sex *was* stupid," Lisa says. "We both admitted that. Why is it so different coming from him?"

Because he got no room to judge me. "How was school today?"

"Wow, avoiding the subject, are we? Okay, cool. I'll let you slide. School was fine. I found out I aced my calculus exam last week. Bam!"

"Ooohwee! That girl killing it!" We bump fists.

"That's what I do." Lisa unwrap a Blow Pop. She addicted to them. "How was your day off? With your lucky public-school ass."

I laugh. "It was a'ight. I caught up on some sleep. You know me, I'm always tired. Then I visited Dre for a while. You and Connor hung out all day?" Hell yeah, I'm back on that.

Lisa smirk as she take her headphones and her Discman from her backpack. She wear them headphones around school to block out the gossip and whispers. Pregnant girls catch it bad.

"I'm gonna listen to some music and rest my eyes," she says. "Let me know when the bus is here."

Lisa slide her headphones over her ears. She never answer my question.

This Lisa and Connor shit really bugging me.

I swear, I'm doing everything I should to get her back. Like when we get to the Garden, I buy her a rib plate at Reuben's since that's what she craving. I check on her daily, walk her home from school, give her money, buy stuff to help her with all the aches and discomfort pregnancy bring. I'm being a good-ass boyfriend without being her boyfriend. Now this white boy sliding in with a teddy bear, and she grinning in his face?

I can't win.

I walk Lisa from Reuben's to Ms. Rosalie's. She swear she can walk herself home but the streets too wild for her to be alone. A li'l girl got struck by a bullet a couple of days ago over some shit P-Nut started with the Garden Disciples.

There's a red Honda parked in Ms. Rosalie's driveway behind her Oldsmobile. "Tammy got a new car?" I ask Lisa.

"No," Lisa says with a slight frown. "I don't know who that is."

I follow her onto the porch and hold the front door open. Lisa gasp. "Bren!"

Tammy's older sister hop up from the couch and meet Lisa with a big hug. "Leelee!"

"Oh my God, stop calling me that," Lisa whine.

"Never." Brenda hold Lisa in front of her to check her out. "I don't care that you're having a baby. You're Leelee and Tam will always be Teetee."

Lisa roll her eyes. "What are you doing here?"

"Momma's been bugging me to bring Khalil to see her."

"I sho have," Ms. Rosalie says. She cradle a tiny baby boy in the recliner as Tammy shake a rattle over him. Lisa told me Bren had him last month.

Suddenly, he all Lisa care about. "Aww! Hi, Khalil! Bren, he looks exactly like you."

"You think so? He's Jerome's twin to me. Hey, Mav."

I set Lisa's food on the coffee table. "Whaddup? Ain't seen you in a minute."

"Me and Khalil's daddy moved outta town, but we're coming back to be close to Momma and Tam. We hope to find an apartment this week."

"That's dope," I say. Only thing Brenda and Tammy got in common is their dimples and hazel eyes. Tammy quiet. Bren? Never. She the life of the party when there ain't a party. Last I heard, she got pregnant by some dude and moved in with him. Lisa said that Tammy and Ms. Rosalie don't like him, but Bren gon' do what Bren gon' do.

"You want your room while you're looking for a place?" Lisa asks.

"Nope. We're getting a motel. I don't want Momma all up in my business."

"Somebody needs to be," Ms. Rosalie mumbles.

"Momma," Brenda groans.

"I'm leaving it alone." Ms. Rosalie give Khalil to Brenda. "I'll go take those pork chops out the freezer. Somebody begged me to cook for them despite the fact I'm all in their business."

"I love you too," Bren says to her back and look at Khalil. "Grandma knows she was gonna cook for me regardless. I don't know why she's catching an attitude."

"Hold on, Ms. Rosalie," I say as I dig in my pocket. I count out a couple hundred dollars and give it to her. "A li'l something to help out. I 'preciate all you do for Lisa."

"Boy, I don't need your money. We're fine."

"Then you can put it aside for a rainy day," I say.

Ms. Rosalie roll her eyes, but she stick the money in her shirt. She bad as Granny, keeping money in her bra. "Mmm-hmm. I'll put this aside for *Lisa*."

"You do whatever you wanna do with it," I say.

She shake her head at me and go to the kitchen.

Lisa stare me down, all frowned up. "You sure have a lot of money lately."

"Oh, you know. I took on a couple of odd jobs around the neighborhood."

"Go 'head then, Maverick," Brenda says. "Nothing wrong with a man hustling to provide for his. That's how my boo do."

"I guess," Lisa says, biting her lip. She turn to Bren. "Can I hold Khalil?"

"Of course."

Lisa take Ms. Rosalie's spot in the recliner, and Brenda carefully give her Khalil. I sit on the arm of the chair. I forgot that newborns be so tiny—I didn't get Seven till he was three months old. Khalil small as a doll. He seem to be looking at us or at the lights, I don't know. He stretch and make li'l grunting sounds.

"He a'ight?" I ask.

"Yeah," Brenda says. "I'll probably have to change him soon."

"Don't you poop on me," Lisa coos at him. "No, sir, don't you do that."

"Good luck," says Tammy. "He got me earlier."

Ay, I'm just glad it wasn't me. I run my finger along Khalil's slick black hair. He got a head full of it. "Dang. We gonna have one of these in a few months."

"Y'all ready for it?" Brenda asks.

"No," me and Lisa both say. Brenda and Tammy laugh.

"He's so little and fragile," Lisa says. "Don't you get scared that you'll break him?"

"Word," I say. I toss Seven around, and he fine. I'm scared to hold Khalil.

Brenda chuckles. "I used to be. He's not as fragile as he looks. I promise, your baby won't be either. Y'all know what you're having yet?"

"Maverick thinks it's a boy. I *know* it's a girl," Lisa says.

She can get outta here with that. "Andre Amar ain't a girl."

"Dang, y'all picked out a name already?" Tammy asks.

"Just for a boy," says Lisa. "It made sense to name the baby after Dre. We wanna do something different for a girl."

"I'm sorry about your cousin, Mav," Brenda says. "He was a real sweet guy."

Months later, and the sympathy still hurt. "'Preciate it. You knew him?"

"Yeah. Jerome used to be one of his customers. He was one of Jerome's customers, too."

A door open down the hall, and somebody yawn loud.

"Man oh man," a dude says. "I needed that nap after that drive."

I know that raspy voice.

Red the hustler come into the living room, stretching and yawning. "Thanks for letting me catch a couple of z's in your room, Tam."

Tammy go "Mmm-hmm," with a strong stank eye.

Hold up. *Red* is Brenda's boyfriend?

He go over to her and kiss her on the lips. "I slept so good, I'm ready for whatever now." He wiggle his eyebrows at Brenda.

She giggle. "Jerome, behave."

I should've known his parents didn't name him Red. Sometimes you don't find out folks' real names in the Garden until you go to their funeral and see the program. Red notice me and Lisa on the recliner. "My bad. Hey, y'all."

"Hey, Red," Lisa says, dry as hell.

"Whaddup, Mav? How you living?"

"I'm chilling. Long time, no see."

"Oh yeah. I'm a man on the move. Gotta make that money after the damage you and your boy caused when you knocked over my shit." He laugh, but it sound forced. He still mad.

"You gave me some fake sneakers," I say. "We had to let you know that won't fly."

"Y'all lucky I'm forgiving." He come over to the recliner. "How daddy's buddy doing?"

Red lift Khalil from Lisa's arms, and that's when I see it—a gold watch with diamonds, glistening on his wrist. There's a scratch on the face from the time it fell off during a water gun fight.

How I know? That's Dre's watch. The one that was stolen the night he was killed.

TWENTY-ONE

Dre's watch is all I see.

I ain't bugging, I know my cousin's watch. I always wished Granddaddy gave it to me. I only got one of his brimmed hats 'cause I was the youngest. Dre would rub that shit in my face too like that annoying big bro he was.

He wore it everywhere and all the time. What the hell is it doing on Red's wrist now?

Red's eyes follow mine to it. He step back. "Um, baby, I think Khalil need his diaper changed."

Brenda come get Khalil, saying that Red could change the diaper himself. Red say something to Brenda while staring at me, but his eyes won't meet mine . . . almost like he nervous.

What he nervous for?

He clear his throat. "I'll be back in a little bit, baby."

I snap outta it. Brenda beg Red to stay a little longer. He already heading for the door.

I hop up and start after him, but somebody grab hold of my wrist.

"Mav."

I look down at Lisa. I forgot she was here that fast. "Huh?"

"Are you okay?" she says.

I gotta go after Red. Gotta go after Red. "Yeah, I'm straight."

"Are you sure?"

A car door slam shut in the driveway.

"Yeah, I gotta go to work," I tell Lisa. "I'll holla at you later."

I tug away from her and rush out the house, but I'm too late. Red disappearing down the street.

Mr. Wyatt got me working in the store today. This probably the easiest shift I've had on this job. I bag customers' groceries as he ring them up. Simple. Yet I'm almost too distracted to do that.

Everybody in the Garden know that Red crooked as hell. That's why he always got the hookup on good stuff—he get it dirty. He'd definitely buy a stolen watch, so he could've bought it from Ant.

There was this look in his eyes though. When he noticed me staring at the watch, dude was straight-up nervous. Would he be that on edge over a stolen—

"Dammit, boy!" Mr. Wyatt snap. "Pay attention to what you're doing!"

Oh shit. I dropped a carton of eggs. The yolks and the whites ooze near my kicks.

Mrs. Rooks, one of our neighbors, set her hand on her hip. "Now how the hell I'm gon' make red velvet cake if all the eggs on the floor?"

"I'm sorry, Elaine," Mr. Wyatt says. "Maverick, go get her two cartons. They're coming out of your check. That'll teach you to pay attention. Then clean up that mess."

The one part of this job I hate is dealing with his mouth. I bite my tongue every day.

I grab two cartons of eggs for Mrs. Rooks. She pull out her glasses and examine each egg, as if she don't trust me to get good ones. I guess they fine 'cause she let me bag them.

Mr. Wyatt wait till I finish cleaning the floor and my sneakers to say something to me. "Where in the world is your head at? You've been on another planet since you got here."

"I'm sorry, Mr. Wyatt. It's one of them days."

He fold his arms. "You keep this up, you're gonna lose half of your check. What's more important than your job right now?"

I'd be a fool to tell him any of that Red stuff. "You know how my life is, Mr. Wyatt. I got a lot on my plate."

Mr. Wyatt take a deep breath. "Yeah, I suppose I understand. You have to keep your eyes on the prize, son. Tackle one thing at a time until you reach your goals."

"Goals?"

"Yeah, goals," he says. "Don't you have some?"

"I mean, I wanna buy a ride soon. Oh, and one of them double strollers that I can use for Seven and the baby."

"Son, that's a to-do list. I'm talking about real accomplishments. What do you wanna do with your life?"

I look at him.

Nobody ever asked me that.

A'ight yeah, back in the day when I was little, teachers would ask what I wanted to be when I grew up. I'd say stuff like an astronaut or a doctor or a vet. But at some point, I stopped imagining myself being any of that. Ain't no astronauts, doctors, or veterinarians around here. Everybody I know just tryna survive, and that's all I wanna do.

I shrug at Mr. Wyatt.

His forehead wrinkle. "You don't have any kind of dream?"

"Dreams can't buy diapers."

"Maybe not immediately, but they can eventually. When you were a kid, what did you wanna be?"

"Mr. Wyatt, c'mon. This silly."

"Humor me for a bit," he says. "What did you want to be?"

I stuff my hands in my pockets. "I wanted to be like my pops."

"Is that why you're in that gang?"

"That's for protection, Mr. Wyatt. These streets can get

rough. You gotta claim gray or green to survive."

"I don't believe that. There are young men around here who don't gangbang. My nephew doesn't. That Montgomery boy, Carlos, he didn't. Now look at them. Jamal's at community college and about to head to a university, and Carlos is in college, too."

Them the worst examples he could give. "No offense, Mr. Wyatt, but your nephew seem like a nerd. As for Carlos, his momma kept him and Lisa in the house. Of course they didn't need protection. Anyway, I'm Li'l Don. Everybody expected me to join."

"Because the apple doesn't fall far from the tree?" Mr. Wyatt asks. "However, it can roll away from the tree. It simply need a little push."

"Yeah, a'ight."

Mr. Wyatt shake his head. "It's going in one ear and out the other. Did you have any other dreams, Maverick?"

I had one when I was a kid that I never told anybody. It was gon' sound stupid, but it was the only thing I really wanted to be. "A Laker."

"One of them basketball players?"

"Yeah. I wanted to join the team and convince Magic to come outta retirement and play with me. We were gon' be better than the Bulls. That ain't happening. I can't ball for nothing."

"Have to agree with you there," Mr. Wyatt says. "I've seen

you play, and that's definitely off the table. What dreams have you had lately?"

I shrug again. "Sometimes I think it might be cool to own a business like you do. You ain't gotta answer to nobody. That's dope."

"An entrepreneur," he says. "That's doable. What kinda business do you have in mind?"

"Maybe a clothes store? I could sell jerseys, sneakers, caps, all the fly gear. Or a music store. Everybody love music, and CDs and tapes not going nowhere." I look at him. "You think that could work?"

He smiles. "I do. You can make it happen, but you have to come up with a plan."

"What kinda plan?"

"Well first, you need to get your high school diploma or a GED. I have the latter myself. Next, I'd recommend taking some community college courses or going to a trade school."

"Wait, what for? I'll be my own boss."

"You're gonna need a business loan, son," Mr. Wyatt says. "As a Black man, you walk into a bank without some type of education, they're gonna laugh you out of there. Then let's say the store ends up closing or it's not bringing in enough money. You'll need something else to fall back on. Plan for that ahead of time and increase your education."

I shake my head. "That won't work, Mr. Wyatt. I barely got time for school as it is."

"Good luck, then. You might find yourself selling stuff out the back of your trunk like that ol' hustler with the Impala."

Red. For a few minutes, Mr. Wyatt distracted me from my distraction.

"Hey, I've got an idea," he says. "I had a couple of errands I planned to run in the morning, but if I get out of here now I can handle them today. Why don't you run the store while I'm gone?"

My eyes widen. "For real?"

"Only for an hour or two. It'll give you a taste of what your dream will feel like."

For him to do that, he must really believe in me. Worse, he trust me, not knowing I'm using this job to keep my drug dealing a secret from Ma.

Mr. Wyatt grab his wallet and keys outta his office. He remind me to check for counterfeit bills and to keep an eye on the security monitor before he leave.

I look around. For the next two hours, this all mine. Ain't nobody here to tell me what to do or when to do it.

This the life.

I grab the broom. Mr. Wyatt says sweeping give him time to think, and that's what I need. Up until today, I was sure that Ant killed Dre. He said my cousin deserved to die. That's as bad as bragging 'bout taking him out. But what if he didn't do it?

I don't get to think on it long. A couple of snot-nosed kids from the projects come in the store. They grab chips, cookies, and Little Hugs juices and dump a sock full of change on the counter to pay. I make them count it out. Their li'l badasses need to know how to count money.

Mrs. Pearl come in next. She live across the street from Lisa's momma. She buy bunches of turnip greens, and even though I don't ask, she tell me that if you put baking soda in the pot it makes greens more tender. I promise her I'll keep it in mind.

When nobody in the store, I check the aisles and shelves to make sure everything where it's supposed to be. The bell will ding on the door, and I'll get back to the cash register as another customer come in. I ring them up, bag their stuff, and they're on their way.

It honestly don't feel like I'm working. That first hour go by real fast. Things slow down a bit, so I grab the Windex and wipe down the door. All them fingerprints on it don't look good.

A gray SUV park in front of the store. I tense up.

P-Nut and three big homies hop out in their gray and black clothes. P-Nut rock a couple of chains that you can spot a block away. Pops used to say that flashy shit only bring unwanted attention. It's the reason Shawn kept a low profile for the most part. P-Nut act like he want everybody to see him and know what he do.

I hope Mr. Lewis's nosy behind don't notice him. He'd love to tell Mr. Wyatt that I'm up to something.

I hold the door open for P-Nut and the homies. "What y'all doing here?"

"Look at this! Old Man Wyatt got Li'l Don cleaning the doors," P-Nut says. "Who you supposed to be, Mr. Neat?"

The big homies laugh like they would do at Shawn's jokes. Difference is, Shawn's jokes made sense. "It's Mr. Clean, P-Nut," I say.

He wave me off as he and the homies wander up an aisle. "Fools always focused on technicalisms. You work on them floors and doors, playboy."

Technicalism?

Forget it, that ain't important. P-Nut's dumbass is the crown for the time being, and he oughta know 'bout this Red stuff. "P-Nut, I need to holla at you."

"Aw, damn!" he groan from the snack aisle. "Can a man quench his hunger first without being approached about operationaltivities?"

He dump an arm full of snacks on the checkout counter and hand me a hundred-dollar bill. "What you want, Li'l Don? You better give me the right change or I'll beat your ass."

He lucky he the crown or I'd snap on this fool. "We don't take bills over fifty, P-Nut."

"What kinda establishment is this?" P-Nut pull out his wallet and slap two fifties on the counter. "I still want my change."

"Fine," I say, and start to ring him up. The big homies add more snacks to the pile.

P-Nut hop up on the edge of the counter. He rip open a bag

of Doritos and munch on them. "What your li'l punk ass need to holla at me for?"

I swallow down what I really wanna say, for Dre's sake. "I saw Red the hustler earlier, P-Nut, and he was wearing Dre's watch. The one that was stolen when he got killed."

"So?"

My stomach drop. "So, don't you think that's a problem? What he doing with my cousin's watch?"

P-Nut lick cheese dust off his fingers. "That bitch Ant probably sold it to him. Big deal."

"Nah, P-Nut. What if he the one who killed Dre?"

P-Nut bust out laughing. "Yeah right! Red cowardly ass ain't no killer. He weak as you."

The big homies laugh.

I grind my teeth. "I ain't weak."

"That's a goddamn lie if there ever was one. For the past couple of months, you been hiding in this store and your momma's house while the rest of us earn our stripes in the streets. You lucky I respect Dre's wishes for you to stay outta the drug game or else I'd make you put in the work."

"Look, P-Nut. I think you need to check out Red, for real. He got real nervous when he noticed that I—"

"Li'l Don, you finna get on my nerves. I said Red ain't no killer. You tryna make me look dumb?"

You don't need me to do that. "No."

"Then stop arguing with me. It makes me think you taking

advantage of my niceticity. You don't wanna do that."

The big homies all stare me down, and I feel like fresh meat in a lion's den. This ain't Shawn's set no more, this P-Nut's, and he'd love to tell them to whoop my ass.

I don't say anything else. I ring their stuff up and let them go.

For the first time in my whole life, I ain't sure I can depend on the set. It look like Dre can't neither.

TWENTY-TWO

I couldn't sleep last night for thinking 'bout Red.

Red.

Red.

Red.

It's the same thing the next day at school—I'm sitting in the front office with Red on my mind. I'm one of like twenty students waiting to see Mr. Clayton, the counselor. He meeting with all the seniors one-on-one this week to discuss our "futures." For me that's probably summer school with the way my grades looking.

I don't really care at the moment. I'm almost dizzy from the tug-o-war happening in my head.

Red was wearing Dre's watch.

But what if it wasn't Dre's watch and simply looked like it?

Why did Red get nervous when he saw me staring at it?

He a crooked dude, no doubt, but like P-Nut said, he not the type to kill.

But he disappeared right after Dre died.

"Maverick Carter?" Mr. Clayton call out.

I shake Red out my head at least for now, and go over to Mr. Clayton. He meet me with a strong handshake. Mr. Wyatt says you can tell a lot about a man by his handshake. Mr. Clayton don't take no mess. I already knew that. He look like a Black "Stone Cold" Steve Austin, bald and wide-shouldered. Bet he lift weights bigger than me.

"Nice to see you, Mr. Carter," he says. "I'm glad you finally stopped by."

Oh yeah. I forgot he wanted to talk to me after Dre died. "My bad."

"Not a problem. Come in, have a seat."

His office kinda dope. He got framed black-and-white pictures on the walls of all these important-looking Black people. I only recognize Malcolm X and Huey Newton, the founder of the Black Panthers. Pops put me onto them. I never heard them mentioned in a history class.

I take the chair across from Mr. Clayton's desk. He pull a folder from his file cabinet and join me. "Word around the school is that you've had some life-changing developments this year," he says.

I wait for the *look*. I swear, when grown folks know I got

two kids, I see myself become trash in their eyes. It's like they see my babies as trash, too, just 'cause I made them so young. Hell nah.

"Look, if you gon' come at me 'bout my kids—"

"Calm down, Mr. Carter. There's no judgment. I'm here to help you, young brotha."

He look over the files in the folder. My name typed out on the tab on the top. "I can see how becoming a father has affected your grades this year. Your GPA is down drastically."

"Yeah, but I ain't dumb."

Mr. Clayton look at me over his glasses. "Then why haven't your grades reflected that?"

He pulled that one outta Ma's playbook. "I got a lot going on, you said it yourself."

"I understand that, Mr. Carter. However, there are teen parents who stay on top of their grades. Barring a miracle that would require a lot of hard work on your part, you won't be graduating in May."

Shit. "I gotta do summer school, huh?" Damn, I don't really wanna deal with that, but I guess I'll do it.

"I wish it were that easy."

"It's not?"

"No, sir," he says. "You would have to take *all* of your classes in summer school, and we don't offer them all in the summer. The district can't afford it. Now, you could hope you raise your GPA enough to graduate. Otherwise, you have to repeat the twelfth grade in order to get a diploma."

Shit, man. I thought—I know my grades bad, but I figured—

"Mr. Clayton, I can't repeat. What I look like, coming to high school every day when I got two kids?"

"You'll have to figure it out," he says.

"Nah, man! I shouldn't have to do the whole year over!"

Mr. Clayton remove his glasses and rub his eyes. "Young brotha, you can't wait until the credits are rolling to decide that you wanna see the movie. You obviously didn't make school a priority this year, judging by your grades and all of your absences. We're a few months away from graduation. Why do you care now?"

You know what? I don't. I push up from my seat. "Fuck this," I mumble.

"Whoa, hold on, Mr. Carter."

"I ain't tryna do another year, Mr. Clayton. Real talk."

"Okay, understandable," he says. "You also have the option of getting your GED. It's the equivalent of a diploma." He pull a pamphlet from a drawer and hand it to me. "The school district has a program for adults. You're the perfect candidate."

Adults. Guess I ain't a kid no more.

"You would take night classes over a three-month period," Mr. Clayton explains. "At the end, you take an exam. You pass, you get your GED. You don't, you take the classes again."

And again and again. "I may as well come back here, then."

"Sounds like you've got good reasons to give it a shot. A

GED or a high school diploma will give you more opportunities to provide for your children."

I already do that, and it don't require returning to this goddamn school or taking a class.

Mr. Clayton hand me a card and tell me to call him if I decide I wanna enroll in the GED program. Then he say I can go back to class. You know, the classes I'm taking for no damn reason at all now.

I drop Mr. Clayton's card and the pamphlet in the trash can on my way out the building.

What's the point of a high school diploma or a GED? Nah, for real. People claim they'll make my life easier, but all a high school diploma did for Ma was help her get two jobs that don't pay enough.

Nah, man. I'm done with this school shit. It's time to put all my focus on making money.

I go to King's crib.

He rent a house near Rose Park. I knock on the front door since the doorbell never work. The lock click on the other side, and Iesha answer with an eye roll. "What you want?"

Man, I don't wanna deal with her today. "Hey to you too. Is King here?"

Iesha look at me like I'm stupid and motion toward the empty driveway. "Do you see his car anywhere?"

"You know when he'll be back?"

"Better be soon. He went to get some breakfast, and we hungry."

"*We?*" I ask.

She proudly caress her belly. "We found out yesterday that I'm expecting. It really is King's baby this time."

One: Goddamn, what the hell in the water around here?

Two: She barely around for the baby she got.

Three: "You tryna replace Seven since he ain't King's?"

The goofy grin disappear off Iesha's face. "Screw you, Maverick! Ain't nobody tryna replace him."

"It sure look that way."

"Shut up! You don't have room to talk. You knocked up your li'l bougie girlfriend. You tryna replace Seven since he ain't hers?"

"Nah, that just happened."

"This did too! I may not have been around Seven for months, but don't ever say I don't love my son."

"A'ight, a'ight. My bad. I'm sorry."

She point her long fingernail in my face. "You should be. You better start letting me see him more. Them li'l Sunday visits won't cut it."

I wipe my face. I didn't come over here for this. "A'ight, we'll work something out. Give me a few days."

"Fine. Don't take forever," Iesha says as King's car turn into the driveway. She whirl around and stomp in the house, talking 'bout, "Oooh, I can't stand him!"

My life, man. I gotta deal with this girl for at least the next eighteen years.

Now here come this foul fool. King come up the walkway, holding a couple of McDonald's bags. "What's good, Mav?"

I stuff my hands in my pockets. I ain't forgot what he pulled on Thanksgiving. "My stash at home low, and I wanna put in some work."

"Cool, I got you," he says, and I follow him inside. King only got a TV, couch, PlayStation, and stereo system in his living room. He don't even have curtains. He hung sheets and blankets from the Dollar Store on the windows. "Yo! I got the food," he calls out to Iesha.

She come and snatch a bag. "Thank. You!" she says, and go back to the bedroom.

King sit on the couch, shaking his head. "Females. You came at a good time, homie. I cooked up some rocks last night. According to one of my regulars, it's outta this woooorld." He laughs. "It had him so gone."

"Cool. I'll take whatever."

King tilt his head. "What's wrong with you?"

"Nothing. Give me some product, and I can bounce."

"What is your goddamn problem lately?" King asks. "Don't tell me you still mad that I moved Iesha in. That was months ago! She ain't your girl, why you mad?"

"'Cause you ain't tell me where she was, and you knew I was struggling with my son!"

"I ain't know you was still looking for her!" he says.

"Just give me some product, King. I'm not in the mood, a'ight?"

"That's why I asked what's wrong, fool! It's obvious you upset." He sit forward. "Seriously, Mav. I'm your boy. Talk to me."

I hold the back of my neck. This school stuff and this Red situation on my mind heavy, and fact is I ain't got nobody to talk to. Lisa not an option; she don't need the stress. Mr. Wyatt not; Ma definitely not. I could talk to Dre's grave, but I'd never get a response.

King all I got left.

I sigh. A'ight, maybe I am tripping over the Iesha stuff. It ain't that big of a deal, I guess. Plus King right, that was months ago.

I may as well talk to him. "I found out I can't graduate. They want me to repeat the twelfth grade."

"What? That's bullshit," King says.

"It's my own fault, King. I accept that. I refuse to do another year though. It would be a waste of my time."

"Hell yeah, it would. Who wanna look in Mr. Phillips's ol' wrinkly face for another year?"

"Word." I laugh with him. "Mr. Clayton said I could take night classes to get my GED."

"Another waste of time," King says. "Once you focus on this drug shit completely, you'll be making more than Clayton and the teachers. Bet that."

"I know," I mumble. I left the school knowing that. At the same time, this ain't what I wanna do forever. I mean what I told Dre. Slinging is supposed to be temporary.

Being a man don't got nothing to do with what I want. I gotta do what I gotta do, and it looks like that's selling drugs.

"Ay," King says, and I look at him. "Don't stress this. You my boy, I'm gon' make sure you good. We homies for life, remember?" He hold his fist over to me.

Now I'm feeling real stupid. "Man, I'm sorry that I—"

"I forgive you," King says. "We cool. A'ight?"

I dap him up. "A'ight."

King reach in his McDonald's bag for some fries. "That school stuff all that was bothering you?"

I see Dre's watch on Red's wrist as clear as I see my own wrist. "Nah," I say, through my teeth. "I saw Red yesterday. He was wearing the watch that was stolen off Dre when he was killed."

King look up from his bag. "What? You bullshitting me."

That's what P-Nut should've said. "Not even a li'l bit. On top of that, when he saw me staring at it, his ass got shook."

"Yooo! That's suspect as hell. You tell P-Nut and them?"

I sit beside King. "Don't get me started. I told that dumbass yesterday. He gon' tell me Red probably bought the watch from Ant, and he too much of a coward to kill Dre."

"What the hell? We talking 'bout the same crooked Red?"

King shake his head. "P-Nut dumb ass don't need to be the crown."

"Who you telling?" I fold my arms on top of my lap. "He threatened to jump me if I kept pushing the issue. Said I was making him look stupid."

"He looked in a mirror lately? Stupid written on his forehead."

I smirk. "Don't you know? P-Nut full of intelligisms that have preparized him for the situonalization at hand."

Me and King crack up. It feel good to laugh with him again.

"You know what this mean, right?" he says, after a minute.

That's one reason I couldn't sleep last night.

I stare ahead at the floor, and I can almost see Dre. I'll never forget holding him in the middle of the street as blood leaked outta his body. It's tatted on my brain for life.

If Red did that to him, I swear on everything I love he ain't got much time left.

I look at King. "I gotta kill that nigga."

TWENTY-THREE

Seven don't care 'bout Red or that I can't graduate. He giving me hell tonight.

I wipe his face for the fifty-leventh time. I'm tryna feed him this jar of pureed peas and carrots with a li'l applesauce mixed in like Mrs. Wyatt taught me. This boy here . . . he shake his head to dodge the spoon with his lips shut tight. When I do sneak some in his mouth, he spit it right out. There's splatters of green and orange mush everywhere.

"C'mon, man," I groan. "I know peas and carrots not the best, but give me a break, a'ight? Dada had a rough day."

"Da-da-da-da-da!" he repeat. He first said it on Christmas. Best gift I ever got, for real.

As he saying "Da-da," I put a spoonful of food in his mouth.

This boy look right at me, and I swear to God he spit it dead in my face.

Don't let the cuteness fool you. Babies straight-up thugs. They don't give a damn what you going through.

I grab a paper towel and wipe off the mush. "Stop spitting your food out."

Seven blow raspberries, sending spit flying in my face, too.

I rest my forehead on his high chair. I give up. He too stubborn and smart for his own good. Yesterday I gave him pancakes for breakfast, and he wouldn't let this one li'l piece go for nothing. Acted a fool when I tried to take it from him. I was like forget it and took him to Mrs. Wyatt's, gripping that pancake.

Ma think he sense that another baby coming and acting out. I don't know, but this need to quit for real. I'm dealing with enough tonight. For one, I gotta tell Ma I can't graduate. She might kill me, which would stop me from handling the other thing on my plate—Red.

King said he'll get me a gun. This should be easy-peasy once I have my piece. Yet my stomach knot up every time I think 'bout shooting Red.

Seven pat the top of my head. "Da-da-da-da-da!"

I look at him, and my lips turn up. "You tryna cheer me up, man?"

He stick his hand in the baby food and hold it toward me.

"Ahhh," I say as I open my mouth wide. I let him feed me the baby food, then I act like I'm gon' eat his hand. He pull away, giggling.

That sound always get a smile outta me. "You know what, man?" I say to him. "I get why you spit it out. That baby food nasty. Let me see what Daddy can give you instead."

I get his favorite—rice cereal. It look like mush and it's not really a dinner food, but ay, cut me some slack. I had a day. Seven buck in his high chair as I bring it over.

"Aww, snap," I say, doing a li'l dance. "We got rice cereal, ay! Rice cereal, ay! Daddy coming through with the save!"

He open his mouth wide for every spoonful. That full belly later put him right to sleep. Thank God for rice cereal.

Now I wait for Ma to get home. She don't get off from her second job till around ten thirty. I pace the kitchen. I sit down. I get back up. I peek in on Seven. I turn on the TV. I turn it off. I don't know what I can tell Ma to make this better. I can't graduate, the one thing she always wanted from me. Ain't no "better."

She can't ever find out that I'm going after Red. I'm more afraid of her than the cops.

I sit at the kitchen table and rub my temples. Red really going around wearing Dre's watch. That piss me off so much. Whether he killed Dre or not, it's disrespectful as hell. He gotta know it's Dre's. He gotta! He wasn't nervous for nothing.

I should've said something to his ass. Better yet, I should've snatched it off his wrist, then popped a bullet in him.

Let me stop, I'm getting ahead of myself. I need proof that he did it. Otherwise, I'd be killing Brenda's boyfriend and Khalil's daddy for nothing. Bet Red didn't think 'bout Keisha and Andreanna though.

Wait a minute. Keisha was on the phone with Dre that

night. She might've heard something that could help me out. It's a long-ass shot unless she flat-out say it was Red, but I owe it to Dre.

I can talk to her this weekend. Keisha helped me set up Lisa's surprise tour of Markham, and she meeting us for lunch afterward. The timing kinda perfect.

Headlights flash through the kitchen windows. A minute later, the front door groan open. Ma never announce it's her in case I'm asleep. Her purse thud as she toss it onto the living room sofa, and her feet thump toward the kitchen.

"Hey, baby." She kiss my temple. "You didn't have to stay up and wait for me."

"I wanted to. How was work?"

Ma roll up her sleeves and open the refrigerator. "Things were pretty quiet at both jobs. How was your day? You were supposed to talk to Mr. Clayton, right?"

My mouth dry all of a sudden. Three words—"I can't graduate"—that's all I gotta say. But they stuck in the back of my throat.

I swallow them down even more. "It was fine. He told me what I need to do in order to graduate." That's sorta true.

Ma take out a container of food and sniff it. Her nose scrunch up. "Whew, Lord. Gotta throw that out. Glad it went well. You do whatever he said to do, Maverick. I have faith in you."

I really ain't shit compared to what she think. "Yes, ma'am."

Ma take out a container of leftover spaghetti. "Before I

forget, did you see the light bill in the mail? I need to pay it in the morning."

"I already took care of it and the water bill."

Ma look up from sniffing the spaghetti. "You did?"

"Yes, ma'am. I went to the bill-pay place earlier and paid them both."

"Okay, Mr. Man," she says, all impressed. "You're spoiling me, helping me with these bills. Thank God for Mr. Wyatt and that job. How was my Seven tonight?"

"Fine. He put me through it."

Ma chuckles. "That's his job. You earned it for all that you put me and Adonis through."

I push away from the table. "I only stayed up to say good night. I'm gon' head to bed."

"Hold on," Ma says, closing the refrigerator door. "I need to talk to you."

Her tone make me do a double take. "You okay, Ma?"

She pull out the chair next to me and sit. "Yeah. It's nothing bad. Only long overdue."

I sit back down. "Oh. What's up, then?"

Ma's fingers fumble with one another, then they drum the table, then they fumble again.

"I . . ." She snap her lips shut. Her eyes too. She take a deep breath. "I have a date on Sunday."

Valentine's Day is Sunday. "Oh. You seeing some dude behind Pops's back?"

I ain't mean to put it like that, but Ma and Pops *are* married. How else could I put it?

"No, actually. I'm not going behind his back," Ma says. "Adonis knows. And it's not a man. It's Moe, Maverick."

It take me a second. A lot of seconds, to be honest. Shit, I'm still stuck. "Moe?"

"Yes. Moe and I have been in a relationship for a few years."

Relationship? "I thought y'all were just friends."

"We—*I* thought it was best to appear that way," she says. "Not everyone can be so accepting. Lord knows your grandmother isn't."

"Granny know?"

Ma sigh again, scratching through her hair. "She suspected. She's always thought I was 'funny,' as she calls it. Your aunt 'Nita knows, and like I said, your father knows."

"That's why he don't want you hanging with Moe?" I ask.

"Right."

The kitchen get real quiet.

I got a million thoughts in my head. Hard to pin down one. "You always been like this?"

"Have you always liked girls?"

"Yeah."

"Then you've got your answer," Ma says.

"Do Pops know?"

"Yes, I told your father early on in our relationship that I was bisexual. He accepted it."

"Oh."

Lisa said I needed to pay attention. I guess she figured it out way before me. Now that I really think on it, Ma and Moe do go out a lot, and Ma always happier after she been with Moe. Her face light up when that woman come around. At Dre's repast, Moe held Ma's hand whenever they were close, and I thought it was just for support.

It was in my face the whole time.

I look at Ma. "Do you love her?"

Ma's eyes get that sparkle I've seen before. "I do. In fact, we've discussed her possibly moving in one day. Not without me talking to you first, of course, but yeah. It's come up."

"Oh." They serious then. "Do you love Pops?"

"I do," she says. "I'll always love Adonis, and I'll always be there for him. I also have to love myself. All of that 'ride or die' stuff, it's nice until you feel like you're dying from not living. Adonis made choices that put his life at a standstill. He didn't have to sell drugs; he chose to. I shouldn't have to put my life on hold because of his decisions."

I shift in my seat, thinking of my own decisions.

Ma look up at the ceiling, blinking real fast. "I've wanted to tell you for years. But I—I wasn't sure you'd—"

The crack in her voice do me in. I hop up and hug her in her chair. "Ma, it's okay."

She wrap her arms around me just as tight. It's almost like I'm holding a sobbing little girl. "I'm sorry I didn't tell you."

"You ain't gotta apologize. Are you happy?"

"I am," she says. "Happiest I've been in a long time."

I kiss her hair. "That's all I care 'bout. Promise."

I don't know how long we stay like this. I'll hold Ma long as she need me to.

But there's a twinge in my chest for Pops. I hadn't thought that his life was at a "standstill" until Ma said it was. He went away almost a decade ago. I was a scrawny eight-year-old. Now I'm almost grown with two kids. We out here living our lives while he stuck in prison, hoping we'll visit.

Or at least talk to him when he call.

I did him real wrong.

Ma pull away, wiping her eyes. "You smell like baby food."

I crack a smile. "Blame your grandson. He spit his dinner in my face." I kiss her forehead. "I'll heat you up some food."

I go to the cabinet and grab a plate. I'm happy that Ma happy. For real, I am. Considering all the stuff she put up with from me and Pops, she deserve it more than anybody.

She should also have her moment without me breaking her heart.

TWENTY-FOUR

I lie to Ma for the rest of the week. She think I go to school every day. Really, I drop Seven off with Mrs. Wyatt, and I watch Red from afar.

I know his schedule like I know my name. He start his mornings at his spot in the Cedar Lane parking lot. Around noon, he get lunch from somewhere around the neighborhood, then head to Rose Park to set up shop. I pick up Lisa and go to work. By the time I get off, he packing up his things in the park.

I'm almost addicted to watching that fool, like I'm scared he'll disappear before I get my chance. I hate that I won't be able to keep an eye on him today. I'm taking Lisa on her surprise tour of the Markham campus. It's a two-hour drive one way. Ma letting me use her car, but not without a lecture first.

"Bring my tank back on full. I'm not playing, Maverick,"

she says. "Put premium gas in it. I don't want that regular shit—stuff. Got me cussing in front of the baby."

I smirk as I pack snacks at the kitchen table. Seven drink his morning bottle in his high chair. I took today off from work, and Ma agreed to watch him for me. I'll have him all day tomorrow while she spend Valentine's with Moe.

"While we're on the subject of gas, do you need money for it?" Ma asks.

"No, ma'am." I haven't needed money from her since I started slinging. That's life-changing damn near.

"Okay, good. Wear your seat belt at all times and use the signal lights when you switch lanes. The left lane is for passing, the right is for slower traffic. Stay in the right as much as possible, and don't go over the speed limit."

I look at her. "Says the part-time NASCAR driver."

"Who isn't a Black boy, driving down the highway," she says. "Don't give the police a reason to pull you over. If they do—"

"Keep my hands visible, don't make no sudden moves, and only speak when they speak to me." I know the talk by heart. Ma and Pops drilled it into my head since I was seven.

"Exactly," Ma says. She watch me pack snacks. "Are you okay, baby?"

"Yeah. Why you ask?"

"Lately . . . I don't know. It seems like you have a heavy heart, beyond the normal stuff."

"My life not normal, Ma."

"You know what I mean," she says. She run her fingers through my hair. "Is something going on?"

Red headed to Cedar Lane by now . . . with Dre's watch on his wrist. "No, ma'am. I'm fine."

"All right. Well, it'll probably do you good to be out of the neighborhood for the day. I think you'll really enjoy Markham. It could be your home one day."

"You still think I can go to college?"

Ma cup my cheek. "I think you can do whatever you put your mind to."

It's hard to look her in the eye. The son I am is nothing like the son she think she got.

Ma hand me a piece of paper. "These are directions to Markham from that MapQuest site. I printed them off at work. It has gas stations marked. Lisa may need a couple of restroom stops. Don't let her go in alone, and don't you go in with your hands in your pockets. You know what? I should just take y'all myself."

"Ma, chill. Why you tripping?"

"You're a parent, you'll understand soon enough. Wait until Seven starts walking and you realize everything he can get into."

A'ight, yeah, that is a scary thought. I look at him and point. "Ay, don't be walking no time soon."

Seven chuck his bottle my way.

What the— "Boy, stop talking back."

Ma laugh and pick him up. "You tell him, baby. Daddy don't know what he's in for. You're gonna do him the same way he did me and his daddy."

Funny she bring up Pops. "Ay, Ma, can I ask you something?"

"My chunka-chunka-chunk," she says to Seven as she move his arms with the words. He laugh and laugh. I don't know what "chunka" mean. Half the stuff people say to babies don't make sense. "My chunka-chunka-chunk! What, Maverick?"

"If I do good on this trip, can I take the car to go see Pops one day?"

She look at me. "By yourself?"

"Yes, ma'am. I figured I should see him in person since we ain't really talked lately."

That stuff she said 'bout his life being at a standstill kinda stuck with me. After a day or two, I realized I oughta be a man and go see him.

Ma smiles. "He'd like that. I'll work on setting up a visit."

"Cool, cool," I say, but I'm already nervous.

She kiss my cheek. "Y'all will be fine. Now, back to my car—"

Around eight o'clock, I back outta the driveway.

The sun shine bright in clear-blue skies. Perfect weather for a road trip. It's kinda cold today, but I got the heat on and brought a blanket in case Lisa need it.

I make a detour first, just to see if Red ain't left town again. No, he at his usual morning spot at Cedar Lane. King supposed to hit me up on my pager today once he get me a gun. He asked if I wanted a certain type of piece. Long as it take out Red, it's fine by me.

I got a strong feeling that whatever Keisha say today gon' confirm it was him.

I honk my horn in front of Ms. Rosalie's house. Lisa come outside, yawning in a hair bonnet and slippers with jeans and a sweatshirt. Girl look barely dressed.

I get out to help her with her backpack and Hello Kitty blanket. "You just rolled outta bed, huh?"

"Shut up. Your baby kept me up all night. Here." Lisa place my hand on her sweatshirt. Her stomach quiver, as if something rolling around under there.

My eyes get big. "Oh, dang."

"I know, right? It was fascinating at first. After the third hour, I just wanted to sleep."

I kneel in front of her. Some days Seven and the li'l baby in Lisa's belly be the only things to make me smile. I tap Lisa's stomach. "Ay, this your daddy. Chill in there, your mommy dealing with enough."

Lisa snort. "I doubt that'll work. She's as stubborn as you."

"Well, *he* ain't mean to keep you awake." I straighten up. "He know we got a busy schedule today."

"I want extra sauce on my rib plate when I win this bet. Will you finally tell me where we're going?"

I open the passenger door. "You gotta come and see, madam."

Lisa tilt her head. "How do I know you're not kidnapping me?"

"You think I wanna be stuck with you?"

Her mouth drop, and she punch my arm.

"I'm playing, I'm playing!" I laugh. "It's a surprise, a'ight? You gotta trust me."

Lisa study me hard. "Fine," she eventually huffs, and hop in the car.

I close the door behind her. "Violent ass."

I drive past Cedar Lane one more time—Red still there— and I head out the Garden. There's not a lot of cars on the highway this morning. Most people sleep in on Saturdays. I drive the speed limit like Ma asked and nod with the stereo. It's an Outkast kinda morning.

Lisa unwrap her sausage McMuffin. She made me stop at McDonald's before we got on the highway. "Dang! I should've asked for mustard."

What the hell? "*Mustard?* On a McMuffin?"

"I like mustard, okay?"

"A'ight, Dre."

We both laugh. It feel good to joke 'bout him again.

"Whatever. This a pregnancy craving. Dre was just weird," Lisa says. She nibble her McMuffin and watch the sub-urbs pass by her window. Fancy shopping centers and gated neighborhoods everywhere. "Hard to believe this isn't that far from the Garden, huh?"

"I guess. It's a li'l too 'sophisticated' for me. Bet everybody out here bougie as hell."

"You don't know that," Lisa says. "Would you be bougie if you lived out here?"

"I don't live out here, so we'll never know."

"What if you did though?" she asks. "What if you had like a trillion dollars and could live out here in a gigantic mansion. Would you be bougie?"

"Nah, 'cause I wouldn't live out here. I'd live on a private island somewhere so I ain't gotta be bothered by nobody."

"A private island, huh? All right." She turn toward me as much as her seat belt will allow. "What else would you do?"

"You serious?"

"Yeah," she says. "What would you do if you had a trillion dollars?"

Pay somebody to find out if Red killed my cousin and kill him.

I sit up. I gotta get that fool outta my head. "I'd, um . . . I'd probably rebuild the whole Garden and make it nice. Nobody would have to pay for their new house. Then I'd start some kinda company and hire everybody so they can make big money. If I'm rich, my whole hood gon' be rich."

Lisa tilt her head. "Why would you live on a private island, then?"

"I ain't finna let nobody take me out. Fools get jealous."

She laugh. "Okay, makes sense."

"Exactly. I'd live in a mansion with a lot of windows to see the ocean and elevators, forget stairs. I'd drive a Bentley and a Rolls-Royce. All my furniture would be made outta gold."

"*Ill!* That sounds tacky as hell."

"Okay. Then I'd move you in and let you decorate."

She roll her eyes, but I see that grin playing at her lips. "Whatever."

"What 'bout you? What would you do with a trillion dollars?"

"End world poverty and world hunger and destroy the system as we know it. Then I'd build a house with the rest, I guess." Lisa shrugs.

"Dang. Now I feel bad for my island and cars."

"Um, don't get it twisted. I'd have a Bentley. Also, lots of shoes and diamonds." She look at her McMuffin. "I'd also hire a personal chef. Ugh, why didn't I ask for mustard?"

"You want me to go to another McDonald's and get you some mustard?"

"No, I'll deal. You're always going outta the way for me."

"You worth it, why wouldn't I?"

She keep her eyes on her sandwich, but she smiling. She look out the window again. We're out the suburbs and surrounded by trees. "Still won't tell me where we're headed?"

"Nope. I told you it's a surprise."

"I hate surprises." Lisa mess around with the buttons in the ceiling until one of them open up the sunroof.

"What the hell? You letting cold air in, girl!"

"It smells so good though!"

"Air don't got a smell, Lisa."

"Air outside of the city definitely smells different. Give it a try."

She lucky I love her. We take in deep breaths and exhale together. Dang, it do smell different.

"See!" Lisa says. "You can smell the pine trees, can't you?"

"That's what that is?"

"Mmm-hmm." She rest her head back and close her eyes. "It's like being in an entirely different world."

She quiet for a few minutes. Soon, soft snores come from the passenger seat. I turn the stereo down and close the sunroof. Then I reach over and rub Lisa's stomach.

"Chill out in there," I whisper. "Let your mommy get some rest."

Baby boy—or girl, I guess—listen. Lisa's stomach stop quivering.

Lisa sleep peacefully the entire drive. I hate to wake her up when we arrive at Markham.

I gotta say, this campus real pretty. It's exactly like them colleges you see on TV: the big brick buildings, the perfect lawns, and the statues and fountains. Only difference from the colleges on TV is that all the students are Black. Ma said that Markham is a HBCU, historically Black college and university.

I park in the visitors' lot like the lady on the phone told me. We meeting our tour guide at ten thirty, but I'm early.

I gently shake Lisa's shoulder. "Wake up, sleeping beauty."

She stir a little, but her eyes don't open. "Are we there?"

"Yeah. You gotta wake up to see your surprise."

She stretch and yawn. Slowly, she open her eyes. "Where are we?"

"Markham State. I got you a private tour of the campus today."

"What?" Lisa glance around some more. "Oh my God, you didn't!"

"Yeah, I did. I know this the top school on your list and—" Lisa hug my neck.

I wrap my arms around her. Damn, I missed holding her. She smell better than any fresh air I've ever breathed.

"Thank you," she murmurs.

"You're welcome," I say as she pull back. "Plain-Ass Connor never surprised you like this, huh?"

Lisa roll her eyes. "You're ridiculous."

She take off her bonnet, letting her braids fall around her shoulders. She grab a toothbrush and some hair gel outta her backpack and use them to comb down her baby hairs. She slide lip gloss across her lips. Then she press them together and make a *pop* sound. "Okay, I'm ready."

Girls.

We supposed to meet our tour guide at the fountain in the quad. I follow the directions I wrote down and lead Lisa there. She can barely walk for looking around. "Holy shit, this campus is gorgeous."

"I can definitely imagine you here, with your backpack on and your kicks, all fly."

"You know how I do," she says matter-of-factly. "I can imagine you here, too."

I ain't had the guts to tell her I can't graduate yet either. "Today not 'bout me. This your tour of *your* school."

"It may not even be my school. I'd obviously take the first semester off and enroll in the winter, but I don't know how I'll manage a two-hour drive every day when we have a baby—"

"Ay, don't stress. Enjoy being here. We'll figure out the rest later."

A Black girl in a Markham hoodie greet us with a smile in the quad. She introduce herself as Deja McAllister. She a senior here at Markham. She also pregnant.

I didn't plan that; I swear I didn't. Ay, maybe it's a good thing for Lisa to see somebody like her doing what she wanna do.

"You know what you're having yet?" Lisa ask her as we walk around the quad.

"A boy in June. My husband and I are naming him Justyce with a *y*," Deja says. "You would think we're prelaw students, but no. I'm studying biology. What do you have in mind?"

"For my baby or my major?" Lisa asks.

Deja chuckles. "Your major."

"Oh. I don't know. I wanna go in the medical field, but the whole doctor thing? Med school and a toddler would be a lot."

"I will say that Markham has a fantastic nursing program. They offer courses here as well as at our satellite campus back in the city. It would allow you to work in the medical field without all of the years of med school."

Lisa go, "Huh. Hadn't thought about that."

"See?" I say. "You don't know everything."

She elbow the shit outta me.

Going on a campus tour with two pregnant girls is a trip. They both need a lot of restroom breaks, and when they not talking 'bout the school, they complain 'bout aching backs, swollen ankles, and how bullshit it is that men don't deal with none of that. I'm smart enough to keep my mouth closed.

It's wild to see only Black people at a place like this—Black people who ain't that much older than me. We pass some guys in matching letterman jackets and that could be me, King, Junie, and Rico.

Stupid as it is, I imagine myself here. I'd join a fraternity, fa'sho. We pass the Omega Psi Phi house—dudes got their own house!—and a couple say whaddup to us. They tell me I oughta pledge in the fall. I nearly psych myself into thinking I will.

Until King page me three numbers during the tour—132. *I got it.*

Markham ain't meant for drug dealers who flunk outta high school and plot to kill people. I didn't come here to dream no way. I need to talk to Keisha.

Deja wrap up the tour a little after noon, around the time Red headed on his lunch break. Deja give Lisa her phone number, and they promise to keep in touch.

I drive me and Lisa a couple of blocks from campus to a Chinese restaurant. The hostess wanna seat us, but I tell her we're meeting somebody. I start to look for Keisha and Andreanna when a tiny voice go, "Mavy!"

Andreanna rush toward us. The bobos on her ponytails clink and clack. I catch her and swing her around. When I put her down, she fold her arms with a pout. "Where's my Sevy?"

I pretend to gasp. "I ain't enough?"

Andreanna shake her head. Lisa bust out laughing.

"That's right, baby girl." Lisa give her a high five.

"Haters!" I say, and tickle Andreanna. She giggle and run back into the restaurant.

We follow her to a table in a corner. Keisha meet us with hugs. Of course she gotta check out Lisa's belly. Everybody do that.

"So, how was the tour?" she asks.

"You knew about it?" Lisa says.

I hold her chair out for her. "Yep. Who you think helped me plan it?"

Keisha raise her hand. "Guilty as charged. I thought it was

a sweet surprise. I didn't realize y'all were back together till Mav called me."

"We not. I can do something special for my friend, can't I?" I look at Lisa. "I'll do *whatever* she want."

That's *whatever-ever*, if you get what I mean. Yeah, I went there. Can't knock your boy for trying.

Lisa fumble for the menu and clear her throat. "Um, what dish you recommend, Keisha?"

Oh, hell yeah. I still got it.

We order egg rolls and crab rangoon for the table. Keisha tell us what she been up to for the past few months, mainly school and work. Andreanna give us a whole rundown on pre-school. She claim some li'l knucklehead boy is her boyfriend.

"I'm gon' have to roll through and have a talk with him," I say. "We don't play that."

"Goodbye," Keisha laughs. "You're as bad as—"

Her voice die. Dre oughta be here with us.

Lisa touch her hand. "How are you really doing?"

Andreanna sway her head as she eat an egg roll. Kids love to dance when the food is good. Keisha run her fingers through her hair. "Day by day, that's all I can do. I miss him so much it hurts. We should be getting ready for a wedding."

That's the worst part of this. Dre had a whole life ahead of him that he won't get to live.

Lisa push back from the table. "Ugh, I'm sorry. I gotta run to the restroom. Pregnancy bladder is the worst."

"I remember those days," says Keisha. "It's only gonna get worse."

"Don't tell me that," Lisa groans. "I'll be right back."

This my chance. I wait until Lisa disappear into the women's restroom.

"Keisha, you mind if I ask you something?"

She try to get Andreanna to drink the water in her cup. Andreanna want juice. "Sure, what's up?"

I shift in my seat. "Look, I ain't tryna upset you, but I wanted to ask you 'bout that night. Is there anything you remember before the gunshots?"

"Mav, I don't know if I can—"

"I get it. I try not to think on it much myself. But the set tryna find out who did this." I can lie so easy nowadays.

Keisha stir her straw around her glass. "We were talking about our plans for the next weekend. He was gonna take us to the aquarium. Andreanna had been begging to see the 'fishies.' Bus Stop Tony came and joked around with him and—"

"Whoa, hold up. *Tony?*"

"Yeah. He asked Dre for money for liquor. Dre laughed and told him to leave him alone. A few minutes later, the robber showed up."

I thought Tony was long gone when Dre got killed. He came back though, so he was most likely in the area when it happened.

I look at Keisha. "You remember anything 'bout the robber?"

"Mav, I told the cops everything I heard. It must not have been enough. They're not investigating the case anymore."

Of course they not. Dre just another "ghetto casualty" in their books. "That's why I wanna—I mean the set wanna take care of this. Anything you remember would help."

Keisha blink and blink.

Shit, I shouldn't have asked her any of this. "I'm sorr—"

"It was a raspy voice," she whispers. "I've heard it before, I swear I have. It's been driving me outta my mind, trying to remember where."

I stiffen.

Red's voice is raspy.

The waitress bring the rest of our food to the table. Andreanna clap for her noodles. My stomach churning too much for me to eat.

I got little doubt that Red killed Dre, but I oughta talk to Tony before I make my move.

Lisa come back to the table, and I let her and Keisha do most of the talking for the rest of lunch. I take like a bite of my orange chicken. The waitress box the rest up for me and put it in a doggie bag. Lisa eat all of her food, order another plate to go, and walk out the restaurant with an ice cream cone. She act like she eating for four. I pray to God she ain't.

We hug Keisha and Andreanna goodbye in the parking lot. I don't get in Ma's car until I see that they safely in theirs and going down the street. Dre would've done the same thing.

The sun still out, so me and Lisa should get back to the

Garden way before dark. Ma don't want me on the highway at night. She said the cops more likely to stop me.

I go through her checklist—put on my seat belt, crank up the engine, turn on my lights, make sure the stereo ain't high, and have my wallet in the cupholder so I don't have to dig for it if I'm pulled over. I'm good to go.

Lisa buckle up and wrap herself in her Hello Kitty blanket just to eat her ice cream. If she so cold, why she eating that? "Soo . . . what's up with you?" she says.

I slowly back out the parking spot. "What you mean?"

"You were super quiet during lunch. Maverick Malcolm Carter is anything but quiet."

I poke at her side. "Oh, somebody got jokes."

"Stooooop," she whine. "You're gonna make me pee, and my bladder's weak as hell thanks to your baby."

I laugh and turn onto the road. "My bad. I'm a'ight. Just didn't have a lot to say."

"You looked like you had a lot on your mind. Wanna talk?"

I don't know how she can read me so good. "It's nothing. Did you enjoy your surprise?"

"I did. I can't believe you pulled it off," she says.

"I told you, I'll do anything for you . . ." I drum the steering wheel. I may as well go ahead and ask. "Do this mean I got a chance now?"

Lisa sighs heavy. "Mav, I appreciate what you did today, but I told you there's no us."

"Wait. So corny Connor give you a teddy bear and he good, but I give you this—"

Lisa sit all the way up. "Whoa, hold up. First of all, I didn't ask you to do anything. You did this on your own. Secondly, who I'm with has nothing to do with what I can 'get' outta them. I'm not a gold digger like your other baby momma."

The car go silent.

"I shouldn't have said that," Lisa says.

"It's okay. You mad and—"

"It's not fair to Iesha. You were the idiot who had sex with her. What, did you think doing stuff for me would make *me* have sex with you?"

"Of course not! I don't think of you like that, Lisa. But goddamn, I *am* doing a lot. I buy you stuff, pick you up every day, bring you food. You won't even give me a chance."

"That kinda shit doesn't matter to me!" she snaps. "What are you doing with your *life*?"

"My bad. I'm sorry I ain't got it figured out like you do. Some of us tryna make it day-to-day. Not that you'd understand."

"That's what you wanna do? Play the 'Lisa's too bougie to understand the struggle' card? Don't give me that bullshit, Maverick. You don't have to have it figured out. You should at least wanna better yourself. But nooo, you're still in a gang. And I should wanna be with you?"

"This what I be talking 'bout! You don't know how it

work," I say. "I can't just walk away from the set. I gotta either put in some major work like taking a big charge for somebody or get jumped out. Dudes end up dead and close to it after them beatings. It ain't worth it."

"You could distance yourself from them!" Lisa says.

"But they my boys! King, Junie, and Rico look out for me more than you'll ever know."

Lisa stare at me real hard. "You're selling drugs with King again, aren't you?"

I sigh. "Man, look—"

"You know what? Don't answer that," she says. "Do whatever you want, Maverick. Me and my baby will be all right."

"There you go, acting like I won't be around."

"Because you won't!" Lisa says. "I make plans, knowing that. My baby needs one of us to think about the future."

She don't get it. She really don't get it. "Lisa, hear me out—"

She turn her back to me and pull her blanket over her head. "Leave me alone, Maverick."

We don't speak for the rest of the drive.

TWENTY-FIVE

I ain't shit.

I'm a drug-dealing, gangbanging, high school flunk-out—that's worse than a dropout. I got two kids by two different girls at seventeen. I hurt my momma, and I hurt Lisa, two of the main people who care about me only 'cause I made them think I'm somebody I'm not. Truth is, I'm the kinda dude who end up in the news or in one of them PSAs they show at school on what not to be.

Since I ain't shit, I ain't got shit to lose. I may as well kill the person who killed Dre. First, I gotta make sure that's really Red.

Monday morning, I look for Bus Stop Tony. It can be easier to find crack around the Garden than it can be to find a crackhead. They stay on the move. I go to Tony's bus stop first, and I find his shopping cart and a dirty blanket. No Tony.

I walk over to the swap meet. Tony known to ask folks for money in the parking lot, but he ain't there today. I go to Magnolia next. He sometimes offer to wash windows at the intersections for money. No Tony. I got one other option, the White House.

Not the one in DC. I mean this run-down crack house over on Carnation. It used to be white, the paint peeling now, so everybody in the Garden call it the White House. Let's be real though—half these politicians act like they on crack anyway, selling pipe dreams and shit. Calling it the White House make perfect sense.

I used to be scared to walk by it when I was little. All the people coming in and out had red eyes and scaly skin, like dragons. I came up with this story in my head that it was a dragon dungeon, and I was a knight, Sir Maverick, Prince of Garden Heights. I figured I was royalty too, since my pops was the crown of the King Lords. My mission every day was to sneak past the dungeon without the dragons spotting me. Them crackheads ain't care 'bout me, but I would hide behind trees and bushes. It was my own li'l game.

I miss my wild imagination.

Today, I walk right up to the house. The yard been missing grass for a minute. These days it's just dirt covered in trash. A lady in dingy clothes curled up in a corner of the porch. I'm glad she snoring. As still as she is, I almost thought she was dead.

The White House don't belong to any one person, it's more like the neighborhood's spot for junkies to hide. I walk right in, and goddamn, the stench hit me head-on. It's the strongest piss mixed with this burning plastic smell. I pull my shirt over my mouth and nose.

Several people lie around the dim living room on raggedy couches and in corners on the floor. Wisps of smoke rise in the air near some of their mouths and their skin scaly like the dragons I used to imagine.

Now, I've seen crackheads before, like on a corner acting a fool or around the neighborhood asking for money. I done laughed at plenty of them and sold product to a couple. I ain't laughing now.

There's no sign of Tony in any room or in the backyard. After a while, I figure I may as well go wait at his bus stop. I head back to the living room, and guess who happen to walk through the front door?

Tony freeze. His eyes get big. Just as his name reach the tip of my tongue, he take off.

"Ay, Tony! Wait up."

Crackheads fast as hell. Tony haul ass down the sidewalk. He start to dart around a corner, but I grab his shirt.

"Let me go!" He try to shake me off. "I didn't do nothing!"

I put my hands up. "Ay, ay, chill. I didn't say you did."

"Them cops told you they questioned me, didn't they? I told them I ain't do nothing! They wouldn't listen to me!"

He almost in tears. Cops get real dirty when they want some info. Who knows what they did to a crackhead? "I believe you," I say. "You wouldn't kill nobody."

"I wouldn't! Dre was a good fella. I wouldn't do that!"

"I know. But Tony, did you see anything that night?"

He scratch himself. Them look and smell like the same clothes he had on the night he snuck up on me and Dre. "I don't want nobody coming after me."

"Nobody's gonna come after you. You got my word."

"I don't want a word! I want a hookup!"

"Tony, man—"

"I know you got something on you. You Li'l Don! You just like your daddy! He used to hook me up all the time. Gave me my first crack rock!" Tony flash a gummy grin.

He right, I could easily hand him something to get him to talk. My hand drift toward my pocket.

I stop myself. Fast as he is, he may take off without talking. "I'll hook you up, but first you gotta tell me what you saw."

Tony stare at my pocket, licking his lips. "You promise?"

"I promise. What did you see?"

"I was down the street from your house, near Mr. Randall's house. That ol' mean man. Ain't he mean, Maverick?"

I nod. Mr. Randall got one of the prettiest front yards in the whole Garden, and he'll cuss kids out if they get too close. Me and King egged his house once for the hell of it.

"What happened next?" I ask.

"I was minding my business. Minding my business, I swear, and I heard the gunshots. Liked to scared the mess outta ol' Tony. Had my heart racing! I dove into Mr. Randall's bushes. Ended up pissing myself right there."

That's what Mr. Randall get. "Did you see the car?"

"I did. It was red. Looked like an ol' Impala."

And there's my proof. That's the same kinda car Red used to drive.

That son of a bitch. I swear, I could choke the life outta him. Make him stare at nothing at all like he made Dre—

"Now give me my hookup!"

I'm snapped back to the corner with Tony. He got a hungry glint in his eyes as he stare at my pocket.

I dig in my other pocket for my wallet and hand a couple hundred to Tony. "Go get you some new clothes and a meal, then get a room at a motel for a few nights, a'ight? You need to clean up."

His eyes light up more and he reach for the money. I hold it back. "I'm serious, Tony. Don't go blowing my money on drugs. Go get some food, some clothes, and a motel. Don't make me come looking for you."

"I'll do it, I'll do it!" he claims, and snatch the money. He count it out and go, "Oooohwee! I can get me some name-brand clothes with this. Ol' Tony gon' be sharp!"

He whistle down the sidewalk.

That was the first time in a long time that anybody ever said that I'm like my pops. Straight up? It don't feel as good as I thought it would.

TWENTY-SIX

There's a lot of things I never wanted to know 'bout my pops. It come with the territory when your father is Big Don. I'd rather hear that he bought kids' shoes and fed families at holidays. Not that he got people hooked on crack.

Sometimes one person's hero is another person's monster, or in my case, father. Yet it's hard for me to judge him when I'm plotting to kill somebody else's father. But see, taking Red out is the best way for Dre to get justice. It ain't much different from a judge sentencing Red to death row.

I think.

I ain't real sure why, but I drive three hours to Evergreen Prison. Ma let me use her car like she promised. It's real weird looking for a table in the visiting area without her. I grab one in a corner with only two chairs so I don't take one a family could use. There's lots of mommas here with their kids. It kinda surprise me, since it's Friday, a school day. Then again, Ma would sign me out early so we could come see Pops. You visit when you can, not when you want.

All the kids look real nervous or real excited. I remember them days. First time we came to see Pops, I couldn't sleep the night before. I told everybody all week that I was gonna see my daddy. Ma explained that I wouldn't be able to play with him. It didn't matter to me. I bounced in my seat the whole drive up here.

Until I saw the prison. That big mountain surrounded by barbwire drained the excitement right outta me. The stone-faced guards with their guns made me think I was in trouble. Any kid who can still be excited just don't know better.

The buzz go off, and the inmates come in. Today, Pops one of the first ones out.

I stand up. My heart seem to beat along with his footsteps. He look older, but that ain't possible. It's only been a couple of months. I think it's the bags under his eyes that age him.

He reach the table. "Hey."

"Hey."

We just look at each other. I can't hug him after how I did him. He obviously don't wanna hug me either, since he ain't moving.

I sit back down. "Thanks for agreeing to see me."

Pops take the seat across from me. "I'll always see you, you know that. Faye said you wanted to talk."

I watch my fumbling fingers. "Um, yeah. I um—"

Pops dip his head so I can see him. "My name not 'Um,' and my eyes not down there."

I look at him. This man oughta go off on me. Let Seven treat me how I treated Pops, and I'd put his behind in check real quick.

In Pops's eyes, there's a whole lot of things he ain't saying, like *I love you* and *I missed you*. *I'm pissed at you* ain't one.

It make my throat close up. "I'm sorry, Pops. I shouldn't have cut you off like I did."

"Aw, Mav Man, I'm not tripping. You were right that day. I had a lot of nerve coming down on you after all I've done. I wouldn't have talked to me either. I forgive you. I'm willing to forget too. A'ight?"

He reach his fist across the table even though he not supposed to. I lightly bump it.

A smile stretch across his face. "My main man. What's going on with you? How's baby boy and Lisa? Her pregnancy okay?"

"Ma didn't keep you updated?"

"She did. I wanna hear from *you* though. My son. Don't tell me you forgot how to talk these past few months, big as your mouth is."

"Who I get it from?"

He let out one of them gut-busting laughs. "Okay, you got me, you got me."

"I know. Seven good. He crawling now. I dread when he start walking. He already wanna get into everything. Lisa good. Her pregnancy fine, in fact." I dig in my pocket and put the sonogram picture on the table. I got it from Lisa's appointment last month. The baby ain't a li'l blob no more. It's starting to look like a real baby.

Pops pick up the sonogram. "Would you look at that? That's definitely the Carter family apple head."

"Maaaan. He just gotta grow into it, a'ight?"

"*He?* Y'all found out it's a boy?"

"Nah, but I know it is. Lisa think it's a girl."

"Then it's a girl. Always listen to a woman's intuition. Won't ever lead you wrong." He hold the picture toward me.

I wave him off. "That's yours. I thought you'd want a picture of your new *grandson.*"

Pops laughs. "A'ight, stubborn. How's your momma? She told me she fine, but I know she don't want me worrying if she not."

"She good. Ummm . . . Moe might be moving in with us."

"Oh." Pops quiet for a minute. "You cool with that?"

It feel like he drew a line in the sand with that question; he on one side, and Ma on the other, and I gotta pick who I'm with.

I tiptoe down the middle. "I'm cool with whatever make Ma happy. That's nothing against you—"

"I know." There's another pause. "You think your momma's in love with her?"

I picture that light in Ma's eyes that she only get when Moe around, and that's all the answer I need. It may not be what Pops wanna hear. He and Ma been together since they were my age. That's twenty years of love I could be messing with. "We shouldn't talk 'bout this."

"I'm fine, Maverick. Be honest with me. I can handle it."

"A'ight." It take me a moment regardless. "I think Ma is in love with her."

Pops let out a long sigh. "I had a feeling."

"She love you, Pops, but—"

He put his hand up. "This isn't for you to deal with, Mav Man. I shouldn't have asked you no way. Me and your momma can work through this ourselves, a'ight?"

"A'ight."

Pops tiredly wipe his face. "Man. Enough of that. What did you wanna talk to me about?"

I tried to figure that out the whole three-hour drive up here. I honestly ain't sure why I came in the first place. I know I gotta kill Red, no question, but it's like *I need* to talk to Pops. Need to hear him say that I'm doing the right thing. Need him to tell me that I'm being a man.

My foot won't stop tapping. It don't help that we sitting in a prison, surrounded by guards. "I just . . . I wanted to tell you I got some business to handle for Dre."

"What kinda business?" Pops asks.

"I found out who shut him down."

Pops's eyes get big, but only for a second. He straighten up, sneak a quick glance at the guards, then look at me. "Was it green?"

In other words, Garden Disciples. I shake my head. "Red, actually."

"Red," Pops says, slowly, and he seem to figure it out. "You sure?"

"Positive."

Pops sit back in his chair, stroking his chin. "Do you wanna take this . . . *business* on?"

"You know the code, Pops."

"That's not what I asked you," he says.

All I gotta do is remember Dre slumped over his steering wheel to know what I want. "I can't let nobody get away with it."

"Then why you come all this way to tell me?" Pops says. "You don't need my approval or my permission."

I want it though. But if I said that, I'd sound like a li'l-ass kid who need his daddy. I can't be that no more. Instead I say nothing.

Pops sit forward. "Listen, Mav Man. I been in your shoes plenty of times. I can tell you that it ain't something you forget. Every time you close your eyes, every time your mind wander a little bit, you'll be back at that moment. You sure you wanna deal with that?"

My eyes start to burn. "Dre was my brother, Pops."

"Hey, hey, hey." He cup my cheek. A white guard bark at us 'bout contact, but this Latino guard tell him to leave us alone. It would take all of them to get Pops to let me go anyway.

"I'm here, man," Pops says. "Daddy's here. It's okay."

Them few words do me in. I say them to Seven all the time, but I ain't heard them myself in years, and they everything I ever needed. "Dre should be here," I blubber.

"He should be."

"He deserved better," I say.

"He did."

"I wanna do this for him. I got to."

Pops smile so sad it's hard to call it that. "There were a lot of things I thought I had to do, too. Reality was, I only had to be there for you and your momma, and I failed at that."

"Carter," the Latino guard near us says. "That's enough."

Pops lift his hand off my cheek and sit back.

"I won't give you the permission or the approval you want, Maverick," he says. "You're becoming your own man. This is your choice to make. You just make sure it's one you can live with."

Yeah, but what 'bout what I can't live with? I can't go on, knowing Red got away with murdering my cousin. I can't.

Another loud buzz go off, this one signaling that visiting time is over. Inmates and their families stand and say their goodbyes around the room.

I only rise when Pops do. This time, he don't hesitate to wrap me up in his arms.

His hugs got power. Nothing else exist beyond them.

Eventually, he have to let me go. He hold my shoulders. "Take care of yourself, a'ight?"

"You too, Pops."

He turn around real fast. Not fast enough. I catch a glimpse of the tears in his eyes.

TWENTY-SEVEN

Two days later, I'm ready to kill Red.

I close my bedroom door. Ma and Moe watch *Waiting to Exhale* in the living room for like the fiftieth time. Seven asleep in his crib. He don't see me go in my closet and pull the Glock that King got me outta my FILA box.

I tuck it in my waistband and pull my hoodie over it. Red close up shop at the park once the streetlights come on. The park be pretty empty on Sunday nights, 'cause most of the homies watching whatever game on TV. Tonight it's my Lakers versus the Supersonics. I'm taking a gray bandana to hide my face in case somebody walk by. From the park, I'll run to the cemetery. I'll toss my hoodie and the gun in the lake in the back. Then I'll go home and go on with my life.

I got my plan, and I'm ready.

Yet my legs won't stop shaking.

I grab the cordless phone off my nightstand and start to dial the number I done learned by heart, but I stop. Lisa know me real good. She'd figure out something is up quick.

I set the phone back down.

Ma and Moe cuddled up on the couch with a bowl of popcorn. The living room smell like the first bag Ma burnt. Ma go, "Show his ass, girl," as the lady on the TV grab a bunch of clothes from a closet.

I lean against the doorway. "Ay, Ma? Can you watch Seven for a while? Lisa want me to bring her some food. You know how them pregnancy cravings can be."

"Do I?" Ma says, eyes glued to the TV. "You had me craving ice cream all the time."

"What's your excuse now?" Moe asks.

"Hush!" Ma says, and they laugh. Moe kiss her to try to make up for it, but Ma go, "No. You gotta do more than that. We'll keep an ear out for Seven, Maverick. Be careful out there, baby."

Them words hit harder than usual. I swallow. "Yes, ma'am."

I almost kiss her cheek, but that would seem like there's a chance I'm not coming back. That's not an option, just like getting caught ain't. I throw my hood over my head and walk out the front door.

The Garden a different world as the night fall. Shadows start to creep in, and stuff that usually lurk in the daytime suddenly ain't gotta lurk. Stray dogs, crackheads all making their way out. It's way quieter, but that just mean when a siren blare or a bullet blast, it's loud enough for the whole neighborhood to hear.

I hope that wherever Dre is, he hear the gunshot when I pull the trigger and know that his li'l cousin always got his back.

The sun gone down by the time I make it to Rose, and darkness taking over the park. Most of the light poles been shot out by the set. You can't do the kinda work they do under a light or the cops might see.

The only pole that works is at the basketball court. I stare that way too long, and I swear there go me, Dre, King, and Shawn hooping a few months ago. That seem like another lifetime.

In this one, I got unfinished business to handle. I watch from behind a tree as Red load his trunk up with merchandise in the parking lot. He whistle a li'l cheery-ass tune that got no business coming from a killer's lips. His last customer pulled off a few minutes ago, leaving just me and him in the park.

I'm meant to do this.

I wrap my bandana around my face from the nose down and take my gun from my waist. It's cold and heavy; so is the feeling in my gut.

But when it comes to the streets, there's rules.

Nobody will ever write them down, and you'll never find them in a book. It's stuff you need in order to survive the moment your momma let you out the house. Kinda like how you gotta breathe even when it's hard to.

If there was a book, the most important section would be on family, and the first rule would be:

When somebody kills your family, you kill them.

My heart race like I'm on the run from something. Instead, I walk to it.

Red don't see me coming up behind him. He lift a box of CDs off the ground. As he straighten up, I press the Glock to the back of his head.

"Don't make a fucking move," I growl.

The box fall outta Red's hands. He raise his arms high, like he praising the Lord. "Shit! Don't shoot, don't shoot!"

"Shut up!" I say, deeper than I normally talk "Get on your goddamn knees and keep your hands up."

He slowly drop down with his hands raised above him. "Please, don't shoot me," he whimpers. "I'll give you whatever you want. I got a kid, man."

The shakiness in my legs find its way to my fingers. I grip the gun tighter. "You should've thought of your kid before you killed the homie!"

I can't say Dre's name or my voice might give me away.

"I don't know what you talking about!"

"You shot the homie in the head!"

"Nah, man! I—I—I—I didn't—I didn't—"

I cock my gun and press it harder against his skull. "You

gon' stand there and lie to me?"

Red let out an ugly sob. "Please, don't shoot me! I got a kid!"

"The homie had a kid, too!" He also had a brother. "You took him over some dough and a watch! Matter of fact, hand me that watch now. I swear to God if you make a wrong move, I'll blow your brains out."

Red shake from all the crying. He slip the watch off his wrist and hold it up. I snatch it outta his hand.

"Your time's up," I tell him.

"Oh God," he cries. "Please, God. Please, Jesus."

While he beg for mercy, I pray that God let me forget this.

I rest my finger against the trigger. I got the power to make Red stare at nothing. Have his blood and his brains leaking onto the concrete.

I just gotta do it.

I just gotta finally be my father's son.

I.

Just.

Gotta.

Squeeze.

TWENTY-EIGHT

Even killers can get their prayers answered.

TWENTY-NINE

The neighborhood blur past me as I run with tears in my eyes. The gun, back on my waist. The bandana, I ripped it off a block ago. Red . . .

Gone.

The lights glow in Lisa's window at Ms. Rosalie's house, and muffled R&B music play inside. I knock against the glass twice.

The curtain pull back, revealing Lisa with a frown. "Maverick?"

She lift her window. I pull myself up and climb through, headfirst. I scramble to my feet and hug her, sobbing.

"Maverick," she croaks. "What's wrong?"

I cry too hard to talk. Lisa lead me to her bed, and we sit down together. All I can do is bawl my eyes out.

"Mav, talk to me," she pleads. "I've never seen you like this. What happened?"

"I can't," I hiccup. "Ms. Rosalie and Tammy might hear—"

"They're at a church program," she says. "It's just you and me. Talk to me. Please?"

It's the "please" that break me. I swallow hard. "I . . . Lisa I . . . I know who killed Dre."

Her eyes widen. "What? Oh my God, who?"

"Red."

Lisa just blink at first. "Wait, hold on. Do you mean—Red as in Brenda's—"

"Yeah."

Silence.

I wipe my face on my sleeve. "That day he came over here with Brenda and Khalil, I noticed he was wearing Dre's watch. I went and did my own investigation. He did it, Lisa. He killed my cousin. So tonight, I walked up on him in the park."

She take in a sharp breath. "Did you—"

I stare at my kicks. "I had the gun pointed to his head and everything. And I . . ." My voice crack. "I couldn't pull the trigger."

Silence again.

Ain't no coming back from this one. I'm worse than she thought. I'm the thug her momma and her brother always make me out to be. I'll be lucky if she ever look me in the eye again.

Minutes that seem like days pass.

Lisa fold her arms under her chest. "Why didn't you do it?"

"I thought of my kids, my momma, and . . . and you. What it would do to y'all if I got caught or killed." I close my eyes. Tears slip outta them. "I'm such a fucking coward."

"No," Lisa murmurs. "You sound like a man to me."

I look at her. "How? That fool murdered Dre, Lisa. And what I do? I *let him* run away. What kinda justice is that?"

"It wouldn't have been justice if you threw your life away to kill him."

I almost laugh. "My life ain't worth much. I just didn't wanna put my babies through that. I know what it's like not to have a father around."

"So, you're saying your kids deserve to have you?" Lisa asks.

"Straight up? They deserve better."

Lisa take a deep breath and rub her little bump. "You know . . . I still believe in you, Maverick. I—*we* need you to believe in yourself."

I look at her. "You do?"

"I do."

It trip me out that she can say that after what I almost did tonight. It's like Lisa see this version of me that nobody else do. This Maverick who ain't worried 'bout the set or the streets, and who do something worthwhile with his life. I wanna be that dude. Not the one sitting in a prison, telling my kids that I got regrets.

I guess it's like Mr. Wyatt says. The apple don't fall far from the tree, but it can roll away from it. It simply need a little push.

I place my hand on Lisa's stomach. It's quivering again, like a fish swimming around in it. My lips turn up a little. "He real active tonight, huh?"

"Yeah, *she* is."

I laugh and roll my eyes. "Yeah, a'ight."

I rub her belly. Months ago, Dre told me the story of the first time he held Andreanna. He said he cried, 'cause she was stuck with him for a father. I understand that more every day.

He also said he wanted to be the father she deserved.

I think I get that now, too.

I got some things to handle.

Ma and Moe asleep on the couch where I left them.

Moe stretched out with her back against the arm of the sofa, and Ma cuddled up alongside her. Their arms tangled up like they fell asleep hugging. I grab the throw blanket from the recliner and lay it over them. Then I head to the bathroom and close the door behind me.

My drug stash should be under the cabinet where I left it. I get on my hands and knees, and I grab the Ziploc bag from behind the pipe. It's full of smaller Ziplocs that have coke, crack, and weed in them.

I may not be shit, but there's some shit I don't wanna do

anymore. Selling drugs at the top of that list. I'll give this back to—

Two loud knocks rattle the bathroom door.

They scare the shit outta me.

The Ziploc bag fall from my hands.

And land in the toilet.

Weed start to float around in the toilet bowl.

And some of the coke and crack rocks start to dissolve.

"Shit!" I hiss.

"Maverick?" Ma calls on the other side of the door. "You all right?"

Oh shit, oh shit, oh shit.

I fake a moan. "Yeah. Give me a minute. My stomach kinda to'e up."

"I keep telling you to eat more vegetables," she says. "Don't forget to spray. Other people use this bathroom besides you."

"Yes, ma'am," I say as I stick my hand in the toilet. Half the goddamn bag either floating or dissolving. I save what's left and dry the Ziploc off with paper towels.

I can't just walk outta here with it. I stick it in the front of my pants and pull my hoodie over it. God, please don't let Ma notice.

I flush the toilet, sending half my stash swirling down the pipe, and I spray the air freshener. I open the door with the best smile I can manage. "My bad, Ma."

"You're fine," she says.

We stare at each other. She raise her eyebrows.

"Oh, my bad." I step aside and let her in.

I'm frozen outside the bathroom. I swear, my lungs done stopped working. Please God. Please, please, please don't let her see anything.

The toilet flush again. The bathroom door open. Ma come out, wiping her hands with a paper towel. "Why are you still standing here?" she asks.

I breathe again. "Nothing. I wanted to say good night."

"Oh, all right. You sure were gone a while. What took so long?"

"Lisa needed me," I say, which is the truth. She still do.

"Is she okay. Is the baby—"

"Everything's fine, Ma. You can go back to sleep." I kiss her cheek. "Good night."

"Good night, baby."

I watch her go back to the living room. I'll let her get her rest tonight. Tomorrow, I'll tell her I can't graduate. It's time to own up to that.

I carefully open my bedroom door, so I don't wake Seven. It don't matter, he standing in his crib, sucking his pacifier. He see me and start bouncing, reaching his arms out.

I tear up. Man, I done turned into a crybaby. I need to get my shit together, for real.

I pick him up. "Hey, man. What you doing awake, huh?" I kiss his temple. "You waiting on Daddy?"

He play with the string on my hoodie. Can't lie, I'm as scared as I was that first day I held him. Don't know if that feeling gon' ever go away. Forget the world; he should have the sun, the moon, and all the stars, and they wouldn't be enough.

I'm definitely not. I'm a gangbanging, high school flunk-out who only seventeen. But you can bet that I'm gon' do my best to be whatever he need.

I press my forehead against his. "Daddy almost messed up tonight. You saved me, man. You and your li'l brother—or sister. I thought of y'all and I couldn't do it."

Seven more into my hoodie string than anything I'm saying. Good. He shouldn't know how close I came to failing him.

I kiss his eyebrows. "I won't let you down. You got my word."

I lay him back in his crib and turn on his mobile, so he can watch a moon and stars like the ones that should be his.

Damn, I'm tired. The adrenaline rush from earlier must've drained me. I untuck the Glock and the Ziploc bag from my waist, and I hide them in the shoebox in my closet. I throw myself onto my bed and close my eyes, but they quickly open again.

I gotta tell King what happened to his drugs.

The sun not fully out when King park in front of my house. I called him last night and asked him to meet me first thing this morning.

He gon' be beyond pissed that I flushed his drugs. I doubt *pissed* even the right word. That had to be a couple grand's worth of product. If this was anybody else but King, I might end up six feet deep. He probably gon' beat my ass, homies or not.

Goddamn. I'll have to pay him back, but I got no idea how the hell I can get that kinda money. I'm in deep shit.

I wipe my clammy hands on my shorts and close the front door behind me. Ma, Moe, and Seven asleep. There's a damp spot on my tank top from where Seven drooled on me. He didn't wanna stay in his crib last night, and I let him lay on my chest. It was the only way either of us was gonna fall asleep.

I hop in King's Crown Vic and dap him up. "Thanks for coming over so early."

"Fa'sho," he says hoarsely. He must not've been woke long. "I need to be up and at it anyway."

Pops used to get up before the sun rose. He'd say, "Fiends don't sleep, and neither can I." It's wild how normal he made some stuff for me.

"So what's up?" King asks. "You said it's important."

"Yeah. First I wanna return this to you." I set the Glock in the cupholder. "I don't need it anymore."

King pick it up and examine it. "Did you use it?"

"Red didn't do it," I say.

"What? But you—"

"Drop it, King." I look at him. "Red didn't do it."

Don't get it twisted—I'm not doing this for that coward.

Red gon' get his one way or another, that's how karma work.

"If you say so." King set the gun on his leg. "I'm honestly glad you hit me up. I wanted to talk to you."

"Word?"

"Yeah. I want us to take over the set's drug operations."

I do a double take. "What?"

"P-Nut don't know what he doing, Mav. That's fact. He running everything Shawn did into the ground. We can go to the supplier ourselves, tell him we can handle it better than P-Nut, then bam! We move the product and make the money."

I stare at him for a long time. "You tryna be the crown?"

King shrug and lean back in his seat. "Whatever come with it, come with it. I got a baby on the way. I need to make major moves."

"Dawg, this a death wish," I say.

"I dare any of them to come after us."

Us.

"Nah. Count me out," I say.

"Aw, hell! C'mon, Mav! We can pull this off!" King says. "It would take a little time, but a year from now, we'd run the whole Garden just like our daddies. Li'l Zeke and Li'l Don, doing the damn thing."

Yeah, and Big Zeke in a grave with his wife while Big Don in a prison.

I shake my head. "I'm done selling drugs. For good this time."

King chuckles. "Here we go again. You talking big shit for somebody who got their second baby on the way. What you gon' do for money? Work that sorry job for Mr. Wyatt?"

"I guess so. I'm sorry, but I gotta do it, dawg."

"This not the Mav I know talking. *My* best friend down for whatever. Let me guess, your momma found out you were slinging. Or was it Mr. Wyatt's old ass? Wait, nah." He snap his finger and point at me. "It was Lisa, wasn't it? That ho say jump, you say how high."

"What the hell you call her?" I yell.

King bust out laughing. "Damn, you whipped!"

"I'll show you whipped, keep talking!"

"A'ight, a'ight." He put his hands up. "Chill, *Li'l Don*. Getting pissed over a female that don't want you. You'll be begging me to let you back in the game soon enough. Watch. I'll take your stash for now."

This the part I dread the most. I take the Ziploc bag from my pocket and pass it to King.

He look from it to me. "Where the rest?"

"There was an accident. I dropped it in the toilet."

King slowly sit up. "It's too early for April Fool's 'cause I know—I know—ain't no goddamn way you flushed my stuff, Mav!"

"I said it was an accident, a'ight? Give me a couple of months, and I'll pay you back every penny. You got my word."

"Your word ain't worth nothing! I did *you* a favor"—he

poke my chest with the Glock—"by bringing you on, and you repay me by flushing my money?"

I eye the gun, then him. "I get that you mad, but you better get that thing off of me."

King cock it and point it sideways. "Or what? You won't do nothing! Everybody know you a bitch. I bet Red did kill Dre. You was probably too scared to shoot him."

"Stop. Pointing. That. Gun. At. Me," I growl.

A smile slowly form on King's face. "Chill, *Maverick*." He says my name like it's a joke. "I'm messing with you, homie. Goddamn, you on edge." He snickers as he put the gun down.

"Don't you ever point a gun at me again in your goddamn life!"

"Don't give me a reason to," he says through his teeth.

I don't know the person staring at me. It damn sure ain't my best friend.

If I'm honest with myself, me and King done had a crack between us for a while, ever since the DNA tests proved Seven not his. That crack feel like a canyon now.

I think I'm losing another brother, and this hurt just as bad as putting one in the ground.

I stare ahead. "Don't worry," I murmur. "I'll get your money back."

King suck his teeth. "It's all good, Mav. I'm willing to let bygones be bygones. I don't want no money."

I look at him. "You don't?"

"Nah." King's lips turn up again with a dark glint in his eyes. "You'll pay me back another way one day."

Whatever he got in mind, it ain't good. That's real clear now.

I swallow the lump in my throat and get out the car. "See you around, King."

THIRTY

Here's the thing Mr. Wyatt taught me 'bout gardening:

.   Flowers, fruits, and vegetables can grow anywhere, among anything. They were made for that. I mean c'mon, when God made that sh—stuff, I gotta stop cussing so much—when he made that stuff, he didn't put them in garden plots. He put them out in the wild or whatever and gave them everything they needed to survive. I shouldn't be surprised to see Mr. Wyatt's roses blossoming before winter even over.

They catch my eye from the walkway as King drive down the street. They so pretty that I go over.

I unlock the gate and let myself in the Wyatts' backyard. We put chicken wire around a lot of the plots weeks ago and packed them with pine needles to protect them till spring. We left the roses untouched. I expected them to be dead by now, but they got blooms as big as my palm.

I bend down for a closer look. "Dang. Y'all doing real good, huh? I might need to cut these canes. I think they dead. Y'all cool with that?"

Man, here I go, talking to the flowers like—

The Wyatts' back door squeak open. "Dammit, boy!" Mr. Wyatt says, with a deep breath. "You oughta know you can't sneak into folks' yard this early in the morning! I thought you were a burglar."

I look back over my shoulder. "What would a burglar steal from back here? Plants?"

"Who knows?" he says as he come down the steps. He pull his robe together tighter. "You're lucky I didn't have my pistol."

"Whaaat? Deacon Wyatt pack heat?"

"Heaven yeah!"

I bust out laughing. This man really don't cuss.

"What you doing in the garden this early?" he asks.

I turn back to the roses. "I was outside and noticed that these starting to bloom. Had to check them out myself."

Mr. Wyatt grunt as he bend down beside me. "Oooh, these ol' knees. What I tell you? Roses can bloom in the hardest conditions."

"No doubt." I run my finger along some of the petals. "I can prune them if you want. These canes don't look good."

He pull his head back a little. "You sound like you know what you're doing."

340

"I should by now, as much as you talk."

"Yeah, I suppose. I'm surprised you were listening." He check out the roses himself. "Looks like you're right. These canes need to be snipped."

"Because they won't help them grow, right?"

"Mmm-hmm. It's kinda like how we have to do with ourselves. Get rid of things that don't do us any good. If it won't help the rose grow, you've gotta let it go. Hey, hey! Look at me rapping again."

I snort. "A'ight, MC Wyatt."

"That's got a nice ring to it." He straighten up with another grunt. "The bride and I have been talking, Maverick. You've been a big help here in the garden and at the store. Jamal's heading off to one of them four-year colleges soon, and I'll need somebody to pick up the slack. What do you think about becoming a full-time employee?"

"For real?"

"Yeah. I know that the pay is nothing compared to what your li'l friends make out in the streets—"

"Fast money lead to a fast end."

Mr. Wyatt raise his eyebrows. "You really have been listening. I thought it all went in one side of that big head and out the other."

"Dang, Mr. Wyatt. You ain't gotta diss me."

"A little early-morning humor never hurt nobody. You can start full-time after you graduate. What do you say?"

I hold the back of my neck. "Um . . . I'm not graduating, Mr. Wyatt. I kinda flunked out."

"What is flunked out?" he says. "Do you mean you dropped out?"

"Yeah. The other week, I found out I was flunking all my classes and would have to repeat the twelfth grade. That won't work, so I stopped going to school."

"I see," he says. "Does Faye know?"

"No, sir, not yet," I say, and he real quiet. "But I'm gon' get my GED," I add quickly. "The school counselor said they got classes downtown. I just gotta sign up for them."

Ay, I told Seven I won't let him down. Getting my GED is the first step.

"I see," Mr. Wyatt says again, and I don't know if he disappointed or what. He take a deep breath. "I tell you what. You go downtown this morning, sign up for those classes, then come to the store to start as a full-time employee."

My eyes widen. "The job still mine?"

"Why wouldn't it be?" he says. "I'm not the one you need to worry about. That title belongs to Faye."

True.

He pat my shoulder. "Go do what you need to do, son. I expect you to come straight to work afterward. Don't be—"

"Lollygagging around," I finish for him. "Yes, sir, I know."

"Since you're listening so well, I oughta start reciting scripture so you can repeat that."

Aw, damn. "Let's stick with the work stuff for now, Mr. Wyatt."

He chuckles. "That's what you think. I ain't done with you yet, boy," he says, and climb his back steps.

I finally told Ma the truth about school.

Was she pissed? Hell yeah.

Did she go off on me? Fa'sho.

Did my lies make it worse? Oh yeah.

Am I glad Moe was there as a witness? You damn right. She probably saved my life.

Once I swore to Ma that I'd get my GED, she calmed down a little. She marched outta the house to work and barely said two words to me. I deserve it.

I get dressed to go downtown. Seven in his playpen in the living room, babbling to the Teletubbies on the TV. I don't understand why li'l kids love them creepy-looking things.

The phone ring throughout the house. I grab the cordless off my nightstand. "Hello?"

"Hello!" the automated voice says. "You have a collect call from—"

"Adonis."

I accept the charges. "Pops?"

"Mav Man?" he says. "I wasn't sure anybody would be home. I got some calling time and figured I'd try. You . . . you good?"

That's his way of asking if I went through with my plan.

"I'm good, Pops," I say. "Nothing going on; nothing went on."

He let out a deep breath. "Good."

I sit on the side of my bed. "Hard for me to say that. I almost feel like I let the family down."

"Nah, man. The family needs *you*," he says. "I'm stuck here; Dre gone. You gotta stay around, you feel me? By any means."

"I know," I mumble as I pick at a thread on my comforter. That's my main goal. It's not really the kind Mr. Wyatt told me to have, but yeah. Thing is, I don't see how I can accomplish that long as I'm a King Lord. "I think I want out the set, Pops."

The line fall silent.

"That's nothing against you or Dre or none of y'all," I say. "I know this part of our blood. But this not the life—I don't want my kids to—"

"Hey, hey. You don't owe me an explanation," he says. "Like I told you the other day, you're becoming your own man. You don't need my permission or approval."

"Yes, sir."

Pops take another deep breath. "On some real shit, son? There's a lot of grown men in the game who don't wanna be in it. They don't have the guts to admit it like you do. They too caught up or too scared of what people will think. They end up accepting that they stuck."

For a second, it sound like he describing himself.

"For you to admit that you want out? It means you're think-ing for yourself, like a man should," he says. "They oughta start calling you Big Mav instead of Li'l Don."

"Quit playing." I laugh, as he do. "I'll always be Li'l Don around here."

"Yeah, we'll see," Pops says. "Do what you need to do, son. I love you. Regardless."

I smile. "I love you too, Pops."

Signing up for GED classes wasn't too bad. The lady at the school district office already had my info courtesy of Mr. Clayton. She put me in the class for "young people, nineteen and under." Said it would be good for me to be with other kids.

That's the first time in a while anybody called me a kid. I figure I got a couple more months of that, 'cause once you got two kids, you grown. I'll enjoy it while I can.

The classes meet Monday, Wednesday, and Friday nights. The school district got some career development courses for young adults, too. I signed up for the landscaping class. I can earn a certificate when I get my GED, and it would allow me to professionally care for gardens. It's something, I guess.

I caught the bus and came straight to the store like I told Mr. Wyatt I would. I run the cash register while he take a "break" across the street with Mr. Reuben and Mr. Lewis. The way he laughing, he ain't concerned with this long line of customers I got over here.

I ring up Mrs. Rooks, and I don't drop her eggs this time. Best believe she watch me real close to make sure I don't. The li'l snot-nosed kids from the projects count their change out themselves, and when I ask why their behinds not in school, they ask why I'm not either. They got me there.

"Have a good day," I call after the last customer around half an hour later. Ol' girl talked my ear off, man. She showed me a picture of her sons and proudly told me she named them Dalvin and DeVante after the dudes in Jodeci. I looked at her funny. I can't talk though. I named my son after a number.

As she walk out, Mr. Wyatt come back in. "Everything all right, Maverick?"

"Yes, sir," I say, opening my bag of salt-n-vinegar chips. Now that I'm full-time, I get an employee discount. "I survived that afternoon rush. Didn't think I would, huh?"

"Now, hold on, I didn't say that."

"C'mon, Mr. Wyatt. You know you were testing me. I ain't stupid."

"Okay, maybe it was a teeny-tiny test," he says, with two of his fingers inches apart. "The fellas and I had a bet going. Cletus thought you'd be hollering for me two minutes in. I said five. Reuben said ten. We all lost."

"Gah-lee! That's what y'all get. Ain't got no faith in a brother."

"I'll admit, you surprised me," Mr. Wyatt says. "If I'm honest, I'm surprised you've lasted this long at the job. I thought you would've had your third strike by now."

I can't lie. I expected to get it, too.

But maybe it's time I start surprising myself.

EPILOGUE

BUD

Lisa eat her barbecue at my kitchen table, smacking extra loud. "Dang! Mr. Reuben did this right! You sure you don't want some, loser?" She wave a rib in front of me.

I lightly push it away. "Man, if you don't go on somewhere. You won the bet, a'ight? You ain't gotta rub it in my face."

"Yes, I do actually. I don't wanna say I told you so but . . ." She snort. "Who am I kidding? I. Told. You. So! Bam!"

Maaan. Lisa ain't let up since Dr. Byrd told us we having a baby girl. I took her to Reuben's to buy her prize, and she told everybody in the restaurant that I lost our bet. As we walked to my house, she told every neighbor we passed. Gloating for no reason.

I reach over and rub her belly. "Baby girl, please don't come out acting like your momma."

"Excuse you?" Lisa says.

"I'm playing, I'm playing. I hope our daughter is exactly like you."

"Our *daughter*. Because guess what? I was ri-ight!" she sings.

I flip her Braves cap off of her head.

"Stopppp," she whine, and quickly put it back over her ponytail. "You know I don't have my hair done!"

I laugh and check on Seven in his high chair. He tearing up that mac and cheese I got for him. I sneak a li'l for myself. Ma says you ain't a real parent till you eat your kid's food. "You lucky I'm not a sore loser."

"Ha! Since when? You sulked through the rest of the appointment."

"I wasn't sulking! I was surprised."

Lisa twist her mouth. "Suuuure."

"I was! I'm cool with a girl. I can do tea parties and baby dolls."

"Hey, she could love sports. I used to throw my baby dolls like footballs in the backyard." Lisa trace her finger along her sonogram picture. "She's so stinking cute."

"Even with my big apple head?" I tease.

"Yep, although God help me during labor. I hope she has your eyelashes. And my eyes. I like my eyes. Is that conceited?"

She crack me up. "Nah, not at all. Our li'l girl gon' be perfect, no matter what."

"She will," Lisa murmurs. She look away from the picture and pat the table. "All right, no more distractions. You asked me to help you study."

"Yeah, yeah, yeah." I sit at the table and open my GED prep book. "They foul for this quiz they giving us tomorrow. Class only been going on a week, dang."

"You like it so far?" Lisa asks.

I shrug. "I like that it's faster than a regular school day. My landscaping class real cool. I know more than anybody in that joint except the teacher." I grin.

Lisa roll her eyes. "Lord help the teacher, then."

"Forget you." I laugh. "I like the classes mostly. I gotta get used to going to class at night though, and it's weird not being around my homeboys."

"Understandable," Lisa says. "Have you told any of them what you told me?"

"That I want out the set? Not yet." I run my hand over my durag. "I gotta work my nerve up to that, Lisa. It's gon' cost me. I already owe King that money."

"Yeah," she mumbles. I told her everything. She the only friend I got left. "It'll work out."

"Fa'sho. I'm gon' make sure it do."

Lisa get a small smile. "Look at you, believing in yourself."

"Well, you know." I pop my collar.

Lisa crack up.

"I'm home!" Ma call from the living room. She come down the hall, taking her heels off. "Whew! My feet say, 'Yes, Lord.' How was the appointment?"

What she really mean is, "What y'all having?"

"Lisa won the bet," I say.

"Yes, yes! I knew it!" Ma hug Lisa at the table. "I was scared we'd have to deal with three Mavericks."

What the— "Ma!"

Lisa laugh. "Nope, baby girl is coming to the rescue."

"Hallelujah!" Ma rub Lisa's belly. "Grandma already bought you some of the cutest outfits, Pooh Bear."

"Dang, Ma. She ain't out the womb yet. Let us give her a name before you give her a nickname."

"Hush, Stinka Butt."

"Oh my God. *Stinka Butt?*" Lisa says.

"Ma, you said you'd stop using that name! C'mon!"

"You'll be all right." Ma step around me to get to Seven. He buck in his high chair, reaching for her. Ma scoop him up. "Do y'all have a name picked out yet?"

"No, ma'am. We were gonna name her Andre if she were a boy," Lisa says. "We could name her Andrea, I guess."

"You could, but we already have an Andreanna in the family," Ma says. "Baby girl should have her own name. Something that'll tell her who she is."

"We could name her after me." I cheese. "Mavericka."

"What?" Ma says, and Lisa go, "Oh, heck no!"

"Dre named his daughter after him!"

"Andreanna is cute," Lisa says. "Mavericka is a mess."

"The biggest mess," Ma adds. "Sounds like a damn spice."

How they gon' gang up on me? "Y'all some haters."

Ma hand Seven over to me. "Keep telling yourself that. I'm gonna go take a bubble bath and drink a little something-something to wind down from the day I had. Those folks at the hotel almost made me lose my mind."

"You not going to your other job?" I ask.

"Nope, I'm taking tonight off. I'm actually thinking of quitting altogether. With Moe moving in and bringing in more money, things won't be as tight."

I feel bad, man. Me and my son are the main reasons things get tight in the first place. My money looking funny again since I'm not slinging. Ma and Moe shouldn't have to help take care of us.

"One day, I'll get my own spot, Ma. That'll make it easier for you and Moe."

Ma set her hand on her hip. "Who said you have to move out? We're making it work, aren't we?"

"My son is my responsibility. So is my daughter. I'm gon' get on my own two feet and take care of them."

Ma cup one of my cheeks. "Focus on getting that GED and that landscaping certificate. We'll worry about the other stuff later." She kiss that same cheek. "Dre would be proud of you."

It don't hurt as much to hear stuff like that no more. I can actually smile.

Ma grab a bottle of wine outta the fridge and take it her toward her bedroom. "Night, y'all!"

"Don't you need a glass?" I ask.

"Not after the day I had," she calls. She close her bedroom door.

I shake my head. That wine gon' have her knocked out.

I settle Seven in my lap. He watch Lisa every move as she eat. "Sooooo . . . where should we live?" I ask.

"What do you mean? You want some, Punkin?" Lisa put a little barbecue sauce on one of her fingers and hold it toward Seven. Boy grab it and put it in his mouth like it's a rib.

"You heard me. I told Ma that I'm gon' get us a place. I'm thinking we oughta get that mansion on a private island, with the elevators and the Bentleys."

Lisa get a little more sauce on her finger and hold it toward Seven again. He open his mouth wide. She laughs. "Somebody likes barbecue. Who says we'll be living together, Maverick?"

"I say so. I bet that one day, you'll be Mrs. Carter."

Lisa scoff. "Here you go, making bets. Didn't you learn from the first one?"

"I got no doubt this time."

"Umm, we're not even a couple, sooo . . ." Lisa shrugs. "You have a ton of work to do to make that happen."

"I'm up for the challenge. I got a plan."

"Oh, really?"

"Yeah. A wise, beautiful girl told me I oughta have one. Don't tell her I complimented her. She'd let it go to her head."

Lisa roll her eyes. "What's your plan, smart aleck?"

"First, I'll get my GED and my certificate while I work for Mr. Wyatt. Then once I get them, I'll get a second job at night. I'll use money from that to get my own place and save up for business courses. My endgame is to be an entrepreneur. I don't have it completely figured out but—"

"It's a start," Lisa says, with a small smile. "However, I don't see what it has to do with me."

"Well, hopefully, I'll show you that you can depend on me." I grin.

Lisa fight one herself. "We'll see . . . *Stinka Butt*."

"Gah-lee! Not you too!"

She laugh, and that got Seven laughing in my lap. "I won't *ever* let you live it down," she says.

"I'll remember this." I pretend to eat Seven's jaw. He squeal. "I'll remember this!"

Lisa adjust her Braves cap. "Dang. Tammy needs to do my hair ASAP."

I look up at her. "Let me do your hair."

She stare at me, her mouth slightly open. Then she bust out laughing. "You can't be serious."

"Yeah, I am. I gotta learn before baby girl get here since I'll be combing her hair."

"You will, Mr. Conditioner-Is-for-Girls?"

"Yeah, I will. I'm all in," I say. "That mean *all* in. Combing hair, giving baths, clipping toenails, whatever. Everything won't be on you."

Lisa slowly nod, as if the idea sinking in. "Okay, Stinka Butt. I guess I can let you practice on my hair tonight. Tam can fix it tomorrow. God help her."

"Just for that, I'm gon' have you looking to'e up from the flo' up."

I get Seven ready for bed and put him in his crib. He suck his fingers and his forehead wrinkle like he don't understand why they don't taste like barbecue.

I kiss right in the middle of that wrinkle. "Sweet dreams, man. Don't try to solve all the world's problems tonight, a'ight? Let the rest of us handle that."

Lisa wait for me on the back porch with a comb, brush, and some hair products she borrowed from Ma. I sit behind her on the steps. This the first warm night we done had in a while. The Garden quiet enough that I hear the cars rumbling on the freeway. The moon glow big in the sky, and stars twinkle all around. Gotta be hundreds of them tonight.

Lisa flip through Ma's latest copy of *Ebony* magazine. "No matter what happens, Mav, don't panic. It can be fixed."

"Dang, girl. You make it sound so serious."

She tilt her head back and look up at me. "A Black woman's hair is *always* serious."

"Okay, okay. What you want me to do?"

"I'm gonna teach you how to plait. Take my ponytail down and comb any tangles out."

I pull the rubber band—wait, this ain't rubber—the hair-tie thingamajig from around her ponytail. I grab the comb and run it through.

Lisa wince. "Ow!" She turn all the way around. "Don't be so rough!"

"What is it you always tell me? 'I wasn't rough, you just tender-headed,'" I say, in a high-pitched voice.

This girl grab my shirt and twist one of my nipples.

"Ow!"

"Was that rough?" she asks. "Comb my hair like you would comb baby girl's hair."

"Okay, okay!" I'm real careful as I run that comb through again. "We can't call her baby girl forever. We gotta think of a name at some point."

"Yeah, I know. We could use Dre's middle name, Amar, and make it Amara. But Amara Carter doesn't really roll off the tongue. . . . It feels like something else should be there."

"It could be her middle name," I point out.

"Then what's her first name?"

I gently—*gently*—comb a tangle outta her hair. "My folks named me Maverick 'cause it mean independent thinker. That's who they wanted me to be. Who do we want her to be?"

"Intelligent. Independent. Outspoken. I doubt there's a name that means all of that."

"A'ight. Let's think 'bout what she already is to us. I gave Seven his name 'cause it mean perfection. He perfect to me. What is she to us?"

Lisa caress her belly. "One of the few good things during all the bad stuff."

I wrap my arms around her, placing my hands over hers. "She been that for me, too."

Lisa rest her head against my arm, and it's like we just

created our own world where it don't matter that we two kids who don't know what the hell we doing. All that matter is us.

I look up at the night sky. It's pitch black, and yet that somehow make the stars shine brighter. Hundreds of lights in all that darkness.

Wait a second.

A light in the darkness.

I smile, and I look at Lisa. "I think I got a name."

ACKNOWLEDGMENTS

In a lot of ways this book itself has been a rose, and it took a lot of gardeners to help it grow:

My mom, Julia, who is the reason the rose even exists. Thank you for nurturing me and, in turn, it.

My editor, Donna, who saw the potential in all of the concrete that I brought to her and chipped it away so that the flower could bloom.

My agent, Brooks, who watered the buds and reminded me that it was a flower even when it looked its worst, along with my Janklow & Nesbit team: Roma Panganiban, Emma Winter, Stephanie Koven, and Cullen Stanley.

My film agent, Mary, who is sunshine personified.

My Balzer + Bray/HarperCollins family, who are willing to pull the weeds and nurture the rose so it can blossom into